They thought the tsunami was the worst of their problems—until they saw what it brought with it...

From the balcony outside, Bruce heard Liz give off a small, almost frightened shriek. He knew how she felt. He had suspicions this place would never be the same again.

"Bruce!" she said, coming up behind him.

He turned, hearing something strange in her voice. "What's wrong?"

Her eyes looked frozen and more terrified than at any point during the hour-and-a-half tsunami.

"Outside." She paused, swallowing hard. "There's something outside—on the balcony"

He walked over and wrapped his arms around her.

"I know, it's awful. We'll leave here as soon as we can."

She pulled back and looked at him. "On the balcony there's...something—not real—" She shook her head. "It can't be real."

Not understanding, he frowned. "Not real? What do you mean, not real? Don't you mean unreal?"

Liz shook her head no.

Stepping away from her, he headed toward the balcony. How could something be *not* real? But with everything Liz had been through today, her reaction was normal. Bruce just hoped some wreckage had found its way to them, not a dead body.

"I'm sure it's just mangled debris—" He stopped cold in mid-sentence, even colder in his tracks. He now saw what she had—he now saw what lay on the balcony.

Welcome to the quiet town of Harrow, a picturesque community found in New Hampshire's White Mountains. To the outside world, this charming little town was a dreamland vacation spot.

UNTIL SORROW FELL UPON IT...

Hidden deep within the Harrowing Hills is a secret pathway to the realm of mist and darkness—an unsanctified land where a dark enemy seeks to destroy everything in existence.

NOW ALL MAY BE LOST...

What can this normally-sleepy village harbor that could not only devour this close-knit community, but the universe itself?

KUDOS for Harrow

Henson seemingly fuses religion, science, and philosophy in a horrific tale that will keep you turning pages into the night. – *Christopher Allan Poe, author of The Portal*

The beginning has a strong hook and the ending was a stroke of absolute brilliance. – *Mike Kingsly, editor*

Have to say I'm surprised. I had no idea Henson could pose the pen like this. – *Elvis Thompson*

Harrow gave me goosebumps. Scared the be-jesus out of me, actually. Still, I couldn't put it down until I'd finished...The story was almost too well-written. – *Taylor Jones, reviewer*

It is a chilling story, made more so by the quality of Henson's writing. – *Regan Murphy, reviewer*

HARROW BOOK 1

Large Print

ERIC HENSON

A Black Opal Books Publication

GENRE: PARANORMAL THRILLER/ HORROR

HARROW ~ BOOK 1 ~ Large Print
Copyright © 2012 by Eric Henson
Cover Design by Eric Henson
All cover art copyright © 2012
All Rights Reserved
Large Print ISBN: 978-1-626942-26-4
First Publication: OCTOBER 2012

FOR MY PSYCHOTIC PUZZLE PIECE

PROLOGUE

Using the Crescent Realm to conceal his actions, the cacodemon Báalzbub conspired with an unimaginable adversary to destroy the very existence he helped create.

Believing, although cruel and unfair, existence deserved to be saved, a small group of fallen angels decided to act. Fully aware that forgiveness was unattainable, these former Messengers-of-Light, reached out for help from those they once betrayed, sending word to their one-time ally—and now enemy—the archangel Gabrielus.

Unable to ignore the information, Gabrielus replied that Sariel agreed to meet them in the human realm. Hearing this, Abaddon and his small number of followers attempted to escape the realm of Hell.

Only to discover one of their own had betrayed them.

Báalzbub slaughtered them as they fled.

1

Only Abaddon and another named Ezziel survived the massacre. Forced to separate in battle, the two, now fatigued and wounded, had to regroup in the realm of man to find Sariel—the dreaded Angel of Death.

PART I

ARRIVAL

"The oldest and strongest emotion of mankind is fear, and the strongest kind of fear is fear of the unknown."

H.P. Lovecraft

CHAPTER 1

October 12th:

In the Indian Ocean, just off the western coast of North Sumatra, about one hundred miles north of the Simeulue Islands, an entity of negative energy caused a colossal earthquake nineteen miles below on the ocean's floor. Lifting the seabed up twenty feet and forcing nine hundred, ninety-four miles of fault line to slip fifty feet along the subduction zone, where the India plate slides under the Burma plate, this slip happened in two phases over a period of several minutes.

The first rupture proceeded at a momentum of six thousand, three hundred miles per hour, beginning off the coast of Aceh, proceeding northwesterly over a period of about one hundred seconds. The split stopped, paused, and then continued on as a second rupture begun to move northward at a speed of four thousand, seven hundred miles per hour, heading toward the Andama and Nicobar Islands. This first rupture was about two hundred fifty miles long and sixty miles wide—the longest rupture ever known to be caused by an earthquake, and reaching a moment magnitude of nine-point-three on the seismograph, making it the second largest tremor ever recorded.

It was also the longest duration of faulting ever observed, lasting between five hundred and six hundred seconds, and large enough to cause the entire planet to vibrate as much as half an inch, triggering earthquakes as far away as Alaska. And tremors were felt in Bangladesh, India, Malaysia, Myanmar, Thailand, Singapore and the Maldives Islands.

The total energy released was equivalent to 0.08 gigatons of TNT, about as much energy used in the United States in eleven days.

On the Mai Khao Beach in the northern part of Phuket Island, Thailand, Bruce Wren and his girlfriend, Elizabeth Bernhardt, were on a working holiday. Bruce, an Investment banker, had come to Phuket for a client, the owner of one of the largest rubber tree plantations on the island.

There was a time when tin mining was the major source of income for the island, but since the price of tin fell, the local economy had used two other sources for its income. One of those resources came from their rubber trees, making Thailand the largest producer of rubber in the world. The other resource was tourism, and Bruce happened to be on the island for both.

The decision came easy to ask Liz to join him on the trip. It had been awhile since either one of them had gotten away. The last trip the two of them took together was to New York City last year for New Year's Eve. The packed Times Square was freezing, but with the two of them being New Englanders, and with the amount of alcohol they consumed, the cold was not a problem. They kept warm just fine. They had a good time, but this trip to an exotic beach was a little more special, and Bruce took advantage of the opportunity handed to him. When the business trip came up, by some miracle, Liz, a tax lawyer working for a mid-size firm out of Boston, was free to join him.

They were now on the amazing five and a half miles of Mai Khao Beach where sea turtles came to lay eggs on the pristine white sand. Bruce had hoped for a remote and isolated place, and he found it. After all, he had special plans this week.

He walked out onto their room's balcony at the Mai Khao Resort & Spa, a five-star hotel right off the beach, to have a quick smoke, and saw the oranges and reds of the early morning sky that foretold the heat of the coming day.

He turned and looked into the room, just as Liz rolled over in her sleep, and smiled as he watched her. The two of them had been together for almost three years. He remembered the moment he became infatuated with her at a mutual friend's birthday party, how helpless he was in keeping his mind and eyes off her. The way her blue dress perfectly embraced her body, how her hair fell across and framed her face. And then there was that smile of hers.

He became so besotted he had trouble engaging in conversations with friends. Every time he heard her voice and laugher his blood ran cold. Just the sound of her shoes walking across the floor caused his heart to race. He had always heard the expression "love at first sight" and thought it was just that, an expression. And then at thirty-three years old it happened to him.

When someone kindly introduced him to her, he fell head over heels in love with just a touch of her hand, reducing him to nothing and her into everything.

Last night, he took her to the southern-most point of the Island, the popular Brahman Cape, to watch the sunset. This was where he'd planned to take advantage of the rare vacation and scenery.

Packing a picnic, he led her up a small lush hillside, and while the two watched the sunset melt into the blue sea, he asked her to be his wife, to which she had ecstatically responded, "Yes."

He walked back inside and closed the screen door, allowing the morning sea air in. With no intention of going back to sleep, he climbed into bed, slid over to his still naked fiancée, and started kissing her neck.

She slowly came around with a smile, let-

ting him move on top. Liz had always enjoyed making love in the morning most of
all.

CHAPTER 2

Within the deep waters of the Indian Ocean, barely noticeable and harmless looking waves traveled at an unusually high speed of six hundred twenty miles per hour, en route to the surrounding seacoast areas with absolutely no forewarning. The radar satellites orbiting above recorded the heights of the waves, but these observations would not provide any warning. This was not their intended function.

There was no network of sensors in this area necessary for detection like in the Pacific Ocean's Ring of Fire, where ninety percent of the world's earthquakes and eighty-one percent of the largest earthquakes occurred. Beneath these small fast moving ripples, the wounded Ezziel unintentionally advanced toward unknown land to change Bruce and Liz's kismet forever.

After making love to Bruce, Liz got out of bed to get ready for her ten-thirty appointment with the spa downstairs. She still couldn't believe Bruce proposed last night. She hadn't seen it coming. She thought she could always tell when he was up to something, that he could never surprise her. That was up until the big one and then—wham, he got her. She'd actually lost her breath for a moment.

She could not help but look at her new ring. It all seemed like a dream still. She half expected to look down at her hand this morning and see just her plain bare finger, but the ring was there. It really happened.

While making love her eyes kept falling on it. She loved the way it made her feel. She'd never felt more complete than when looking at that ring while making love to the man who gave it to her.

After freshening up, she walked to the balcony to catch the morning sky before it disappeared. The landscape looked stunning in the early dawn light, the sea was smooth and blue and already people were swimming, boating, and taking their morning stroll along the beach.

Liz then looked around the resort where she and Bruce had spent the past few days. She loved the way it looked here and wished there was somewhere like this back home. As a little girl, she fantasized about being a princess.

Too bad, she couldn't have visited this fairy-tale palace back then.

Smiling, she left for the spa.

Due to how close the northern regions of the Indonesian Islands were to the epicenter, the three phases of the tsunami hit there first. It only took fifteen minutes for the first wave to reach them.

On the Island of Simeulue, local legend spoke of an earthquake and tsunami from 1907, and after the initial shaking the islanders fled to the hills, being one of the few coastal areas to evacuate before the tsunami struck.

Not all were so lucky.

In the minutes before the tsunami, the sea

receded temporarily from the coast. This rare sight induced people, especially children, to visit the coast to investigate and collect stranded fish. It ended with lethal results.

In Indonesia, there were over one hundred, thirty thousand people killed, thirty-seven thousand missing and another one hundred, sixty-seven thousand people injured. In some regions, the water killed four times more women than men as they waited for their anglers to return home, and searched the beaches for their children.

Two hours later waves started to enter the waters of India and Thailand. Slowing down in shallow water, these waves started to form into large destructive tsunamis.

Bruce opened the fridge. His original plan was to get a glass of ice tea, when the bottles of Corona caught his eye. Normally he wouldn't drink beer this early in the day, but his work with the rubber tree man was over and this was his last full day here. He was on vacation and he had reason to celebrate.

With the Mexican beer in hand, he walked through the large apartment-sized suite and entered the bedroom, picked up his laptop, and stepped out onto the terrace. This was by far his favorite part of the room. He laid the computer on the table. Even on semi-vacation, he checked work e-mail and the stock market. Citigroup might be able to go without him for a few days, but Bruce could not go without Citigroup.

Finished, he logged off and heard people yelling on the ground. He walked over to the balcony and recognized the family from a few rooms down.

The majority of the commotion came from their ten-year-old daughter, something about geography class and a tsunami.

"What's going on out there?" asked Liz as she entered the terrace.

"Not sure, how was your appointment?

"Great, you should give it a go."

Not the least bit interested, Bruce smiled.

She glanced out at the ocean and frowned. "Does the water look weird to you?"

"A little, it receded a bit earlier, but seems to be coming back now."

"Could it be some kind of storm coming in?"

He shrugged, uncertain. "Could be. The water has begun to bubble and boats on the horizon are bobbing."

"What kind of storm starts like this? Sure looks different from anything I've seen in New England."

They watched a yacht tip vertically in the bay.

"Hold on a second." Bruce ran inside for a pair of binoculars.

Putting them to his eyes, he watched the yacht.

Coming in beyond it was what looked like a large wave.

He mentioned this to Liz and she looked at him questioningly.

"Did you just say large wave?"

"Looks like it, yeah, in fact, it looks like a *very* large wave."

CHAPTER 3

October 13th:

The New England town of Harrow was a small, friendly community found in the State of New Hampshire's White Mountain region. The kind of place you could imagine Norman Rockwell would love. Whether Mr. Rockwell ever made it up to Harrow was unknown, but the town was that sort of small New England town. Unfortunately, just like the *Saturday Evening Post*, those days were long gone, but that spirit and atmosphere could still linger in a few communities and this was one of them.

Harrow was a beautiful town with colonial era buildings and small narrow roads, an old-fashioned township that never totally caught up with the times, and that was part of the charm. The kind of place where fuel station attendants pumped the gas for you, men

opened doors for women, homes were unlocked, and everybody knew everyone.

Where else would hayrides and a covered
bridge look so natural and part of life.

Bordering beautiful mountains, forests,
and lakes, the town was a gorgeous and cap-
tivating sight admired by the area's camping
and skiing culture for over a hundred years.

In summertime, Harrow looked picture
perfect with its deep green trees and sparkling blue watering holes. Winters had an
amazing way of transforming the town into
the ideal snow globe, a wintry wonderland
covered in snow and ice. Come autumn, the
area became a canvas painted with bright,
multicolored leaves that shone unlike anywhere else on the planet.

However, not all traveled to Harrow, or
the region for that matter, for its natural
splendor and beauty.

In fact, some made the journey in search
of the complete opposite. They sought the
hidden unnatural ugliness believed to be
lurking somewhere within the Harrowing
Hills.

These sightseers scoured the Hills year
round, but come fall they arrived in abun-

dance, trampling carelessly through the woods, stomping mindlessly over the dead and fallen beauty so many had come to see.

Scores of these tourists unwisely ignored the town's superstitions, and instead of avoiding the Harrowing Hills as the skies darkened, they entered them, chasing after twisted tales that had become modern day legends.

Of course, many of these adventurous investigators got themselves lost each year by trailing off marked paths and into the woods unknown. Fortunately, most of these misguided explorers were found, but not all.

The community had a double-edged view of these tourists. Harrow needed the revenue generated by these people, but hated dealing with them for income. Many were mortified that they had gotten into the position where the Harrowing Hills helped support them.

There had always been rumors circling around the township of Harrow. The most legendary being the myth of the Black Forest, a mysterious patch of woodland said to be a source of haunts. Although no one had ever verified the actual existence of this hidden place, they still claimed to hear low screams and cries mixed within the wind blowing from of them.

Many believed these eerie sounds belonged to the long-lost, still crying out for the help they never received. The more level-minded believed them nothing more than wind blowing through simple trees, and snickered at fools cursed with overactive imaginations. They insisted there was no evil in the Hills.

Whatever their source, those tempests of shrieks and squeals could be disheartening to those who heard them.

Reverend Jack Levi was one of these so-called level-minded people. He had lived in Harrow all forty-seven years of his life, and loved the town and his flock. Unsurprisingly, he could not claim the same for the Hills and had avoided entering them most of his life.

And then today happened.

It was not the source of those phantom cries that brought him back into the Hills again, but the very real ones from Mrs. Jane Moore.

Her son Thomas was lost, wandered off in the way most ten year olds did. Probably went off looking for bugs, or perhaps chased after some animal into the bushes—either way, while the Moore's were in the Hills' picnic area having dinner, they took their eyes off Thomas for a minute. The wrong minute it turned out.

That was over four hours ago. For Mrs. Moore, it was a lifetime.

The sun had started setting half an hour ago and Jack knew then he should have turned back, but the thought of that little boy kept him going.

Suddenly Jack stopped and looked around. When was the last time he had seen or heard any of the other volunteers? Had he gotten himself separated and not realized it? Jack strongly hoped this was not the case. It had been almost thirty-five years since he last saw this woodland, and he'd more than forgotten the area.

He turned and walked back in the direction he'd just come. Nothing looked familiar. Every tree and pile of rocks looked the same. He turned in a small circle trying to decide the best direction.

Being from the area, he fully understood the dangers of getting lost in the woods of New England. Even if not, all he would have to do was watch television. The local six and eleven o'clock news was full of people getting lost in those mountains—people heading north in the belief they were walking south, following the wrong paths, or getting caught by surprise weather. There were a number of ways to get lost in mountain woods, and many of them were life threatening.

The sky continued to darken, increasing Jack's odds of spending the night out here. When he came across a fallen tree, he decided to stop and think.

The call of a raven broke the silence. Jack glanced left, found the large black bird looking down at him, and was glad he no longer was alone.

Sharply from the right came another call—this one louder, harsher than the first one. Jack glanced toward this new raven, as it aggressively spread and shook its wings with enough force to wobble the large limb.

Realizing he had upset the birds in some way, Jack decided it was probably best if he stood and walked away.

Up ahead, three more ravens were perched together, and as he walked through the small cluster of white birches, he noticed all three move their heads in unison following his movement. When he got several yards away, he turned and looked back. Not only were the three birds still watching him closely, but the two from before had joined them.

Then something happened that made him realize just how worn out and tired he actually was. What other explanation could there be? Because he would have sworn on a stack of Bibles that all five ravens just turned and looked at one another in a group tête-à-tête.

He turned back around and quickly walked away as two more ravens landed in a tree beside him. They too seemed to be watching him a little too closely. Jack picked up his pace.

He wanted to get as far from these birds as he could. He understood how intelligent they were, but they were also harmless. Not even starved would these birds turn ravenous enough to attack a human.

Then the phrase *a murder of crows* passed through his mind, and the fact these birds were "harmless" gave him little comfort.

Walking straight ahead, he kept his head low until he reached an odd opening in the trees. Coming across such a clearing was something he did not expect. Up until now, trees and undergrowth covered the land. Then suddenly, the woodsy ground became replaced by a strange greenish-yellow soil that was sulfurous—in both color and scent.

CHAPTER 4

S tepping into this new area was almost surreal. The feeling Jack had was dreamlike, strange and bizarre. This new ground held only a few thick-trunked, creepy trees that split off into several fat branches with small sharp twigs that randomly pointed out. In these twisted dead-looking trees were more ravens.

The woods started up again on the other side beyond the trees. From where Jack stood, it looked as if a path ran down the middle of it. Perhaps it led to a larger path that would carry him out of the woods altogether. If this was so, maybe little Tommy found his way to this path and was now home unharmed.

Jack started toward the trail, and the birds frantically started to shriek.

The noise was almost deafening. As Jack brought his hands up to cover his ears, one of

25

the birds flew past close enough it caused him to step backwards and fall to the ground. Sitting there in this unknown dirt, he realized that if something were to happen out here in the middle of nowhere, it would be his wife Lisa who would suffer for it, not him. He needed out of these woods more for her sake than his own. He prayed this path would lead him home to her.

Picking himself off the ground, he wiped his pants clean and continued on. It was not until he was closer that he noticed how the trees arched into each other, creating a tunneled effect. Jack had seen pictures like this, but never in person. He assumed those photos were Photoshopped, or the trees were forced that way by man. That nature would never naturally lace them together like fingers. Now he knew better.

Resting perfectly at each side of the tunneled pathway were two large boulders. The entrance to the path was dark, almost black, and impossible for Jack to determine how deep it went back, never mind where it led. Believing he would see better once he was inside and traveling down it, he started to step forward. Before his foot touched the pathway, the same raven that nearly hit him landed on the boulder to his left.

The thing spread its enormous wings and jabbed its head. Jack pulled back out of its reach. As another raven landed on the right side boulder, Jack discovered his concern about these birds was valid. As the raven started to thrust its head back and forth, up and down, Jack prayed there was another reason why these creatures of fauna had solid white, pupil-less eyes. Instead, as they stared, his worst fears became reality.

His abdomen started to curl. Taking hold of his stomach, he bent slightly in pain and turned away with plans of retreating into the woodland, only to find a whole flock of these repugnantly sinister birds waiting.

Deciding to chance the path, he turned and found more blocked his way—and any chance of escape. His heart started to race as he spotted someone, or something, fifteen feet inside the darkened path entrance. When this form finally moved forward and Jack could make out what it was, he had all the answers he needed.

He crossed himself, reached down the collar of his flannel shirt, and pulled out the crucifix he worn for longer than he could remember.

As the figure stepped closer, a voice, one Jack easily recognized, drifted from the path. "Hello, Shepherd"

Jack gave no reply.

Little Tommy Moore appeared at the entrance of the pathway. Something had ripped this poor ten-year old boy apart. The front half of little Tommy's skull had been compressed inward like a crushed can. His right eye, bottom jaw, and left arm, from the elbow down, were gone. When he stepped forward, his right leg dragged.

Shocked and horrified, Jack held out the crucifix and recited in a loud and confident voice, "'The Lord is my Shepherd. I shall not want. He maketh me to lie down in green pastures. He leadeth me beside the still waters. He restoreth my soul. He leadeth me in the paths of righteousness for His name' sake.'"

The birds flapped their wings, but did not take flight as Tommy took another step forward.

Jack continued praying. "'Yea, though I walk through the valley of the shadow of death, I will fear no evil: For thou art with me. Thy rod and thy staff, they comfort me. Thou preparest a table before me in the presence of mine enemies. Thou annointest my head with oil. My cup runneth over.'"

A frightening, and much stronger, voice overtook Jack's. A sound more hiss than language traveled within the wind, the trees, and even the birds. This sound, although not Thomas's voice, floated from his mouth as well.

"You have found your valley of death, Reverendus, and you fear the evil in it. Your hopeless devotion and faith are worthless. Nothing can save you here!"

The ravens abruptly took flight, encircling him in a frenzied whirlwind of chaos, diving, and slamming Jack onto the ground. Landing hard, he gasped as the breath was knocked out of him. He tried to get up, working to restore his breathing, as the flock begun to land on him while pecking his back, neck, and head. Able to smell and taste his own blood, Jack wrapped his arms over his head, attempting to block the blows.

The mauled Tommy watched the birds attack as he walked from the pathway. Stopping, he bent over and, as blood flowed heavily from his head, picked up a strong thick branch. After looking the limb over, Tommy started toward Jack. In spite of being a jawless corpse, the boy spoke again. "I have something for you, Shepherd."

The birds continued to brutally peck and tear at Jack, hitting him like small jackhammers, their razor-sharp talons dug into his flesh creating deep fat pencil-sized holes. The amount of blood lost made him weak. He knew his life was over, that he had become another victim of the Harrowing Hills.

Tommy now stood over him. At first the only things Jack saw were the blood drenched Nikes little Tommy was wearing. And then flashes of black as the birds reached in and pulled and tore his eyes out. He tried to scream, but they took hold of his tongue, ripping it out as well. Jack gargled and choked. As blood filled his ears, the only sounds he heard were the ravens pounding on his head and the sonorous beating of his own heart.

Jack waited in terrified agony for it all to end.

He could not see the branch raised over

Tommy's head, nor could he see when it came forcefully down. However, he could feel it—that and the internal sound of his cranium crushing were the last things Reverend Jack Levi knew just before...

CHAPTER 5

Jack woke in a sweat of cold fire, with a substantial-sized headache. He could almost smell and taste sulfur, then it was gone.

As he sat up a dizzy spell came over him. He waited for it to pass then moved the covers slowly off and swung his legs over the edge of the bed. He looked at his sleeping wife hoping he had not disturbed her. Still feeling unsteady and dazed he glanced at the clock, 5:43 a.m., the alarm was set for six o'clock. Turning it off, he climbed out of bed.

Standing up, he could feel some uncomfortable tension in his lower back and legs. He hated the fact he was getting older. He had a good life and it seemed to be going by too fast.

He stretched and thought about the dream that already started to fade, the way dreams do. This was the third such dream in as many nights, but this one had a different quality about it, a more vivid realism. Unable now to remember the whole thing, he was able to recall it had something to do with John Moore's boy Thomas, and again, of course, the ravens. The dreams faded, but the ravens never did.

He could still feel the tension as he walked across the room to the bathroom. A hot shower should help, but that probably would not do a thing for the headache. Stepping into the bathroom Jack flipped on the lights. Their brightness caught him off guard, forcing his eyes shut for a moment. Reopening them, squinting he looked into the mirror over the sink. Both of his eyes were extremely bloodshot and looked as if he spent the night drinking whiskey. Something he had not done in over ten years.

Putting the headache and bloodshot eyes together with the dream, he reached for the bottle of ibuprofen, opened it, and tipped two pills into his hand, looked up at his reflection again, and tapped out another two. Jack hoped he looked better when Lisa woke.

He felt better after the shower. His muscle tension had loosened, and amazingly, even the headache was better. Hungry, he changed into his jogging outfit and walked downstairs to the kitchen for coffee and breakfast. Lisa should be getting up any minute, and he wished to have something ready for her when she did. How many meals had she prepared for him? He was pleased to return the favor.

Lisa decorated their old-fashioned country-styled kitchen with copper-plated watering cans, pottery chickens, and wicker baskets that filled the cabinets and shelves. Hangings on the walls were black and white pictures. Many of her favorites featured young children holding red roses. The concept of the rose being the only thing of color interested Jack. For him it symbolized that even in a colorless world, love could be strong.

Other photos were of gardens, plant life, and foliage. Lisa enjoyed yard sales, always looking for little things for the house and yard. Her latest find was the *home sweet country home* plaque that now hung above the twenty-five-gallon rain urn outside the front door.

Small ceramic figures decorated the countertops. If Jack had to guess, he would say the set of open backed ceramic ducks were Lisa's favorite. Jack thought their straw hats were a nice touch.

The plan was to fix up some eggs and toast, probably some hash browns or sausage as well. As Jack reached the refrigerator, Lisa's last remaining baby rubbed up against his leg. Wolfgang the cat was looking for a bit to eat as well. After getting what he needed from the fridge, Jack fed the house lion.

Just as he finished cooking his favorite finely chopped and seasoned meat, Lisa walked into the kitchen still half asleep. Like Jack, she was average looking, but to him she was the most beautiful woman on the face of the Earth, a vision of true amazement, and the keeper of his heart. The way he felt about this woman, and that she still loved him after everything, simply overwhelmed him at times.

The fact she still existed in his life was all the proof this reverend needed to keep his faith in God.

He gave her a smile warmer than the cup of coffee he handed her. Smiling back at him, Lisa took the cup and sat down at the table.

"Good morning, sleeping beauty. You hungry?" Jack laid a plate next to her coffee cup. Smiling, he leaned over and gave her his first kiss of the day.

Lisa got a glimpse of the redness in Jack's eyes and could tell he'd had another nightmare but chose not to mention it. "Starved, in fact. Do we still have some orange juice left?"

"We do. I'll get you some." He walked back to the fridge. "Did you sleep well? You look as if you did." He returned to the table with the juice and two glasses.

"Not too bad, the breeze coming in the window made it a little chilly, but after I fixed that I slept like a baby. You?"

He poured the orange juice and shrugged. He didn't want to lie to his wife, but saw no point in worrying her, either. "About the same as you I guess, except the draft didn't bother me."

He watched her eat and thought, *Everything she does is beautiful*, as he sat down across the table from her and started eating himself.

After breakfast, Lisa went to the shower. Her plans were to take a quick walk while Jack ran and then open up that new puzzle she brought home yesterday, and think about her husband's behavior the past few days, hoping it was not a sign of things to come.

Jack ran every day. He tried to get in at least five miles, more if he felt up to it. His run started in front of his Winter Street home and continued down the old and weather-beaten streets of Harrow.

Opening the front porch door, he stepped out into the fresh crisp clean autumn air. This was his favorite time of the year, when the summer foliage transformed into a stunning palette of reds, oranges, golds, and browns. And when the leaves fell from their trees, the colors were truly breathtaking.

Just as he was about to shut the door, he noticed a large black bird on one of the railings. He stopped short then quickly stepped back into the house, shutting the door. Moving the door curtain to one side, he looked out at the bird.

He'd reacted this way ever since the raven nightmares began. Jack knew the bird was just a common crow, but his instinct warned him to stay inside. He had to wonder what was next. What if he started dreaming about other animals? Should he count on being afraid of deer someday, or even worse, chipmunks?

Still, he couldn't bring himself to go out there. This unease was real. Something about that thing worried him. He felt his headache threatening a return. Shutting his eyes, he rubbed his temples gently.

He stepped away from the door, turned, and headed for the kitchen. Mercifully, Lisa had moved off to the shower. How could he explain what he'd just done—jumping back into the house like a scared child. He didn't even understand it himself.

Looking down, he suddenly got an idea. He bent over and picked up Wolfgang, and a small smile crossed his face. Jack looked back out the window, and yes, the bird was still there. Turning the doorknob with his left hand while holding Wolfgang in his right, he opened the door about a foot then placed the feline on the floor next to the crack. To get it moving he gave the cat a modest tap and he strutted out onto the porch. At first, Wolfgang did not notice the bird. Then he spotted the feathery trespasser.

Jack knew Wolfgang had no chance of actually catching the bird. The poor thing was just too old. These days the only things the cat could catch were naps, but Jack hoped Wolfgang could at least scare the thing off. And he did. The bird noticed him and flew off with a loud caw, making the reverend's heart jump.

Disappointed, Wolfgang found a sunny patch on the porch and lay down, perhaps to dream he'd made the catch. Opening the door more, Jack once again made his adventuresome journey into the morning light, halfway wishing he could take Wolfgang along for his run.

CHAPTER 6

The waves continued building in size and moved toward the shore. Bruce and Liz could now hear the tsunami coming in from the sea. Bruce realized it might not be safe out here much longer. Not truly believing that the waves were going to, or even could, reach the resort, he couldn't deny their size looked dangerous.

"Liz, go inside."

Looking at him and then out to sea, she did as he asked and turned to go inside.

"Are you coming?"

He nodded his head while looking at Andaman Sea through the binoculars. Watching him from inside the room, she heard a thunderous sound and saw Bruce run toward her.

He grabbed her by the arm, without saying a word, and kept moving. Pulling her along before she understood what was happening, Bruce raced her across the room and slammed into the bathroom door, hard, banging it open. Both of them fell painfully to the floor.

He kicked the door shut and covered Liz as if something was about to drop on her.

"What the hell happened out there?" she demanded.

He looked at the door, got up, and locked it. Returning to the floor, he tried to think of what they should do next. Behind them was a large bathtub. He considered it for a moment then told Liz she needed to get inside it.

"Tell me what happened out there. Why am I getting into this tub, Bruce?" She tried to hide her fear, but the quiver in her voice gave her away.

Putting his hands on the wall, Bruce listened. The only sound he heard was the bathroom fan. He reached over to turn it off, but before he made it to thc switch, the power went out. "That's not good, that's not good at all," he said as he sat back down on the floor.

The room would have been in total darkness if it were not for the light coming in through the window. He looked over at his future wife and saw she had never gotten into the tub.

"Want to tell me what just happened?" she asked

He shook his head. "The sea—it just lifted like a wall, all of it. It dwarfed even the trees. It just lifted. I thought I was seeing things at first."

Liz stared at him. She'd never seen his eyes look so large and terrified. "What do you mean lifted?"

"Lifted—lifted, as in came up and out of the sea. The damn water came right the hell out of the sea—what don't you understand?"

"I don't know, maybe everything. How could water lift from the sea? The water is the sea."

"Yeah, I know, except that's what happened." He gazed at her, his eyes dazed. "A hell of a lot of sea is no longer in the sea."

"Okay, what do you want to do?" Still unsure what Bruce meant, she decided to trust him "Should we leave the hotel, stay here in the bathroom…what?"

"Think we should stay put. I'm going to open the door and see if there's any water in the room."

He tried to open the door and couldn't, and for a moment he contemplated breaking it down, then he noticed the lock. He had no memory of locking it. Had he thought a locked door could stop the force of water?

Unlocking and opening the door, he glanced out into the bedroom. Everything looked normal and dry. Slowly he walked toward the balcony. As soon as he reached the doorway, he saw that nothing was right. Before his eyes laid wreckage unlike anything he'd seen before. The beach was devastated, the resort ruined.

A demolition force had destroyed the tropical forests along with the beach. It looked as if a bomb had exploded. Bruce couldn't believe that just ten minutes ago this was the most beautiful place he had ever seen.

Now it was broken and smashed. Maybe not forever, but it might as well have been, at least for him. Bruce heard Liz carefully move across the bedroom floor. She then joined him in witnessing the aftermath.

"Oh my god, all this is from a wave?" she asked in shock as she wrapped her arms around his waist. She was dumbfounded with awe.

"I told you, the sea lifted. This was no

mere wave. Look over there." He pointed to what was left of a patch of palm trees. In them were the remains of splintered boats, possibly bits and pieces from the flipped yachts. "Waves don't do that."

"How could this happen?"

"Well—I heard the girl from down the hallway say something about a tsunami just before you came in."

"I didn't feel an earthquake, did you? Even one that's under water you can feel—right?"

"Yeah, I suppose, and no, I didn't feel one. But that wouldn't matter, I don't think. It could've happened hundreds of miles from here."

"Is it over?" asked Liz. "Do you think anyone died?"

"I don't know, and I'll be very surprised if no one did. I hope everyone got off the beach."

"You're not sure if it's over? You mean more may come?"

As if in answer to Liz's question, the water receded into the sea again, followed by another huge, destructive wave, coming just twenty minutes after the first.

Once again, Bruce and Liz ran for cover. She ran out of the bedroom and into the kitchen. Bruce was right behind her. He caught up, grabbed her, and pulled her into his embrace. He couldn't allow her to start panicking as he'd almost done. That would only make matters worse, maybe even deadly. "Liz, it'll be safer in the bathroom."

"No more bathroom, okay?"

Bruce nodded and sat her down on the floor, leaning against the cabinet doors. He put his arms around her as they heard colossal waves smash the resort. Screams from other guests followed each pounding.

Cries of fear and panic were everywhere.

Outside the new waves destroyed whatever had survived the first round. Their luck was running dry as they faced the destruction again and again.

"We're going to die. You know that, don't you Bruce? Those waves are just going to keep on coming and coming. They're going to drown all of us—swoosh." Liz swiped her hand. "They'll just carry everyone away. We'll never be found—poof, just gone."

"No, Liz, no, we'll be all right. We're up high enough, the water can't reach us," Bruce told her, hoping maybe she would believe him. The problem was he didn't know if he believed it himself. He assumed the bottom floors were already under water. How much longer before it reached them on the third floor?

Of course, he could not speak of these uncertainties with Liz. She needed his comfort right now and for him to tell her everything was going to be all right.

Her face was red, her eyes swollen up. Her whole body was burning hot. Watching Liz like this was the hardest part, not the thought of dying, but seeing his girl like this. Bruce wished he could make everything all right for her. If this was going to be the end, he wanted it to be easier for her.

The power was still out and like the bathroom, the only light came from the windows. Liz stood up, opened the fridge, and popped open two beers.

"Want one? Might be your last?" she said while holding out a bottle.

Taking it, Bruce said, "This is not my last. For one thing, I'm not on the wagon, and for another, I'm not dying here in a Thailand resort."

"Let's hope your right. I don't feel much like dying on Fuckit Island," she said, giving him the best smirk she had right then.

Bruce was glad to see her relax a bit, even if it was only temporary. He sat on the counter top and patted the spot next to him. She hopped up. Her face was still red and puffy, but she had stopped crying. He noticed her hand shake while she sipped her beer.

CHAPTER 7

When Jack returned from his run, Lisa was sitting at the kitchen table doing one of her covered bridge puzzles. As a girl, she'd believed they stretched across waters to aid animals in crossing. Now, she recognized them for their true beauty, understanding that each bridge reflected the town it was located in, as well as the artist or architect that designed it. Covered bridges spread across waters throughout New England. However, the Vermont bridges were her favorite. She loved all one hundred and seven of them. They reminded her of the trips she and Jack made to Vermont's foliage events, craft fairs, and harvest festivals. They went every other year or so, and she hoped to talk Jack into going again this year. The weather was unusually warm this season and maybe he'd want to go.

She looked up at her husband as he entered. The time away from Harrow might do him some good. Jack had been under an abnormal amount of stress lately. She understood his job could be stressful, but these past few days you would think Jack was a failing stockbroker, not a small town Pastor. She feared the strain was not church related, at least not directly.

It was one thing to have a bad dream every now and then, but Jack was dreaming of the Hills again, of his sister Susannah again. She knew it. Whatever he'd witnessed on that day thirty-seven years ago was so horrifying, his subconscious mind had buried it deep within its mental chest, locking and hiding it away. Except skeletons always find their keys. Nothing could stay hidden forever. Eventually everything surfaces, and for Jack, these emerging bones were the memory of Susannah.

Jack had always blamed himself, and it led to a drinking problem that lasted years.

Lisa was not entirely sure if Jack even realized he was dreaming of her again, but if he did, he was keeping it to himself. She knew the last thing Jack wanted was to worry her. Except that was exactly what he had started to do.

As much as Lisa disliked Jack's emotional disorder, she would gladly accept that over his drinking. She hoped he had not taken to the bottle once more. She couldn't fight that war again. The battles were too strong, stronger than she was now.

Jack sat down. Lisa smiled and gave him a wink. She could tell he was having one of his headaches again. She wanted to ask about them but didn't know how yet.

"How was your run?"

"Not bad, would've gone better without this lingering headache."

She nodded in sympathy. "Been having them a lot this week. Everything all right?"

"Yeah, I'm sure it's nothing serious, just one of those things. If they keep up, I'll see the doc, I promise. Until then, it's just plain old ibuprofen for me."

"Don't you go taking too much. I'll be watching the medicine cabinet," she said, hoping it sounded comical, but at the same time, she meant it.

"I can read the back of the bottle."

"I know you can read. Just don't overdo

it." She placed a puzzle piece and asked, "What should we do about lunch?"

"Why don't we go somewhere, maybe head into North Conway? We haven't eaten there in a while."

"Huh, I don't really feel like getting ready for all that. Can't we just stay home?"

"That's fine. We could eat the chicken that is left. I'll go down to Bradbury's and get what's needed for a salad."

"That works for me. Maybe this weekend we can go out. What do you think about traveling down to Portsmouth? I can't remember the last time we were out of the mountains." Lisa then took the chance and asked about the fall fairs, "Which reminds me, how do you feel about a weekend trip to Vermont soon?"

"Maybe...yeah, we'll see how this weekend goes. The maple fairs, not Portsmouth. Let's go see someone else's mountains for a change," Jack said, giving her a smile.

Getting up, he moved toward the door where Wolfgang waited impatiently. He seemed to feel comforted, knowing someone had finally noticed him. Jack looked down at him with a completely new appreciation and respect. The cat stared back at him, simply wanting out.

"We should get Wolfgang here a friend. Two cats are as easy to care for as one."

Lisa kept looking down at her puzzle, certain now that Jack had lost his mind. "Just go to the store, Tarzan. We'll talk about enlarging our wild kingdom when you get back."

He opened the door to let Wolfgang out, but before he went himself, he looked around making sure it was a bird free zone.

Lisa noticed. If she didn't know better she would suspect he owed someone money, but why would Jack owe someone money, never mind owing enough to avoid them?

It sure looked like he was trying to avoid something anyway. Of course, it could be a sign of something worse

She attached the puzzle piece in her fingers to the puzzle, pushed her chair from the table, and walked upstairs to the bedroom. Jack's sister had disappeared thirty-seven years ago, but her presence had never left Jack. The way she went missing had no doubt contributed to her husband's illness.

Lisa at first protested about naming their

daughter after her. She did not wish to insult Susannah's memory, but she couldn't stop thinking about the impact and effect it could have on Jack—afraid he would treat their daughter differently when she reached the age his sister was when she disappeared.

Jack persisted and won, and as feared, around their daughter's eleventh birthday his drinking hit rock bottom.

There was a walk-in-closet in the back corner of the bedroom. Lisa entered and quickly found her family photo albums. Bending down she took the lip off an old cardboard box and removed an even older picture of Jack's sister. She had seen this photo hundreds of times over the years and still couldn't get over the resemblance between the two Susannah's. They looked like the same person. If only she'd held her ground and named their child something else. Maybe it would have saved both Jack and their daughter some trouble.

Lisa didn't understand the Levi family's management of Susannah's premature death. She could understand them wanting to protect their son—it was a traumatizing experience for Jack, no question—but maybe it would have been better to be more honest with him from the beginning, instead of telling him his sister got lost in the woods. Jack was there.

He'd seen what really happened. He might have blocked it out, but the memories were there just the same.

Then later, his parents told him the truth about the kidnapping.

Jack still blamed himself. Susannah lost was one thing, but to watch her get kidnapped, and not able to stop it, was another. No matter Jack's age, with this issue, he would always be that little boy who woke up confused somewhere in the Harrowing Hills.

Lisa let the picture fall from her hands and, not for the first time, she started to cry.

CHAPTER 8

By the time the third and largest wave came, most of the Mai Khao beach already lay in ruin. The Island of Phuket, along with other parts of Thailand's western coast, suffered extensive damage. The waves destroyed several highly populated areas in the region and killed almost thirty-five hundred people locally, tens of thousands more throughout the wider Asian region.

On Phuket, nearly two hundred fifty people lost their lives. A large portion of those deaths occurred on the west coast side of the island where most of the major beaches were.

In total, close to three hundred thousand people were killed or missing duc to the tsunami. Its path of damage and death reached as far away as the coasts of Africa. It was the worst single tsunami in history and the ninth deadliest natural disaster in modern history.

In many places the waves reached eighty to one hundred feet high and went inland about 1.24 miles. The total energy of the tsunami waves were equivalent to five megatons of TNT, more than twice the amount of explosive energy used in all of World War II, including the two atomic bombs.

When the waves finally stopped, Bruce and Liz were grateful to be alive. The whole event took only about ninety minutes, but it was the longest ninety minutes of their lives. Bruce looked down at Liz sitting on the floor. He held out his hand and, when she took it, helped her to her feet.

"Should we go see what's left of Thailand?" Liz asked.

Bruce gave her a half-hearted smile. He remembered the damage after that first pounding and could not imagine what it looked like after another two. "Might as well. But there may not be much left to see, at least nothing that's going to make us feel any better."

Still holding hands, they left the kitchen. The dining area still looked the same, as did the rest of their room. You wouldn't know anything had happened at all. The sun was coming in through the windows. The world had not stopped or been destroyed, but for many staying in this small corner of it, it sure felt like it had.

Bruce let go of Liz's hand and walked over to the window. She decided to look from the balcony. From the window, he could see what was *not* left of the resort and beach.

The rock walls were smashed, the broad reflection ponds gone. It almost looked as if everything from the first floor, and maybe the second, was out there—mattresses, chairs, tables, everything.

If anyone had been on the beach or outside the building, Bruce couldn't see how they would have survived.

If the water hadn't gotten them, the wreckage would have.

From the balcony outside, he heard Liz give off a small, almost frightened shriek. He knew how she felt. He had suspicions this place would never be the same again.

"Bruce!" she said, coming up behind him.

He turned, hearing something strange in her voice. "What's wrong?"

Her eyes looked frozen and more terrified than at any point during the hour-and-a-half tsunami.

"Outside." She paused, swallowing hard. "There's something outside—on the balcony"

He walked over and wrapped his arms around her.

"I know, it's awful. We'll leave here as soon as we can."

She pulled back and looked at him. "On the balcony there's...something—not real—" She shook her head. "It can't be real."

Not understanding, he frowned. "Not real? What do you mean, not real? Don't you mean unreal?"

Liz shook her head no.

Stepping away from her, he headed toward the balcony. How could something be *not* real?

But with everything Liz had been through today, her reaction was normal. Bruce just hoped some wreckage had found its way to them, not a dead body.

"I'm sure it's just mangled debris—" He stopped cold in mid-sentence, even colder in his tracks. He now saw what she had—he now saw what lay on the balcony.

PART II

ANGEL DUST

"If I must die, I will encounter
darkness as a bride,
And hug it in mine arms."

William Shakespeare

CHAPTER 9

October 14th:

On the second Wednesday of every month, Harrow held a benefit dinner for the voluntary fire department out of Clayton. Like most towns in the area, Harrow and Clayton were too small for their own fire departments, so instead the communities shared one.

Tonight's meal was spaghetti and meatballs, and like always, Father Sean O'Brien was the first in line to help. His chosen place tonight, the meatball and sauce pot.

The Monthly event took place in the grade school cafeteria. Friends and members from almost every neighborhood gather to talk and eat.

Around the room members of the school faculty talk to parents and students, a town selectman teasingly poked fun at the gas station attendant, while a tongue-tied mail carrier awkwardly flirted with a clerk from Bill's Market.

Jack and Lisa sat facing each other half way down the first row of tables. They were fortunate enough to get end seats this time. Sitting next to Lisa was Bill and Rose Watson. Jack could not recall a childhood memory that did not include Bill. But over the years, their paths had gone in different directions and today they were just short of strangers. Even though they saw each other once or twice a week, not much more than the polite hello had passed between the two for years.

Sitting next to Jack was one of the families from his congregation. The Nolans had three children, two boys and a girl, all between the ages of five and nine years old. Mr. Nolan sat next to Jack, his children filled in the spots between him and his wife.

Mrs. Nolan was a chatterbox and talked constantly. From the corner of his eye, Jack could see her sharp pointed chin and lips move endlessly and heard that high-pitched squeaky voice talk incessantly about trivial subjects to *anyone* around the table. Tonight, that voice of hers went right through him.

In the kitchen, Father O'Brien noticed the man responsible for the dinner, Horton Mudgett, in line for some himself. As the line moved forward, Horton made his way up to O'Brien. "Thank you again, Father, for your help. It's much appreciated." Horton reached out his hand. O' Brien shook it as the two exchanged smiles.

"Always glad to help. Looks like a decent crowd tonight."

"Not too bad. Wish more nights were like this. People cannot always make it, I understand that."

"They make it when they can. Let us not think about last month or worry about next. They are here now, that's all that matters," said Father O'Brien

"True, true, we both know they don't have to come. Everyone has a stove at home. I am thankful for each and every hungry mouth, and let's face it, Father, no one comes for the food." He leaned close, covering his mouth. "I eat the wife's cooking every night," he said and chuckled.

"Good evening, Ms. Mudgett."

Horton whipped around, expecting to find his wife standing behind him. "Ha, ha, Father. I'll keep you in mind come the first of April." A friendly smirk appeared on his face.

"I've eaten your wife's cooking many a time, and agreed, she's no Giada De Laurentiis, but she's no Mrs. Lockhorns, neither."

"Mrs. Lockbourne? I'm afraid I don't know her," Horton confessed.

"Lockhorns, as in the comic strip," replied the Father.

"Why am I not surprised you read the funnies?"

Horton looked down the table. The line was getting bigger, and he was slowing things up. He thanked the Father, shook his hand again, and moved on to greet more guests.

O'Brien enjoyed helping with these dinners. It gave him the chance to see everyone. On Sundays, he could not get as much time with everyone as he wished. Here, he could do what he just did. Talk and have fun. He would start to make rounds among the room as soon as he could.

John Moore, the town's Chief of Police, and his family were coming up the line. He wondered how their son, Thomas, was holding up after the disappearance of his friend over the weekend. Jason Benson was the fourth kid, the first one from Harrow, to go missing from the region in the past three months. Sadly, the unthinkable may have happened to them all.

O'Brien hoped everyone here tonight would have the decency not to bring up the somber event, at least not near the boy.

As they reached him, he smiled and welcomed the family warmly. "Well if it isn't the Moore Clan."

"Hello, Father," said Thomas.

"Hello, young Mister Moore. How are you this evening?"

"Wish I was home watching TV,"

"TV—No, that thing will rot your brains," said O'Brien.

"Noooo it won't, that's just a joke. I asked my teacher. It won't make you go blind either," answered Thomas.

Looking at Chief Moore and his son, O'Brien smiled "You should read more Thomas, it's better for you."

"I have to read in school. I want to watch TV at home," Thomas defended. "I also have homework. Mrs. Wentworth gives me too much."

Thomas waited, wondering if he said too much.

"Homework's important, even though I'll have to agree, teachers give too much of it these days," O'Brien said. This seemed to get Thomas back in his corner some.

"Yeah, me too!" said Thomas. "I spend all day at school doing class work. Why do I have to do it at home, too? It's not fair."

"Because you do, that's why," Jane Moore said.

"Why? Dad doesn't bring his work home. Why do I have to?" replied Thomas.

To Thomas, school and his father's job were equal things, except Thomas did not realize just how much his father actually did bring home with him. O'Brien decided it might be a good idea to change the subject. He knew where this could end up.

"So, where is young Candice tonight?" he asked opening another rocky topic without knowing it. He was batting a thousand with the Moore family. Where was the safety net with this family tonight?

"That one, we have no idea. Honestly, I

don't know what to do about her," answered Jane.

"Oh, is something wrong?"

"Yeah, she's sixteen and hates that her father's the police chief," added John.

"That can be a rough age, particularly for girls, and I think most teens would dislike their dad being the town's lead lawman," said O'Brien.

Little Tommy looked at his parents and decided it was worth the risk. "I think she needs an exosist."

His dad looked down. "Did you mean an exorcist, Thomas?"

"That's what I said!"

"Your sister doesn't need an exorcist," said O'Brien, "What she needs is time. The devil of puberty can't be cast out."

Both the adult Moore's showed their embarrassment. They could not believe what their son had just said to a priest, their priest. They apologized and then told Thomas to do the same. Of course, O'Brien told them it was okay, even a little funny.

He finished topping off their plates, and the family started to move on. He made a mental note to avoid that land mine for the rest of the night. Nevertheless, he was glad young Thomas was not depressed over the Benson boy, but then again, he was young and it had only been a few days. Sadly, it would hit him soon enough.

As the Moore family walked down the aisle of tables, they passed Jack. John nodded hello while looking for an opening. Jack raised a hand in acknowledgement, but his attention fell more on Thomas, and he once again thought of the nightmares.

The dreams had been coming and going over the past few weeks, but it wasn't until the past few nights that they became so realistic that he could smell, taste, and feel them after he woke. Jack had begun to fear that madness haunted his mind and projected itself in the form of large, glossy, blue-black birds with raucous cries. Those dirty and vile birds had troubled his every thought and move. These vexatious, wretchedly loathsome creatures had caused him sleepless nights, and now, they followed him into the daylight.

Simply the sight of one drove him into a panic. His heart raced and a cold strike shocked him to the core. A sharp pain to the head made him unable to think, move, or speak, and his eyes burned as if on fire.

Was this fear irrational? Would anyone understand this abnormal fretfulness, this paranoia toward birds? No—not birds, ravens, always the raven.

Jack wished he could speak with someone, but whom, his wife? She would at least try to understand. Father O'Brien? Although Jack and Sean had become great friends over the years, and tried to be the each other's break from the clergy life, keeping their time together separate from their devotion. Talking to O' Brien might cause Jack complications.

No, Jack could not allow anyone to know about this disorder, that he was showing signs of paranoia. How could he give his sermons? He wouldn't be trusted anymore, and in time, he would lose his congregation. He could lose everything to this fear. No, Jack decided he must keep this to himself.

John Moore and his family found an opening near the end of the second row and took a seat. Although this family did not know it, this would be their last restless meal for a while.

Eric Henson

There was trouble on the horizon and the town's Chief of Police was about to have his hands full.

CHAPTER 10

The last of the tsunami waves hit about ten hours ago. In that time rescue personnel had arrived. The resort's damage was not as bad as in other parts of the island. The judgment made was that, for now, keeping the guests in the resort was safer. The first floor guests were now sharing rooms with some of the second and third guests. Liz and Bruce had so far been lucky and were still alone in their room—with the exception of what they found on the balcony.

The discovery had first appeared to be a giant—maybe even Jurassic—sized bird. The thing was five times larger than the foot-and-a-half Archaeopteryx, but it could have still been from the same family and period. However, it ended up being even older, and more incredible, than that. They had discovered something believed to be piously pure and eternal.

The finding of a primitive bird that lived

one hundred fifty million years ago would have been easier to believe and understand than the discovery of an angel. That was just too unbelievable, but nonetheless, there it was.

Candlelight now lit the bedroom. Its golden glow spread across the walls and furniture, and long shadows stretched away from the flames. The remainder of the suite lay in darkness. Outside, emergency helicopters flew around searching for anyone in need of help. With the curtains closed, Bruce and Liz reduced the risk of any one seeing what lay on their bed.

When they first discovered the thing, both of them had been too nervous to go near it. After a while, they decided it was in their best interest to move him inside—something surprisingly harder than expected.

The angel, although looking about the same size as Bruce, weighed much more, and instead of carrying him off the balcony as they planned, Bruce and Liz dragged him off. On the floor near the bed, the two of them rolled the angel onto a blanket. They folded the blanket in two and, together, heaved the being up and laid it on the bed.

Now hours later the shock, and the angel, were still there.

He rested on his back. His grayed left wing stretched across the bed and appeared to be broken, while the other laid flat underneath him. This being was alive. Although not awake, he had moved, and once, his black, marbleized eyes had stared up from his angelic face. If he actually saw anything, they could not tell. He made no reaction other than mumbling in some unknown tongue.

Liz sat in a chair behind the foot of the bed. She did not want to get any closer. She believed it could be an angel, but the word "thing" kept coming to mind. She tried to stop thinking that way, but she could not. To her this thing just couldn't be real. This was not what Cupid looked like. Where was the cute, chubby cherub with his little bow and arrows of love. She had seen angels on Christmas cards, in movies, and in paintings. She'd seen the sculptures and, as most people do, assumed she knew what one looked like.

However, her mental image was not what washed up on the balcony. This thing looked more like a warrior than a spiritual being.

Was this what really acted as an attendant to and messenger of God?

She got up from the chair and walked into the living area. Bruce stood in front of the same window as he had when she discovered the angel.

As he watched people below and copters above, he thought about how they planned to leave the next day. Now they were stuck here awhile. Even if the airport were untouched, the Thailand government would be using it for search and rescue only.

Outside many of the guests were walking around investigating and taking pictures of the destruction. Acting like it was now just another day of vacation. Bruce could almost hear them saying stupid little things like, "Look kids, a boat in a tree," and "Oh wow, that whole patch of forest is down," followed by "Hey guys, remember when a building stood there yesterday!"

Bruce found it interesting how people acted when the danger was over and gone. The same people who just a few hours ago were screaming and crying, fearing for their lives, were now comparing stories, telling what they had seen, and bragging about how much closer to death they came—saying stupid asinine things like, "God must've saved me for a reason" and "He must have some greater purpose for me." They should try telling that to the man a few miles down the beach who just lost his whole family. Explain to him how much more important *they* were than his wife and kids. That man would probably drown them himself, or at least he should.

Liz walked up behind Bruce and wrapped her arms around his waist. She then looked out the window to see what he was looking at.

He glanced at her but said nothing of his current thoughts. She hated his cynical side and he knew it.

"What you looking at? Our great and improved view of the ocean?"

"No, just thinking it was probably a waste of time coming here, from a business point of view, that is. I wonder how our rubber tree man is faring. Think he has any left?" He turned away from the window. "How is our guest? Any change?"

Liz looked back in the direction of the bedroom where low dancing shadows flickered off the walls. Those shadows made her nervous.

"No change."

He wondered how what seemed to be an angel could be on their balcony in the first place. If it was a warning about the quake and tsunami, it had failed.

"Should we call for someone, a priest maybe?" asked Liz. "Even with all that's going on outside, this is bigger."

"I really don't know what to do. I wish we could call Father O'Brien from back home. He's the only person I can think of that we could trust with something like this."

He walked away, stood by the bedroom door, and stared in, wishing he knew what to do. This was something that would change the world. What he was looking at, if it was in fact real, was evidence, actual proof that a supernatural God did, in fact, exist. That could turn out to be very good—or very, very bad. There was no way of knowing how people would react to something like this. Who even knew how the church would react? And what about the government? If they got hold of it first, they would probably treat it as an extraterrestrial and dissect it.

Maybe Liz was right, maybe he was a little too cynical. He stepped into the room. This one had more candles than in any other part of the suite. If this angel woke and decided to get up, Bruce wanted to see every move it made. Maybe this angel was no angel at all. You could not believe everything you heard in Sunday school. Bruce shook his head again and thought, *This will change the world.*

Liz followed him into the bedroom.

CHAPTER 11

The man and woman's conversations seeped into Ezziel's dreams. Horrendous memories of war and death tormented the unconscious fallen angel. The humans' voices flashed out of the flames and drifted within the scent of brimstone as Ezziel's mind tortured itself.

He dreamed of warfare in Hell.

Through bursts of fire, he saw his friends' demise waiting. The sight of Báalzbub replaced their hope with dread and dejection.

Ezziel, with small periods of semi-consciousness, became only slightly aware of the humans in the next room before falling back into unconsciousness.

Hearing screams from the slaughtered, seeing the carnage as Báalzbub and his horde cut them off—and then cut them down. The angel tossed in bed, rocking his head from one side to the other, rehearing the anguishing sounds coming from the front lines. Penetrating shrieks from the Horde filled his head, collapsing his mind farther into fear and panic.

Standing in the back of the bedroom, Bruce and Liz watched their guest. His body language and actions made it clear he was having a nightmare. His movements in this low light added to the creepiness. Bruce sat down in one of the chairs along the back wall. The table he kept his laptop on was to his right, and the door back to the living area was just beyond it.

He wanted to keep as close to that door as he could, just in case. Looking over the table, he reached up to turned on the lamp.

Nothing happened. He could not believe he just tried to turn on a powerless lamp.

"You forget about the power?"

"Watching this in the dark makes me a little uneasy."

Liz sat next to Bruce. It was true, if the power were on, this would be easier. Candle-light could be romantic, but at this moment, they could do without it.

Bruce glanced back at the table.

"You're not about to try that lamp again are you?" she asked.

"No, of course not, but I was just thinking that maybe I can get a signal. I think I'll try the computer." He got up and walked over to the end of the table, opened the laptop, and pressed the power button. Little green circles lit up and the soft start-up beeping sounded as the computer began to boot up. "So far, all looks good."

"What should we do about him? I mean, really, at some point somebody is going to notice him. We have been lucky so far with everyone too busy to pay us any attention, but eventually, were going to have to leave this room, or someone is going to want to come in. At some point, we're going to be flown off this island. So what do we do or say about—" She pointed to the bed. "—him?"

"I don't know! We will figure that out then. Unless we have to, we won't say anything. We'll just leave—let someone else deal with this."

"*Just leave*! I'm not so sure that's even an option. We both know what is resting, and probably dying, on that bed. We need some-one from the church. I wish your priest was here, but he is not. Bruce, we can't leave him here for just anyone to find."

"I know, but—" He lifted both hands up-ward. "—what are we supposed to do? Just walk up to the local holy man, one that may not even speak English, and say, 'Hey, see, we have this angel, and well, we think it is an angel. Could you, maybe, take him off our hands like some unwanted dog? You could? Excellent follow me to my room.'"

"Come on Bruce, we have enough going on right now without you acting like that. I'm only asking. I don't expect you to walk up to just anyone, or e-mail them for that matter, but we have to think of something, and I'm guessing soon, that's all."

Bruce was still working on the computer as he listened to Liz.

He knew how frightened she was. He was, too, and he understood what stress could do to people. He needed to make it a point not to snap and get overly sarcastic with her.

This wasn't her fault.

"I'm not getting anywhere with this damn

thing, but it was worth a try...sorry. And sorry about a minute ago. I'm just a little edgy."

"I know. It's all right."

"...zbub."

Bruce froze in mid-motion of closing his laptop and looked at Liz, hoping she just spoke. He was not ready for anything else. Liz's eyes were wide in shock, looking in the direction of the bed. Bruce slowly started to turn, not knowing what to expect. Maybe the angel would be sitting up, or getting up, maybe walking toward them. He had no idea. Facing the bed, Liz and Bruce both just stared.

Nothing looked different. The angel still just lay there.

"Did you just hear something?" Bruce asked.

"I more than just heard something, I saw something. That thing just spoke. I watched his lips move and everything, but I have no idea what he just said. I think we should go back in the other room, we should ju—"

"*What*? No. I need to hear what he's trying to say. Think about it. It could be really important."

"Yeah, it could. It also could be really

dangerous. We have *no* idea why this thing is even here. If it's the end of the world, I'd rather be surprised."

"Liz, I hardly doubt it's the end of the world."

"*Really*? Have you taken a look outside lately? It's sure the end of something."

"Okay. I'm staying here, at least for a few more minutes. If you need to go into the other room, I understand. That's probably for the best anyway. If this thing wakes and you freak on him, who knows how he might react."

Liz got up from her chair and walked to Bruce. "I'm scared Bruce, and I want this all to be over with. Why did we have to find this thing? I don't want the responsibility. Maybe you're right. Maybe we should just leave it."

He wrapped his arms around her and felt her tremble. The last thing, the absolutely last thing, he wanted to do was upset her, and he wished he could make all this go away for her. He wished she never had to feel as she had this day, and he would do whatever it took to make sure she never did again.

"I know your scared, hon. So am I. This whole thing is unfair, and I promise this will all be over soon. In a few days this nightmare will be over, and the two of us will be back home in Boston, where the only important thing is who we're inviting to the wedding. Just think about that, just think about home and the wedding."

He pulled her closer. She hid her face in his chest. She wouldn't cry again today. Moving slowly back, she looked up at Bruce.

"Sorry about that." She smiled, feeling a little better. "I didn't expect to hear him speak, not even that small amount, but I guess he would. It's only a matter of time before he wakes up. That is unless he dies."

"Báalzbub..."

Both Liz and Bruce's bodies jolted. A feeling like cold electricity ran along their spines and down their legs.

Protective, Bruce moved Liz behind him and watched the winged thing on the bed.

Still, he just lay there, rocking his head back and forth and mumbling. The words were incoherent, but Bruce knew the angel was trying saying something. Bruce moved away from Liz and toward the bed. The words became louder and spoken in a language he couldn't understand.

Reaching the bed, he slowly lowered onto his knees and leaned forward to listen. The candle next to him flickered, causing his already uneasy heart to jump.

"Sariel"

"What is he saying? Can you understand any of it?" Liz whispered from across the room.

Bruce quickly put his right hand up in the signal to stop then moved one finger to his lips quieting her. Then the angel spoke a word that made Bruce more frightened than ever before, a word he would never have anticipated.

"Harrow."

CHAPTER 12

Bruce, think about it for a second. Why would he say Harrow? Harrow is just some small town in New Hampshire. You didn't hear 'Harrow.' Please don't do this."

After hearing the name of his hometown, Bruce had kicked away from the bed and run into the living room.

Now he sat, shaking, on the couch with his hands pressed to each side of his face, leaning over.

"Harrow, he said Harrow. You don't understand Liz. Harrow isn't a normal place. It's haunted. Some even say evil. We need to warn someone."

"Warn someone? And just what do you plan to say? Bruce, please think. Maybe it only said something that sounded like Harrow. You misunderstood. I'm sure it didn't mean your hometown."

He looked up. She saw a look of realization flash across his face and knew something she just said registered with him. A wave of relief ran through her. She needed him strong.

Bruce had always been the strong one, and if he started panicking, there would be no hope for her.

"Maybe, yeah...just maybe. I hope you're right."

"And, even if he did say harrow, harrow is more than just your hometown, right?" She paused for a second. "I believe it's some kind of farming equipment, or something."

Bruce looked at her, trying to decide if she was joking—*farming equipment?* "Ah, yeah, it is, but why an angel would mumble about breaking up plowed land is beyond me. It has to be something else."

"I didn't *mean* he was mumbling about farming. That's as unlikely as mumbling about your hometown. All I meant was it could mean anything." She paused again. She remembered another meaning for harrow. "Well, harrow means..."

"What?"

"Doesn't harrow mean to inflict great distress or torment on?"

"That's harrowing."

"Harrowing means extremely distressing and agonizing, which I suppose pretty much is the same thing."

"You're not making me feel better you know."

"What are we doing? Forget about stupid definitions. Your hometown was probably named after the Borough in London?"

"My hometown is older," Bruce said as he stood up and walked to the bedroom doorway again. A light scent of sulfur mixed in with the dimming sandal wood candles. Had he smelled it before? He guessed he must have. Odd he was only now recognizing it.

"I know you were only trying to help, hon. Thank you, but another question has come to mind." He stopped and looked at the angel. "How do we even know this is, in fact, an angel? We see wings and assume angel, but aren't demons just fallen angels? Who really knows what either one actually looks like? I'm not sure I do."

Liz rubbed her mouth and shook her head. She would not, could not, think about that. She needed this to be an angel, so it was an angel. That was that. "I believe it's an angel. I do not believe we have a demon in our hotel room. I just can't consider that."

"Then why do I smell sulfur, as in brimstone. I'm getting a bad feeling about this, worse than I already had. I no longer feel safe here—What if this thing caused the tsunami?"

Liz saw his eyes starting to water. She walked over, and took him by the hands.

"How many people do you think died today? How many more are hurt and lost?" he asked.

She, too, now smelled sulfur, and she had not before. She chose not to mention this. "I don't know and don't want to think about it." She gave his hands a light squeeze. "Bruce, we have had a very stressful day, and we're both mentally and physically worn out. I think we should try and relax. Everything will become a lot clearer when we can think better."

Bruce nodded his head, knowing there was nothing they could do right now, other than leaving the room. And that was starting to feel more and more like a wise plan. Whether they ended up leaving this hotel tonight or not, regardless of what ended up happening with Harvey Birdman tomorrow—one way or another, he would get Liz off this god-forsaken island.

CHAPTER 13

October 15th:

*Tommyyy...*is what Thomas thought he just heard. Sitting up in bed, listening, he thought at first it was only the wind. Sometimes it would whistle through the sides of the windows, making all kinds of scary sounds. When Thomas was younger he would go running and crying into his mom and dad's room, but that was last year. Now Tommy thought of himself as a big boy, and he was not doing that anymore.

Looking around his room, Tommy really thought he heard his name, not just some noise, his actual name. Then he reminded himself that he had heard things before.

Thomas wished that soft whispering sound had only been the wind. The problem Thomas had with that was that it sounded so much like Jason.

Thomas missed Jay, and wished he knew

where he was. His parents told him something bad had happened to his friend. They said he had gone missing. When Thomas asked what that meant, his father asked him if he remembered those other kids that had been in the news—the ones mommy had talked to him about. Thomas told him that he did, that someone bad might have taken them. That was when his father told Thomas that some bad person might have taken Jason, too.

Thomas did not want to believe him, but his dad was the police and the police would know something like that. His father also told him that he did not want him going near the Harrowing Hills, or its ballpark, for a while.

Thomas did not think this was fair. That was where he, Jason, and Ronnie always played. Where were they supposed to go? Then Thomas saw that his father was upset—not mad, but sad? That was when he figured out where they found Jay's bike.

Thomas still could not understand how his best friend could just disappear.

After listening in the dark for a few more minutes, Thomas decided it had been the wind after all. It was October, and the wind always made noise this time of year. That was what mom and dad told him, last year, when he went running into their room. That was then. He was older now, and he was not afraid of the dark or some stupid spooky wind anymore. He only heard his name because it was his name. If his name were Frank, he would have heard Frankie, if John, then Johnny. That was all it was.

"*Frankiee...*"

Thomas looked toward the window again. Did he just hear what he thought he just heard? Did he just hear the name Frankie? He was older now, so why was he still hearing these stupid little kid things?

Then he considered that maybe someone was playing a trick on him. His sister's friends often came around late at night, like that stupid Bobby Benito. Maybe he and some of the other, bigger kids were just messing around, having a little Halloween fun early this year. His sister Candice could even be out there with them. She had been acting strange lately, even for her, and if that was how teenagers acted, then Thomas didn't want to be one.

Then he wondered how Candice and her friends could have known what he was thinking. Whispering his name, that was easy, it was his name, but whispering something, something he thought. That didn't make any sense.

The wind rattled the windows. This time Thomas felt the coldness come through and hated the fall wind and the chills that came with it.

"*Thomas*!"

The sudden calling of his name again caused him to gasp and jump back, away from the voice. He spun around, looking over his right shoulder. The sound came from right behind him this time, almost in his ear. Though Thomas saw nothing, he still pushed himself to the back of the bed, only stopping because the footboard made him.

The voice came from right in the room— not the wind, or from anything else outside his windows, but from right next to his bed.

His eyes opened wide in fright.

The room was dark and everything looked like something else. Thomas could almost see black shapes floating in the dark—squiggly, zigzag forms that hovered in mid-air. He reached out to touch one, but nothing was there.

Between his heart pounding, and his deep breathing through his nose, he couldn't hear anything else in the room. He reached out again for one of those floating shapes when something moved near his closet door.

"Who's there? This isn't funny anymore!" he said, trying not to sound scared. But he failed.

He got no answer.

Thomas held his breath in hopes of hearing a little better, but it only made his heart sound louder. He looked around the room, keeping the closet area in mind. The room was so dark, the only light came from the moon outside. He regretted now giving up that night light last year—he was a big boy now—and sure wished he had it back.

He brought his attention back to the closet and noticed the door opened a bit. His vision had adjusted since he first woke up. He knew that door wasn't open a few seconds ago. He was certain, in fact.

He remembered his mother closing it after she put away his action figures before he went to bed. Thomas even heard the door click as it shut. No matter how that door got opened, even only a bit, it made Thomas nervous.

He stared at it, unable to move and close it, afraid to go near it. He wanted to yell for his mother, but instead asked, "Is someone in my closet?" Hoping no one was there to answer.

Thomas was so scared his hands and feet hurt. An odd feeling of coldness traveled from his head and down his back as the familiar noise of small metal cars tinkering together came from the closet.

"Is someone in—there?"

A soft little giggle responded as a little metal car rolled out of the closet and toward Thomas's bed.

"Want to play cars with me, Tommy?"

Thomas no longer cared if he was a big boy or not, did not care if his sister made fun of him. He jumped off the bed and ran straight into his parent's room. Later Thomas would not remember jumping off the bed, or even touching his bedroom floor for that matter. He would have no memory of yelling for his mother as he raced down the upstairs hallway.

However, what he would remember was his missing friend rolling a car out of his closet, wanting to play.

CHAPTER 14

The Harrowing Hills State Park was a family camping and picnic area. Come summer time, this park would be booked every weekend, with the long holiday weekends reserved months in advance.

On holiday weekends the population of the area more than doubled. The only benefit of all the out-of-state-annoyance was the money in their pockets. Without this income, many businesses in Harrow would shut down. They could not depend solely on the local populace for business. Still, residents complained all season long about those out-of-staters. The extra people walking around caused more of a traffic jam than their automobiles did.

There were many sensible reasons for picking the White Mountain National Forest for a family vacation. However, the popular stories of the haunted Harrowing Hills should not have been one of them. Nevertheless, these rumors had traveled throughout New England, and beyond, and the people came because of them.

Most of the families that enjoyed the Park did not believe in, or even know about, the urban legends. But plenty of people did and they came, especially around the end of October.

The Park "officially" closed after the second weekend in September, but the State rented out a small section to the town for their haunted Harroween hayride. This hayride was the largest part of the Harrowing of Harrow, which was the town's biggest festival of the year.

A horse and carriage hauled people through the bedecked streets of Harrow, warming them up for the true enticement of horrors, the dark and haunted Harrowing Hills.

Waiting for these unsuspecting buggies were dozens of Harroween spook puppeteers and their "shock n' mock" hands to turn their nights into frights.

Part of the leased area included a limited number of campsites. Those who dared to sleep in Harrow's troubled woods could, at an unpleasant price. These costly spots went fast, but that didn't stop the camping. More than a few sneaked off into the closed areas, wanting to experience the real, non-chaperoned woods of New England's darkest hills, to explore where they believed real evil lurked.

However, not everything of interest happened in the Hills. Some things transpired right in Harrow itself.

First Jason Benson went missing from the park, making him the fourth area-child to disappear. Then there was Simon Allen. His outlandish behavior started as soon as he walked out of his apartment and into Rose Watson's so-called life.

When Rose first saw Simon walking down Sheridan Street, the two things she should have noticed were, one, that Simon was wearing nothing but boxer shorts, in mid-October, and two, how filthy he looked. She failed to notice both of these.

In fact, Rose didn't give the young man much thought at all. She was out walking her dog after all, which was in much need of its morning nature call. The dog, Max, an American Pit Bull Terrier, was in search of the proper spot and did not see Simon at all.

Rose, the dog leash in one hand, and the pooper-scooper in the other, had her mind on the day ahead—and the night before. This by far was her least favorite part of the day, and the slight chill to the October air only made it worse. True, it wasn't as bad as it would become in another month or so, but still bad enough. Slowly Rose and Max headed in the Simon's direction.

If she'd been paying a little more attention to what was up ahead, instead of what the dog was trying to do below, Rose might have noticed the odd stagger in Simon's steps, maybe even how wet and thick the dirt looked. Instead, her thoughts drifted to Billy, her husband, still warm in bed, and she was lost in the wishing that one day he would get off his lazy ass and walk this damn dog himself. Not that Rose ever could, or would, speak up. It was better to walk the dog herself, safer anyway.

Max was first to pay attention to Simon as he walked into their path. The dog became alert, after picking up that something was wrong with the man. Max was able to smell a number of things coming off this human male, two of which were blood and madness. But the third smell—death—was worse.

His instinct was to protect his female master. Standing his ground and growling, Max tried to intimidate Simon. But Simon did not stop or flee, in fact, he increased his pace.

Rose finally noticed what Max already knew as she caught the intense look in the eyes of the undressed, blood-drenched stranger. Focusing on her dog, Rose held the leash as tight as she could when Max—a medium sized dog weighing about fifty-five pounds—started to pull her across the sidewalk.

Her pleas and commands for Max to stop were useless, and Rose did the only thing she could. She let the leash go and watched in shock as her Max attacked Simon.

Watching Max jump at the man was awful, but watching the man leap back was even worse. The stranger kicked Max, forcefully and repeatedly. Rose cried out as Max fell to the ground with a whimper, and she continued to cry out as he stood over her Max and started to stomp.

The strength of this medium sized dog

was no match for the force of this enraged and insane man. Rose saw Max make a pathetic attempt at escape, only to have Simon stop this sad effort with another hard kick, depositing Max back on the cement.

In despair, Rose turned and ran, screaming for help.

CHAPTER 15

Hidden by darkness, a large nefarious horde traveled low and fast above the Andaman Sea, releasing a low buzz as they skimmed the surface. Their reverberation forced marine life to plunge into sudden deep dives, killing many of them.

Báalzbub picked up Ezziel's trail. The hunt led him to a place where talking monkeys believed everything was about them. Where invisible dots, and the invisible dot they managed to survive on, amounted to nothing more than a pebble on the Infinite Mountain called the Universe.

And that incalculable mountain would soon be crumbling down.

As The Black One drew nearer, Báalzbub felt his plans slipping away. For billions of years this devil secretly moved others around like pawns, preparing for what the demons called the final destiny of the Gods.

Knowing energy was indestructible,

Báalzbub theorized it could be converted or neutralized. He started preparations, and those began not with the war in Heaven, but in Hell.

Báalzbub forced an order of demons called the Valkyrja into war. Like the future war in Heaven, all legions of the Valkyrja were cast out. Needing refuge, the Valkyrja swore an allegiance to The Light.

Immediately placed under the watchful eye of Sariel, they were sent into compulsory isolation. This ordered quarantine was to avoid the spread of something considered dangerous, but the segregation was for the Valkyrja's protection as well.

Many of the angels did not trust their loyalty. Members of both the Heavenly Host and the Hierarchy of Angels disapproved of their presence, believing it was only a matter of time before they proved where their true devoutness remained. Seeing the Sariel's demons as an enemy still, divisions of the military and non-military angels alike protested, demanding exile of the newly "risen" demons, proclaiming they were forced out and did not choose to leave. The Mount of Assembly disagreed, announcing the Valkyrja deserved the right to prove themselves.

Some members of the Heavenly Host disagreed, considered their options, and discussed the once-unthinkable. They made a final, and lethal, decision.

Determined not to allow Darkness into The Light, they formed a rebellion under The Light-Bearer, better known as Lucifer. His mixture of energy and emotion, added to his charisma and influence, made him their perfect leader. Under the strength of his command, they persuaded others to join their cause.

As tensions grew between the rebels and the Mount of Assembly, Báalzbub convinced Lucifer that the Valkyrja planned to overthrow the Mount of Assembly and create a realm where they would have supremacy. That was what caused the War in Hell.

Believing action was the only way to save The Light, the rebellion declared war on the Mount of Assembly—to save it. For nine long days, the angels battled one another in civil war, brother killing brother. Carnage saturated the Heavens as flames set it ablaze. Ashen bodies filled the golden paradise.

Sariel ordered the Valkyrja not to get involved. They were only to defend themselves. Sariel, however, battled, and her bloodshed and butchery earned her the title of Angel of Death. But to Lucifer's forces, Sariel was the Death of Angels, massacring them without mercy, without pity. Unable to deny their nature, the Valkyrja's flew above, exhilarated by her bloodbath, but never engaged in the battle. When attacked, which happened repeatedly, they chose to retreat, unwilling to defend themselves. Although many of them fell, they did not want to add to the dilemma. Understanding that if they killed any angel, even in self-defense, it would still be *them* killing an angel and giving the rebellion and, more importantly, Báalzbub, what they needed. The Valkyrja would prove themselves loyal to The Light, to Sariel, even if it led to their own demise.

In the end, the rebellion lost, and those who survived the revolt were cast into exile. Believing Sariel and her demons of death would come for them, and without any other place to go, the banished fled to Hell and to those they hated most of all, making Báalzbub's transformation complete.

Now, some of those very angels could be

his downfall. The Gods of Light and Darkness must not learn of the Phantom God or his messenger. If they did, all would be lost for this devil, the one true betrayer of them all.

Both dreams and nightmares were people's thoughts and imagination at work during sleep. People liked to believed their dreams could come true, but what about their nightmares?

Where did dreams end and nightmares begin?

"Ezziel—Where's Abaddon?"

Jolted, Bruce looked toward the bedroom and listened. Unsure if he'd actually heard something or not.

From the bedroom came a thumbing sound that took Bruce a few seconds to register. The Angel was hitting the mattress.

"I asked you a question, moth!"

Every muscle in Bruce's body froze. Something was in there, something other than the angel. Breaking his temporary paralysis, Bruce looked to see if Liz heard, as more thumping came from the room.

Softy she asked, "What's going on?"

He motioned for her to keep her voice down. "Something else is in the suite—in there!"

"Another angel? Can they find one another?"

Moving closer to Liz, Bruce answered, "I know as much about them as you do, maybe less."

From the bedroom came a terrorized voice, "Don't know...We were separated. Abaddon could be anywh—" Ezziel abruptly gagged.

The pounding sound became louder. Liz looked at Bruce. Something broke—a lamp, a picture frame—Bruce made a bad decision and ran into the bedroom.

As if in a dream, Liz watched Bruce enter the room.

She heard a commotion and an uncanny, echoic voice. "Join your dismembered apostates!"

Then a thunderous blow bent the wall inward, shaking the suite. The ceiling split as plaster fell to the floor. Liz could see blood dripping through the cracked wall.

Remembering that Bruce went in there, she ran into the bedroom.

When Bruce first entered the room, the only thing he could see was that the balcony door was open. Then he noticed the living nightmare holding the angel by the throat above the bed.

Bruce couldn't believe his eyes. Being's such as these did not exist in real life—maybe within mythology and theology—not here in his hotel suite.

But his nose confirmed what his eyes told him as a stronger, more prominent smell of sulfur filled the room. The thing attacking the angel took a step backward, looked at Bruce, then back at the angel. "Join your dismembered apostates!"

The nightmare threw the angel across the room, implanting him into the wall. Before the angelic being could fall from the hole, a spear of flame flashed as the demon stepped forward and drove it under the angels chin, it exited through the back of the head, killing him instantly.

The demon removed the spear, swung left, and faced Bruce. Large compound eyes looked at him as the thing's mandibles opened exposing sharp, rending teeth. Its massive chitinous endo-exoskeletal body readied for attack. As the thing shifted position, the dim moonlight brought the devil better into view. What first appeared solid black became a mixture of iridescent colors, as metallic-blue and emerald-green flickered in the exoskeleton, chitin body.

Heavy breathing and wrath traveled from the beast, its whitened eyes filled with fury.

Movement caught Bruce's attention as other, smaller, hardened, humanoid organisms crawled across the walls and ceiling. As they moved forward, he heard their claws grip and mandibles clatter within the shifting air under their wings.

From behind, Bruce felt Liz's presence as she entered the room.

CHAPTER 16

Liz entered the room and saw Bruce standing ten feet from something with large, black, membranous wings and the arachnid-armored body of a scorpion.

She averted her eyes from the beast toward the long trail of blood leading from the indented wall to the body of the angel on the floor. The wounds in its head spread wider before her eyes, decaying in chemical action. Liz looked back to the insectile fiend. Held in its large segmented arms was the weapon that killed the angel, then the spear capable of burning and corroding living tissue disappeared.

Though the actual word "demon" never entered Liz's mind, she knew that was what stood in the room. Bruce looked back at her. She could see his frightened face even in the dark—how ghost white it was. Now that this monster had killed the angel, what would it do next? What did it plan for her and Bruce?

The creature looked from Bruce to Liz then back to Bruce, as if calculating the changing conditions. From all around the room invertebrate creatures scurried across the ceiling, floor, and balcony. Many of these grotesque things moved to the angel. Liz watched as they edged on top and started to eat.

The things consumed quickly. In a matter of seconds they removed half of the angel's face. Liz heard them chewing and sucking, saw them bite into the angel's cheeks, heard bones crunch. She watched as these monstrous things reached in and pulled brain matter out.

The sight of this caused her to snap. The realization that these things intended on doing the same to her and, more importantly, to her Bruce, sent her into a blind, protective rage. Uncharacteristic of herself—she ran toward Báalzbub.

"*Bruce, No!*" she yelled running past him, grabbing a lamp from the table.

When she went by, Bruce tried to stop her but Liz reacted too quickly and unexpectedly. He had no way of anticipating that she would respond like that, so he did the only thing he could. He leaped forward along with her. Together they launched an attack on the demon.

However, the inexorable Báalzbub was too quick for them.

The beast grabbed Liz first, digging its six-fingered, be-clawed hand into her side, beneath her rib cage. It flung the powerless woman across the room. Her lamp smashed next to her. Báalzbub twisted and swung his left hand up and over, slamming Bruce across the chest and hurling him out and over the third floor balcony.

Báalzbub turned toward Liz and mimicked her, *"Bruce, No!"*

Dizzy from the hit, mixed with how fast everything had happened, Liz did not see Bruce go over the railing. Unable to pull a thought together, she did not notice the blood splatter on the wall and the floor underneath her, never mind that the blood belonged to her.

The beast turned away from the harmless human, walked to the dead, and partly-consumed, Ezziel. His swarm moved away as Báalzbub stepped over, placed a hand on what remained of the angel's forehead, spoke, and stepped back. The body of Ezziel suddenly burst into flames and quickly turned into ash. Nothing was left of the angel but a pile of scorched dust.

Liz felt weak and numb as she looked around, becoming consciously aware that she could not see or hear Bruce anymore. She attempted to call his name but her voice failed. She started to cry as she tried again, but her punctured lung made it impossible for her to create enough voice, and only a soft weep resembling his name whispered from her lips.

She would never see him again.

CHAPTER 17

Darkness
Blackness and Dreams
Beeps and Voices
Voices in the Blackness

Holding hands, Liz and Bruce walked a trail. In his left hand, Bruce carried an old-fashioned wicker picnic basket. They walked up the trail until the lighthouse came into view. A smile formed on Bruce's face. If Liz looked at him right then, she would have known he was up to something. Luckily, the lighthouse caught her attention instead.

Bruce had been looking forward to asking Liz to marry him for a long time. The moment mattered.

It had to be perfect.

Coming to this island presented him the perfect opportunity.

Lights

HARROW

Beeps and Voices
Fades to Blackness
Blackness and Dreams

Liz had wanted to come up to Brahman Cape all week to watch the sunset. The lighthouse was now just up ahead. Even though the sun would not set for another hour or so, the place was already crowded. Bruce and Liz both looked for a clearing that could hold some kind of intimacy and give them the illusion of privacy. As they approached the lighthouse, the perfect site opened for them.

It almost seemed as if it had reserved itself just for the two of them.

Voices and Beeps
Blackness still
Sad Dreams

"Make way for my girl," Bruce said with a big smile as they moved through the slower-walking crowd. Liz gave Bruce that cute little smile of hers, the one that curled the edges of her mouth. He had fallen in love with each and every one she'd ever given him. As they got closer to their spot, Liz started to skip, kicking each leg up as she clapped her hands below them. Her yellow dress blew in the wind as she did. Watching her, Bruce felt sorry for anyone who did not have a Liz in his or her life. Nothing was more important than falling in love.

He feared they would need to compromise on the view for a little privacy, and that would have been fine. However, they didn't have to give up anything. Bruce could not have hand-picked a better location than the one that awaited them.

After laying the blanket out, he unpacked the basket as she set things up. They shared a light dinner of sandwiches and salad. He had brought along a half dozen yellow roses, Liz's favorite, and spread them evenly around the two of them. Inside the basket, there was still a single short stemmed red rose with its thorns carefully removed from its stem, and something special added in their place.

Lights and Beeps
Beeps and Blackness
Blackness and Dreams

At first, Liz did not understand why Bruce had slowly moved onto one bent knee, or why he was handing her this single shortened red rose. Then the light caught the diamond and it sparkled across his eyes. She gasped slightly and clapped her hands over her mouth in shock. He carefully untied the ring from the pin running through the stem and looked at her.

"Liz, I have loved you from the first moment I laid my eyes on you. Since then you have become my best friend, my lover, my whole life. Elizabeth Bernhardt, will you now please become my wife. Will you marry me?"

Liz eyes watered as she told Bruce, "Yes."

Taking her left hand, he slid the ring on her finger and kissed her. Removing the safety pin from the stem, he put the rose behind her ear and watched her blush bring out the blueness of her eyes. And as they sparkled, she put the resort, sunset, and island to shame.

Nightmares
Faces in Death
Death in Faces
Black wings, Red blood

Things crawling on floors, things crawling on ceilings, things crawling on angels, things eating angels, things eating Liz, things eating Bruce, things eating picnic baskets, things eating roses and rings of promise.

Dreams
Dreams and Blackness
Blackness and Beeps
Beeps and Dreams

Liz stood by a cliff. Her sunset was in front of her. Bruce stood next to her holding her hand. Liz's sunset was not for him.

The sunset brightened. Its oranges and reds turned bright white. Liz and Bruce looked at one another. Their hands separated as Liz moved toward, and into, the warm, white light. Bruce reached out for her as he fell into the voices and beeps.

Beeps and Lights
Lights and Voices
Eyes wide open

Open and Alive

PART III

...IF BIRD OR DEVIL

"Words have no power to impress the mind without the exquisite horror of their reality."

Edgar Allan Poe

CHAPTER 18

October 15th:

T he first thing Chief John Moore noticed when he arrived at the scene on Sheridan Street was a man around the age of thirty in nothing but boxer shorts kneeling over a white dog. The second thing he noticed was that this man appeared to be choking the dog with its own leash. John radioed that he'd reached the scene and requested back up.

Parked fifteen feet from the man and dog, John sat there for a minute, thinking. Then picked his hat up from the passenger seat and opened the car door.

As the police chief walked over he could hear a low snarling sound. His original assumption that the dog was dead seemed to be incorrect. The man's face remained hidden as he leaned over the dog. John decided not to get too close until he had a better assess-

125

ment of the situation and stood about six feet back with his baton in hand.

The man had not yet realized John had arrived and continued choking the dog. John decided this had gone on long enough.

"Sir, I'm with the Harrow Police Department. Will you please step back from the animal? "

The man made no response that indicated he heard the officer's command. John took a step forward, prepared to nudge the man if necessary.

"Sir, this is your second warning. I'm ordering you to step away from the dog."

Again, the man did not comply.

"Sir, this is your final warning!"

The man's head slowly rose and looked at him. As soon as the face became visible, John could see fresh blood covered the man's mouth and teeth, bits of fur and skin hung from the sides of his face. The man looked at John for a moment then drove his face back into the dog's throat. The snarling sound started again. The man made the sound, not the dog.

Horror-struck and unwilling to provoke the man, John took a few steps backward. He watched from a safe distance as the individual inhumanly ripped and tore. He returned the baton to his belt and unsnapped his weapon holster.

Carefully, he stepped all the way to the rear of his cruiser and opened the trunk. From inside he grabbed a roll of yellow police line and returned to the front of the patrol car.

Mindfully, he moved to the fence behind the man and dog and tied the end of the line about ten feet away from them. Then walked backwards unrolling, attached the line to the cruiser's front push bar, and carefully repeated this action on the other side of the car, creating a small and weak perimeter.

He expected one of his officers to appear at any moment. It was about five-thirty in the morning. Soon people would be heading off to work and kids leaving for school. John needed help with the proper safety measures.

Standing back by the patrol car, he had time to think about what he was watching. No sane person would do this to a dog. What would drive someone to do such a thing?

When John first received the phone call from Rose Watson about the attack, his thoughts were, *Here we go again.* Every time a dog was involved in an attack, the owner claimed it was provoked. In this case, John had to agree the dog was the victim. Rose also claimed she saw blood on the man before he assaulted her dog.

From what John had seen so far, he had no reason to doubt it.

When the man looked up, all John could see was the fresh blood—clearly from the dog.

That did not mean there was not another dead or, dare he think it, partially eaten dog elsewhere in Harrow, or worse, a human.

This man, as madcap as he was, so far had barely acknowledged him. John also did not recall Rose saying anything about the man ever making an aggressive move toward her personally, only the dog.

As John understood it, the man disregarded her altogether.

There had been no other reports that morning of someone attacking another dog. Until there was reason otherwise, John needed to only deal with the current situation.

Walking over to the patrol car he retrieved a small digital camera from the glove compartment. Photographic evidence, along with the onboard digital video/audio camera, should satisfy anyone's questions about what happened here.

CHAPTER 19

While John spent his morning dealing with the bizarre and the strange, the rest of the Moore family was just beginning their day.

One of the two Moore children had spent a good portion of the night before on the living room couch, while the other, after climbing out her bedroom window, spent it with Bobby Benito.

Jane spent a portion of her night with the same frightened child who slept in the living room and the rest of it worrying about him. Thomas always had a tendency for night scares, but last night was awful. The disappearance of Jason had finally hit hard. Jane knew the nightmares would come. However, she did not expect Thomas to think Jason would be hiding in his closet.

Jason went missing Sunday evening, never making it home from playing with friends. Thomas had been one of those friends. The last anyone saw Jason he was riding his bike near the Hills. Later that night Melissa, Jason's mother, called looking for him. When John heard that Jason had not returned home, he took it upon himself to check the Hills. Jason's bike was there, he was not.

They discussed what happened, and Thomas understood Jason was missing, but he didn't seem to grasp the seriousness of it.

Thomas had always had an over active imagination, and last night it had again gotten the best of him. That closet had been the crypt for so many of his monsters. She probably should have anticipated this. However, Jane's largest concern was not the closet scare, but the toy car.

When she put Thomas to bed, she herself put his toys away. Her husband had built several shelves on the back wall of the closet. She placed the action figures on the middle shelf beside the plastic box of cars. It clearly had a lid, and because of Thomas's past with the closet, she made sure to close the door. There were no matchbox cars on the floor.

If there were, she would have picked them up. Those little hell-on-wheels made her nervous. Jane feared Thomas would wake in the middle of the night and slip on one walking to the bathroom.

When Jane went back with Thomas to his room, she found a tiny red corvette on the floor, slightly outside the cracked closet door. Jane, like most mothers, could tell when their children were lying to them, and this was the confusing part. She did not think Thomas was lying. She could tell he hadn't actually expected to see the car when he returned to the room. So if he did not remove the car from the closet, who did?

If she found out her daughter's had one of her friends in the house and then decided it was a good idea to tease Thomas, Jane would ground Candice's ass until she forgot what her friends looked like outside of school.

Jane sat at the kitchen table drinking coffee. Thomas sat across from her eating breakfast.

She was surprised how well he looked and felt after last night. She thought for sure he'd be over-tired and cranky. She'd considered keeping him home today, but her son actually seemed better off than she did.

"How are you feeling?" she asked Thomas as he pushed his eggs from side to side on his plate.

"Okay, Mom, a little tired. Why?"

"Just wondering. You were up pretty late last night. How did you sleep, after...you know?"

Thomas shrugged his shoulders. "Okay, I guess."

She watched him for a second and then asked again about last night.

"Thomas, are you sure about not playing with your cars after you went to bed?"

"No, Mom, I swear. I haven't played with those cars since..." He stopped—since the last time Jason slept over. Thomas was unable to finish, and he didn't need to, his mother understood.

"It wasn't a nightmare, Mom. At first, I thought it was, but it wasn't. Jay was really in my closet, Mom. I swear he was. That red 'Vette was his. I traded him a black Mustang for it."

That little bit of information did not make this any easier. Jane wrestled with the idea that maybe Thomas was sleepwalking, or in this case sleep playing. It was not impossible. People under stress did it all the time and

Thomas's age wouldn't exclude him from somnambulism. Could there be other times she did not know about. Was Thomas walking around the house asleep in the middle of the night without anyone knowing?

There was no way Candice and her friends could have known about the red Vet, and even if they had, how could they have found that car in the dark? Jane needed to keep a better eye on him.

"A 'Vette for a Mustang, that was a good trade," she responded.

Jane would still have to have a talk with Candice about having friends in the house all the same. She was not accusing her daughter of anything, at least not yet, but the late night visits had to stop regardless. Jane would have preferred to avoid another fight with her daughter, but she could not let Candice run wild doing whatever she wanted for the sake of peace.

Jane was just about to ask Thomas if his sister had known about the trade with Jason when Candice came trotting down the stairs talking on her cell phone. She stopped at the bottom of stairwell, grabbed her jacket and reached for the front door. From the kitchen window, Jane watched a blue Nissan pull up and beep.

Jane got up and walked to the front door, stopping Candice before she jetted off to her awaiting ride.

Jane knew what time her daughter went to bed, and she knew what time she got up, but what Jane did not know was why her sixteen-year-old daughter looked as if she hadn't slept a wink all night.

"Candice, did you stay up all-night?"

"What? No!"

"Don't lie to me. I can tell you haven't slept."

"Maybe you're the one who hasn't slept, or maybe you're still asleep and dreaming. I have to go. School, remember? You always say I shouldn't be late." Candice opened the door and moved quickly outside. Her mother stepped out behind her.

"Were you or any of your friends in Thomas's room last night?" Jane immediately wished she caught that remark before it fell from her mouth.

Candice didn't look back. She just kept moving toward her friends in the blue Altima, and replied, "Oh-yeah, right, like we don't have anything better to do. Get real, will ya?"

"Come straight home, Candice, we need to talk."

Jane watched as the car turned the corner and vanished. Shaking her head, she walked back inside the house.

Thomas listened to his mother. She didn't believe him. She would rather accept anything but the truth.

He sat there and thought to himself, *Why can't she trust me? Just because Jason's mom can't find him doesn't mean anything. Maybe he's hiding from her. Maybe she never believed him either. Jason was in my room, I know it, and if he comes back, I'll play with him. Next time I won't get scared, and I won't tell anyone he was there. If Jay doesn't want anyone to find him, that's fine with me. I'll help him hide.*

Last night, after his mother left his room, Thomas couldn't sleep in there and decided to move to the living room—less closets. Thomas spent the night watching television with the volume turned down—shows and movies his parents wouldn't approve of—avoiding anything scary. He felt there had been enough of that for one night.

Channel surfing, he came across newscasts talking about something they called a tsunami. Thomas had no real understanding of what had happened. As he watched, he thought, *So what?* To him it was just some big wave thing on the other side of the world. Why should he care?

What little Tommy Moore did not understand was that this big wave—the one all the way over on the other side of the world—was connected to Harrow, his Harrow. Tommy was oblivious of the dark and sinister. Of things made in abhorrence, things determined to end the balance between positive and negative.

There was a darker side to cosmogony, the co-creator of the Universe, known by billion different names on billions of different worlds. On earth, Satan was the most popular name.

The connection, however, was not the Deity of Darkness, but one of its agents. This being had been the origin of Harrow's sorrow and pain for centuries, and for the Hills, a great deal longer than that.

Acting out in selfish accord, the devil Báalzbub and his disciples awaited one even darker than them...The Black One.

The Hills of Harrow were hallowed ground for Báalzbub, and coming to this unsanctified land was the envoy from a nameless creator and destroyer: the dark phantom force, accelerating the expansion of the cosmos.

The Black One was everything, and nothing. The laws of this Universe did not apply to this herald—an Entity wrought from thousands of different atoms from thousands of different universes. The freezer of stars, the killer of planets, and the demolisher of galaxies, The Black One was the physical embodiment of the black hole.

Foolishly, Báalzbub had allowed this force, and its God to seep into our Universe with the belief the two Universes would ultimately become one.

The messenger promised Báalzbub the transformation of his energy, giving him, and only him, a place within the new time and space. Báalzbub accepted and then waited in anticipation for the foreseeable sealing of the Creators' fates.

However, the unknowing Báalzbub had been shamelessly deceived. This envoy's phantom God was a Being, not another universe. This wicked devil naively aided not only in the acceleration of the Universe, but also the eventual tearing of it.

The Black One's Deity demolished universes by expanding their "fabric" until there was no gravitational or electromagnetic interaction between their farthest parts, forcing the separation of galaxies and matter at the speed of light. When their gravity became too weak and could no longer hold individual galaxies together, their solar systems unbound, causing stars and planets to rip apart.

Before the destruction of their atoms, this phantom God would feed on them, and whatever remained of these universes would spread off into nothingness.

Little Tommy Moore understood none of this. How could he? Tommy just changed channels looking for some forbidden show and hoped he'd fall asleep.

After a while, Tommy's eyes became heavy and sleep found him. The remote control slipped from his hands and landed on the floor as show after show started and ended. Thomas slept soundly without the voice of his friend waking him. Rest easy while you can, little Tommy Moore. Because just like The Black One, darker days were coming to this postcard town, the darkest days it had ever known.

Thomas finished his breakfast, kissed his mother good-bye, and left for the bus stop. Wondering, hoping, that Jay would be in school today. Maybe that was why Jason hid in his closet last night, Thomas thought as he walked down the street. Jason wanted to tell him he would be in school today!

Thomas started running, only half believing what he'd told himself. In his heart, he knew Jason wouldn't be waiting and smiling for him at the bus stop. Then again, half a belief was more than enough for a boy his age.

Thomas ran as fast as he could. What a laugh they would have talking about how scared he got last night. Jay would no doubt call him a chicken. Maybe make wings by tucking his thumbs under his smelly armpits, peck his head, and cluck. Jay could get silly sometimes.

When Thomas got close to the bus stop, he could see a group of kids. Toward the back of the small cluster, he saw a blue hat. Jason wore a blue Patriots hat like that. Thomas started to run faster. He couldn't believe it. Jay was there. Excited, he jumped into the pack of kids, knocking a few a little too hard, but he didn't care. He grabbed Jay and turned him around. The giant smile on Thomas's face faded when he saw Ronnie Wallace, a friend, but not the friend he wanted.

Thomas apologized and Ronnie turned back to his conversation about video games with some kid Thomas didn't recognize.

CHAPTER 20

O fficer Carl Fisher pulled his cruiser along the driver's side of the chief's car.

John looked back and watched Carl walk to the police line.

"Well, I had a bagel with my coffee, but—I suppose pooch could've worked," Carl said. John glanced over as Carl smiled. "Maybe next time I'll have a beagle instead."

John walked over and handed him the camera. "Move behind that fence and take some from the back." Carl took the camera with a questioning look "That way some smart ass lawyer can't claim his client was looking for fleas or something."

Carl looked at the scene. "You sure that's really necessary? I mean..." He trailed off, realizing John did. "You're the boss, Boss," Carl said and climbed over the fence. "You think he's on bath salts?"

John remembered all the zombie talk

from the incident in Florida. That was worse. "Maybe."

Carl could see someone watching him from inside the house. What a thing to wake up to. He hoped this wasn't their dog. "Whose dog is this anyway?"

John sighed. "Bill Watson's"

"Crazy Bill's dog? Great. This just keeps getting better." Carl looked around. "Is he here?"

"No, I told him not to show up looking for this guy. We have enough on our plate already. I understand how he must feel, it being his dog and his wife walking it and all, but I can't deal with him right now."

"Is Rose all right?"

"She's fine, little shook up is all."

"I'd be surprised if Bill cared. The ass probably preferred it was her instead of the dog."

"Truth—Bill said Rose should've been watching where she walked. He didn't seem very concerned about her."

Taking photos, Carl heard sucking sounds coming from the man and dog. Carl lowered the camera, no longer able to watch this event magnified through the lens.

"Can you hear that?"

"That snarling sound, yeah. It was louder before."

"Snarling, no, I'm talking about a slurping and sucking sound. Think I might get sick."

John had heard it earlier and did not feel the need to listen for it again.

Mark Greene pulled up in his red pick-up. Even when Mark was off duty, he kept his scanner on. His philosophy was he was never off duty, just not at work. If something happened, he felt he should be there to help. When he heard the transmission this morning, he'd decided to check it out, more out of curiosity than responsibility.

You didn't see something like that every day.

"Good morning, boys. What's for breakfast? Can I interest you in my wife's—oh, I see you've found something already!"

"Great, just what I need. Another wise guy. Hello, Mark"

"Can I be of some help?"

"That you can. We were just wondering how to handle this. So far he—" John pointed to the man. "—has been no trouble—other than to the dog, that is. But I also haven't tried to physically remove him yet."

"Any idea who he is?"

"I don't recognize him."

"Has he said anything yet?"

"Not a word, and if he hadn't looked up at me, I would think he wasn't even aware of us."

Mark looked over at the man with his face buried in the dog's throat, wildly shaking his head back and forth. He nodded and said, "Hell of a thing." He ducked under the line and stood next to John.

Carl climbed over the fence, his stomach wishing it had taken the day off. This was the most nauseating thing he had ever come across. How this sicko could be chewing on a dog was beyond him. At some point, no matter how psycho you were, one had to stop and think, "Wait a minute here, I'm chewing on a dog, a dog for Christ sake."

Carl hoped his boss liked the photos he took. If not, John was welcome to fold this camera up nice and tight and stick it where the sun didn't shine. Because there was no way in hell he'd get Carl back behind the lens. He could take the rest himself. Then

Carl recognized the man, and it made everything worse.

"So, Chief, what's the plan here?" asked Mark "Simply asking your new buddy to peacefully step away from the dog didn't work out, so what now?"

John looked over at Carl while answering. "I doubt he'll give up easy." Then to Carl he said, "You feeling all right, Carl? Looks like you took a bite of that dog yourself."

Making his way over to the chief and Mark, Carl shook his head, handed the camera over, leaned against the car, and looked at John like a sick kid needing the school nurse.

"I know who that is. That's Simon Allen. He's from Clayton. I went to high school with him. Allen had always been quiet, nice, you know—normal. What in the hell is happening here?" Carl brought his hands to his mouth. "I'm gonna puke!"

"Hang in there, Carl. This'll all be over soon. Can you do that?" John asked

"Yeah, but can we get this done, before I throw up?"

CHAPTER 21

Simon was unaware of his own actions. These three civil servants might be looking at him, however, he was not present. The man was lost, trapped, somewhere within his head. All they could see was an unbalanced man with a dog. What was actually taking place was beyond their comprehension.

Simon did not notice John as he moved in behind him, nor did he notice Mark move to his right. He did not notice the hand that grabbed him by the nape of his neck or the knee forced into his back as John quickly put him on the ground. Simon never knew that Mark moved on top of him, while John kept his knee placed between his shoulder blades. He also never felt the handcuffs that Mark placed on his blood soaked wrists, or the plastic zip ties Carl used to bind his bloody feet.

Carl took off his braided belt and handed

it to John. Looping the belt, John placed it over Simon's face and into his snapping jaws, fastening it tight at the back of his head.

John wondered if later this would feel like excessive force to Simon. There was no question the use of the belt was unusual. He would have preferred a gag of some kind, however, they did not have one. What they did have was a belt.

News traveled fast in Harrow and people started to show interest. Before long most of the town would know what happened here. If this had been the other way around, the significance of this situation would've had less appeal. All anyone would care about was whether or not John shot a dog. However, today someone had strangled and, rumor had it, bitten a dog to death. Therefore, people would talk and they would come. The dog probably would've favored the bullet over the bite.

Once they restrained Allen, John cut the left side of the police line and opened both of his cruiser's back doors. The three of them carefully picked Simon up and carried him toward John's patrol car.

They decided to put him inside feet first. Carl backed into the cruiser while holding the cuffed feet, and awkwardly slid backward, while John and Mark held Simon by his shoulders. Together they placed him inside.

Closing the door John said, "Let's get this over and done with." He walked toward the dead dog. "There's still a mess to clean up."

John bent down and finally examined the amount of damage done to the Watson's dog, Max. He had seen this dog many times over the years. Memories of it barking at him while he answered calls to the home were clear.

Any one of the injuries could have killed the animal: strangulation, a ripped out throat, and numerous signs of blunt-force trauma. The dog's head had several heel-sized indentations. How could someone barefooted cause so much damage? The unfortunate animal's death must have been horrible.

Removing the camera from his back pocket, John took photos of the injuries. Carl came up carrying a large, black trash bag and duct tape to make a sad body bag for an even sadder death. He cut one of the bags down the side and along the bottom. Placing the bag next to the dog, John and Carl moved the animal's remains on top. Carl quickly moved back to the vehicles afterward, leaving John to wrap and tape the dog himself.

Mark backed his pick-up trunk to the curb. When John finished the unpleasant work of taping the bags, they loaded the dog into the truck's flatbed.

Fortunately for Carl, the resident living in the house behind the attack offered to hose off the sidewalk. Carl was most grateful. Then he noticed the footprints.

"Chief, look!"

John walked over and saw what Carl was pointing at. He sighed deeply and again removed the camera from his back pocket.

"Carl, go with Mark back to the station. Leave the tape line and *do not* hose this off yet." He looked down at the foot trail. "I'm going to follow this."

He started walking down Sheridan Street.

CHAPTER 22

The town of Harrow had a small police force. There was only the Chief of Police and three other officers. With a force this small in Harrow, the State Police covered anything major that might happen.

Mostly, it was up to John to keep things under control.

The Harrow Police Station was a small building. There was a small dispatch area, four cells, John's office, and a small R&R area for the officers. After 11:00 p.m., the station was closed. There was a posted sign on the front door instructing people to call the New Hampshire State police in the case of an emergency. Of course, most people in town had John's home number.

John sat at his desk, confused. He'd returned to the station after his search of Simon's residence. He had not known what awaited him at 85 Sheridan Street, but he expected to discover something. Simon had never been a dangerous person. In fact, most people simply thought of Simon as average, that is, if they gave him any mind at all.

The way John encountered Simon this morning, maybe no one knew him at all. To say the man snapped would be putting it mildly.

John had tracked the bloody footprints from the attack site to a gray three-story apartment house. The property had a history of housing young adults, and the police had responded to several noise complaints over the years. However, things had been quiet here for the past year or so.

The footprints became redder and more complete as John followed them to the low-rent apartment house. The structure, separated into three living quarters, shared a single front porch. On the porch, there were two doorways. One opened into a small hallway with a set of stairs that led to the second and third floors. The other door was for the first floor apartment—Simon's.

John carefully climbed the steps. He noticed the footprints looked smaller. Only the top parts of the feet were visible. It appeared Simon exited his apartment walking on the balls of his feet. It was possible the coldness of the porch caused him to do this, but from what John had seen the weather didn't seem to affect him much.

The door stood wide open and John could see the living room. He moved across the porch and over what looked like a week's worth of newspapers. Stopping at the right side of the opened door John peered inside and was unable to verify if anyone was inside. He announced himself and entered the apartment.

As John stepped inside he noticed that, like the newspapers, an equal amount of daily mail was scattered on the floor. Either Simon had not been home much the past few days, or he wasn't interested in the world outside. John scanned the room and stepped farther in.

The house was a mess. Half-eaten junk food covered the coffee table. The majority of the food wasn't opened before being bitten into, as if removing the item from the wrapper was too difficult, or merely took too long.

The power was out. With what light he had, John followed the bloody footprints toward the bedroom. As his eyes adjusted, he noticed for the first time the writing and drawings on the walls.

Simon had drawn dozens of abstract birds with a black marker on every wall. No two birds were the same, but all had one similar trait.

They all looked evil.

Written all around these iniquitous-looking birds were the words *Ăvis* and *Avi malā*.

Taking out the camera, John photographed the walls and blood trails and proceeded into the bedroom.

The small room had little furniture, only a computer desk and mattress. The blood trail led to the mattress. John approached. There was no one in the apartment—dead, hurt or otherwise—John looked around for a weapon and found nothing. Where had all this blood come from?

He moved closer to the bed and only found blood on the mattress and under the covers. There was no blood above the blankets.

Puzzled, John looked back down at the prints. They only went one way, and they exited the bed, not entered. Whatever happened, happened right here.

More sketches, and the words "Nightmare Birds," covered the walls surrounding the bed. John again looked at the bed and blood trail. If Simon had attacked someone or an animal outside the house and then returned home, there should be a trail showing so. However, there was not. Somehow, the blood came from the uninjured Simon himself.

Bill Watson slammed his way through the station doors.

"Where's my fucking dog, Johnny!"

Bill was a large, mean-tempered man, well known for his rage. John had known it was only a matter of time before Bill showed up. At least he kept away from the scene. That could not have been easy for him and plain old hell for Rose. There was no doubt he blamed her for this morning.

"Where'd you bring him? I want my fucking dog—now!" His large head moved around, searching. "Moore, I want my Max!"

John exited his office and entered the reception area as Rose franticly rushed into the station looking for her out of control husband. She quickly found Bill and moved toward him.

"Billy honey, please don't make things worse, please."

Bill looked back at his wife then returned his attention to John.

"So, where's *my* dog, John? I did as *you* asked and stayed away, didn't I? Now I'm asking you to give me my Max."

"I can't just yet Bill, I'm sorry. Your Max is part of an investigation, and he's considered evidence at this time. I'll release him to you as soon as possible. The—"

"Evidence? He's my dog, not some kind of object or weapon. He's the fuckin' victim here."

It was not even 9:00 a.m. and John could already smell alcohol. "Bill, relax. Let's go into my office to talk. This isn't something we should be discussing out here."

Bill nodded his large head and looked back at his wife.

"Wait here, Rosie. This is men's business. There's no need for you. In fact, you

shoulda stayed in the car where I left ya."
Bill walked toward John "Hell, I shoulda left
ya back home in the first fuckin' place." He
stood in front of John, waiting.

"Well, Bill, actually, I do need her. One,
she still needs to make a statement, and two,
she has a right to understand what's going
on. She was the one walking the dog."

The look on Bill's face said all that needed saying. He clearly disagreed with what
John just said. In Bill's world women—
particularly his woman—had only one right:
to remain silent. That he gladly gave them.
Bill, like his father, believed women and
children should be seen and not heard. He
frowned on anyone that undermined him,
never mind giving his wife a voice over his.

Bill and John had known each other all
their lives, and had not always gotten along.
Even as a kid, John never liked men like Bill.
The kind of man that only felt good while
pushing others around, using intimidation to
get what they wanted. Bill's fist always followed his mouth. His inability to communi-
cate had always driven him to violence and
turned his insecurities into absurdities.

John had always been smaller then Wild

Bill, but never let Watson bully him, and Bill hated when he was powerless and unable to maltreat another.

"I would rather she stayed out of here. I'll tell you what she saw."

"That's not going to work, and you know it. If you like, I can always talk with Rose alone. We won't be long. You can wait out here." John enjoyed pushing Bill's buttons. He looked over at his dispatcher. "Mary, when you get a sec, would you help Mr. Watson here to a cup of coffee?"

"No problem," answered Mary with a big smile. She'd witnessed this sort of exchange before.

Wild Bill, now looking every bit his nickname, took his wife by the arm and said to John, "Thought we were heading into your office?"

John turned, making a "come along" gesture with his right hand.

This was the first time Bill had entered John's office without a charge on him. It would also be his last.

CHAPTER 23

John's office was neat and clean, but it looked worked in. A large oak desk and high-backed leather chair, nicknamed "the throne," almost filled the medium sized space. Two smaller, but matching, chairs were set in front of the desk. John waited as Bill and Rose took their places in them.

From behind his desk, John couldn't help notice the frightened and angry looks coming from Bill and Rose. He understood the fearsome look from Rose. The poor woman had endured the business end of Bill's temper more than once. Regrettably, John could see and feel that rage coming from Bill now. That aggression had led Bill into the county jail on more than one occasion.

John had the feeling this wouldn't be Bill's only trip into the station today. He'd clearly seen anger in Bill's eyes, and later on, after a "few more" drinks to relax and mourn Max, Rose would have the proof on her face and wherever else Bill's blows might land. Guys like Bill didn't care who was to blame. It was more about who was *getting* blamed, and every swallow of beer made it more and more his wife's fault.

"As I was trying to explain, your dog received a number of unusual injuries. We need to understand what happened this morning. Bill, I know you want Max back now, but it's just not possible. I'm sorry."

"This is bullshit John. You know damn well, what happened this morning. Some sick mother killed my dog. What more is there to understand? Who was that asshole anyway?"

"The man's name is Simon Allen. He lives down the street from where the attack took place." John waited to see if they recognized the name. Apparently, it meant nothing to them, still he had to ask the question. "Have either of you two seen or met him before?

"Seen or met him *before*? I haven't seen or met the fuck yet. What you're telling me—" Bill huffed through his nose. "Well, more like *not* telling me, Johnny, is that you don't know a goddamned thing about this piece of shit. I wanna know. What did that asshole do to my dog—and why? God-fucking-dammit, why?" Bill slammed his hand hard on the desk, causing a few things to knock over.

John looked at the fallen picture of his family, and gave Bill a contemptuous look, that only Rose noticed. He observed Bill's Tasmanian devil tattoo flexing on his left forearm as he squeezed his fists. He met Bill's angry red face and wondered, and not for the first time, if Bill realized he had the same long, dirty blond hair as his wife.

"When you showed up, you saw what, huh?" Bill glanced over to Rose. "You buddies with this sick fuck, John, covering for him maybe?"

John did not justify the accusation with a response. He had heard Bill's rants before.

"It's about that blood, isn't it, John, that blood I saw on him?" Rose asked, finally speaking. "Was it that little boy's, the one that went missing the other day?"

Of course, it had something to do with the blood, and yes, it could belong to Jason Benson, not that he intended to reveal that.

Besides, the unanswered questions from Simon's home only made the situation surrounding him more confusing. For obvious reasons, John did not intend to discuss Allan with these two, beyond their dog. Even that he would like to avoid. He disliked Bill and pitied Rose.

"We don't know the source of that blood yet. I assure you, we are looking into it."

"So, it was blood. What's going on in this town, Johnny? Can't you do your job? Missing kids, harmless dogs getting killed, and who knows what you're keeping from us, the taxpayers?" Bill sneered, looked over at his wife, gestured with his head toward John, and said, "See, Rosie? These guys suck, a real fuckin' joke."

Rose looked at her husband for a second and then asked John, "He was in those hills, wasn't he?"

"The Harrowing Hills? No I don't believe so." Knowing what Rose was thinking, John changed the subject, "When can you give a statement Rose? The sooner, the better."

"I can do it now if you'd like."

"Perfect. I'll have Officer Mark Greene take it from you." John leaned forward, tapping the top of his desk with a pen. "I understand this is hard for the both of you, and I'm truly sorry. Nevertheless, I need to ask if the two of you can please keep this quiet— *somewhat* quiet, anyway. We are not trying to hide what happened, Bill. We just don't want people to get the wrong idea. It would be a short jump to the collusion that this morning and the missing kids are connected. We have no real reason to believe that they are. Do you understand what I'm getting at?"

"I don't...what exactly were Max's the injuries, other than being kicked and stomped to death? And how do I know that piece of shit didn't do the same fuckin' thing to those kids?"

"We still need to examine the evidence, but the cause of death may've been either massive trauma to the head or asphyxiation. There may also be the chance—the chance, mind you—that death was the result of bites to the throat. We're sure the dog was dead by the time Allen started...to well, there really is no easy way to put this...before consumption."

"What?" gasped a stunned Bill Watson.

That was probably the shortest response the loud mouth had ever given, John thought. And that look of confusion on his face?

Well, that was almost worth the conversation.

"This town is facing a hard time. We live in a small, close-knit community. What happens here affects the whole region, and vice versa. The region as a whole is trying to deal, and to stop our children from disappearing. We all have a responsibility here, Bill, not just those of us in public service. Things like panic control and false implications rest on those with information, and right now Bill, some of that accountability lands on you."

As much as John enjoyed Bill's awkward and silent moment, he hoped to reason with his better judgment, assuming Bill had any. "It would be too easy for families to fall into a false scene of security. Because they want, need, to believe their children are safe. It would be a mistake assuming Allen is responsible for the region's lost children, and that belief could lead to parents, and the community as a whole, lowering their guard, making it easier for those responsible to take more children."

Unfortunately, for John, Bill lacked common sense.

"Are you telling me some fuckin' sick

vampire wannabe killed my dog? That's what you're telling me, isn't?"

"Come on, Bill, you know I didn't say that. But a very disturbed individual did kill your dog. In a day or so, you will have your dog's remains. Please no vampire talk. This isn't a Stephen King novel."

"Whatever John," Bill said as he got up, Rose watched and followed.

"Can I expect your cooperation?"

"We'll see. I don't know anything yet." Bill paused and then said, "I'll give it to ya, on the condition. I can talk to this Simon Allen...alone."

John unknowingly smirked. "You know I can't do that, Bill."

"Can't or won't?"

"Both"

"Same old John Moore, you want everything, but unwilling to give anything for it."

Bill walked over and opened the door. John felt bad for Rose. She deserved better than what she had, but she was as incapable of changing her lifestyle as Bill was.

"Can I still count on your statement, Rose?" John asked. "We need it."

She looked at Bill. "Will it take long?

"Only a few minutes."

Rose nodded her head. "Okay"

John got up and walked out behind them. Rose looked back over her shoulder and gave John an apologetic look. She was sorry for the way her husband had acted and for the way he was sure to act later on. Rose already knew Bill had no plans of keeping quiet, and knew he would force her to talk as well.

"Prophet," said I, "thing of evil—
prophet still, if bird or devil!"
~ *Edgar Allan Poe*

CHAPTER 24

The cold cell chilled Simon to his bones. The Harrow Police Department had placed a jacket on him. However, this jacket's purpose was not for comfort, style, or warmth. He sat against the back wall of his small cell. Arms criss-crossed over his chest by the long sleeves of a straitjacket. His legs stretched out across the floor, and resting at the ends of those legs were cold bare feet. To protect the officers, and Simon as well, they muzzled him. His unfocused eyes stared off at nothing. Only the cream-colored bolted door was visible before him. His thoughts, still clouded and hazed, lacked any clear definite form.

The small, brightly-lit room did not faze him. He probably didn't even notice. If Simon's mind were ever to clear, he would gladly never spend another moment in the dark. If he spoke, he would surely inform someone of this. However, Simon was not speaking, but he could hear. Simon—or whatever had control of him—could hear very well, hearing voices from the other cells, hearing the officers as they looked in on him. Most of all, Simon heard the tiny little sounds from the unknown speaking and sneaking around him—their soft mutters as they said things Simon did not want to hear. But he was unable to stop himself from listening.

The presence of something unknown was all he understood now—and all he could feel. It flowed through and under his skin, in his skin. And like the coppery taste of blood in his mouth, it would not leave.

The cell was no larger than a nine-by-twelve bathroom and was painted in the same cream color as the door. A seat-less toilet, sink, small table, and a bunk bed bolted to the floor and wall were the only things in the cell with Simon. His head leaned against the hard and unforgiving concrete wall under a single square-foot window.

On the other side of this window was the town of Harrow, Kings Court to be more precise, which was the one-way street running between Main and High Street. There was nothing special about Kings Court. It had all the normal things one would expect to find on a small New England town road: old English-style homes, some going back one hundred, fifty-plus years, nicely kept bushes and landscaping, streetlights, sewer drains—and trees.

Outside Simon's small twelve-inch square window was a beautiful old maple. The tree itself was as normal and natural as any other tree of its kind, probably even the home of a squirrel or two.

However, on this day you wouldn't find any inhabitants. Instead, if one knew what to look for, one would find the very things whispering to Mr. Allen. Perched on one of the branches was a sight our good friend Jack was beginning to know well. A large ebony raven watched Simon. It didn't require seeing through the window. It could observe the now deranged fellow within quite well. Bobbing its head and bouncing along the branch, this fiend placed words into the cell only Simon could hear, moving the inmate farther away from sanity.

Turning its large head to the left, it looked toward the direction of Main Street. Its white lidless eyes now watched two people move toward an old beaten pick-up truck. Taking flight, it traveled over Bill and Rose. As it passed, Bill felt a chill run down his spine, but Rose felt something completely different. She stopped and looked up as the raven headed down Main Street and watched as it climbed higher and disappeared from sight.

With effortless speed, the raven flew over the town and rooftops of Harrow. The natural world's animals fled, dogs whimpered, cats cowered, and plants wilted.

It felt the fear coming from the towns-people below, feeding and thriving off their pain.

It understood the best way to hurt was through loved ones, and the best way to destroy them was through their children.

This baleful thing's purpose was malefaction, to perform any evil deed required, a mischievous servant, loyal to the diabolical, one of a hellish band of Shape-shifting creatures known as Malign. These depravities were the creators of misery and concoctors of lies, the weaver of nightmares and the destroyer of dreams.

This wicked deviance had a little more wretchedness to perform before it returned to The Crescent, its master, and the whole to which this evil thing was only a part.

The Malign descended. The one it must visit next was up ahead.

Patter, patter, patter was the only sound coming from the asphalt as Jack drummed his way along. These morning jogs were his way of getting his thoughts together. He had to get himself under control. His dreams were no longer just coming at night. He found himself experiencing what he thought was called walking dreams—being wide-awake but still dreaming. Jack had seen and heard things he could not explain any other way. His nightmares had somehow joined him during the day.

Jack questioned everything around him. Nothing seemed safe or real anymore. The mere sight of a black bird, whether a raven or not, made him feel threatened.

The trepidation from these birds was making him insane. Jack was unsure how much longer he could hide this emerging phobia.

Running these five miles of back roads every morning was the only thing still unaffected by these visions. The consistency of the road and his familiarly with the families and homes along it seem to help him. The comfort in its consistency steadied his mind. He was at peace. The motion of his arms in time with his legs, the rhythm of his heart and breathing were the only things keeping him sane.

Behind him, a black bird moved quietly and slowly around a curve in the road. The bird lowered from tree top height to street level, flying in Jack's direction.

As it approached, its eyes stayed on the jogging man ahead. The white soles of the reverend's sneakers mesmerized the devilish bird. Up and down, up and down came the flashes of white. The tempo of time, one two, one two, one, captivated it. The bird slowed its pace more as it watched.

Facing forward, Jack was unaware of what was flying behind him. The thing moved as soundless as air. What Jack *could* do, if the wind-shifted directions, was smell it, and then he would become dreadfully aware of the bird's foul stench.

The raven was lost in semi-enchantment as its wings rose and fell in cadence with the running feet—one up, two down, one up, two down, moving in measure. Patter and flap, patter and flap. Synchronized, man and bird traveled down the road.

Jack often thought about his two grown children on his runs. His son Peter lived in Maine and owned a seafood restaurant in Kennebunkport. He had a nice little business going for himself, something he should be proud of. His parents certainly were.

Jack felt his son could have picked a worse place and way to raise his family and live his life. He was glad things were working out for him. He wished his daughter was having the same run of luck.

As Jack jogged down Backwater Road, he couldn't help but let his mind drift to her. He still hoped that someday Susannah would turn her life around. She was their only daughter and youngest of their two children. Jack loved her and wished her the best of luck. She was lost and still needed to find her way through her problems.

Jack could not help but feel responsible for her drinking problem, feeling that his own addiction and battle with the bottle might have contributed to hers. He had been controlling his problem now for almost ten years and knew his daughter would clean herself up before it was too late. He had faith in her. Susannah was stronger than he ever was.

The raven flying behind Jack was now no more than two feet away. It no longer watched the regular repetition of the shoes. It only needed their recurring sound alternations. Its eyes had fallen to something new.

It watched Jack's heart beat through his back, gazed at the muscular pulsations, focused on the blood flowing through the circulatory system. Wanting to feel and taste that very blood, to smell it from the inside.

The homes of friends and parishioners passed by as Jack moved down the back road.

Normally the sound of barking dogs accompanied him along his way, particularly on this part of Backwater. Strangely, no dogs were barking this morning. It had taken him awhile to notice the unusual silence.

Taking a few moments to look around, he saw that nothing other than the lack of barking seemed out of place. Then, as the wind changed, Jack smelled the earthy remains of a dead body, and although he did not see another shadow with his own, he glimpsed something moving behind him. Keeping pace. Jack slowly turned his head and stared into the cold colorless eyes of his nightmares.

Losing step, as one foot stumbled into the other, he staggered and fell, crashing to the hard pavement. The raven soared over Jack as he landed on his hands and knees and rolled across the road to a sliding stop. He laid there on his back for a few seconds before he could manage to sit up.

The raven landed about ten feet to his left. Staring at Jack, the bird picked up the aroma of blood from his scrapes. It crouched, gradually moving closer. Jack sensed movement, looked up, and realized his ordeal was not over.

The horrifyingly strange raven moved toward him with mannerisms more cat-like than bird. It pressed forward almost in a crawl, prowling in his direction. Its white cadaverous eyes were deeply set like a predator's, and within its dull black feathers, a grayish-white to black ashen color became visible as they ruffled. Jack's whole body grew thick and heavy, as sudden sharp and severe pains spiked inside his head and chest.

His day and nightmares had come to life. This was no mere raven. It was *the* raven. The very one that haunted him, the one he had been so afraid of and, unknowingly until now, expecting. Jack had seen this awful raven before. He remembered the thing bouncing and jabbing its large head on top of a boulder before a woodland tunnel.

As the raven moved closer, its head turned slightly to the right, as if knowing Jack's thoughts. Jack could actually feel it looking intently into him. His heart started to beat faster, harder—warning him it might burst from his ribcage. Cold sweat and chills ran down his body as his left arm went numb.

Then the thing spoke. "Reverendus"

At the utterance of that word, hearing it verbalized outside his nightmare, the memory of the path, the attack, and Thomas Moore hurtled back to him, hard.

Jack's eyes locked with the ravens, his heart hammered harder, making the bird more excited as it approached. Its oversized protruding mandibles look ready to stab, tear, and eat Jack's flesh. From the tip of its horn-like beak, a long forked bluish tongue flickered out, picking up particles of fear from the air. As the raven tasted Jack's suffering, its tongue flicked in time with his distressed heart.

Father O'Brien, returning from a women's support group meeting, noticed someone lying on his back with his hands clenched to his chest.

He only knew one person who jogged this road in the morning. He stopped, swung open the door, and jumped from the automobile, leaving it running, as he raced to his friend.

"Jack! You all right?"

When O'Brien reached Jack, he bent down beside him and saw how white and clammy Jack's face was, and then he noticed how much difficultly he had breathing.

"Jack, can you hear me, please...can you understand what I am saying?"

"Raven—watch out for—raven—my heart."

"I know. I think you're having a heart attack, we need to get you to the hospital."

CHAPTER 25

Thomas Moore sat in class, sad that his friend had not returned to school today. He looked over at Jason's still empty desk. Both of them had seized the last desk in the first two rows. Jay figured this was the farthest away from Ms. Wentworth's desk they could get, and if the need for a speedy escape ever came, they could jump out the window.

Jay's getaway windows were to the left of Thomas. The memory of Jay's plan made him turn and look out them. The bright warm sun shone through. Thomas could see no reminder of last night's cold and bitter wind. Then a thought came to him—how could Jay know what name he was thinking?

Hollowed and empty, Thomas started hearing his name called again. This time faint and far away, echoing from a distance or through a tube in another room, like hearing your name before waking from a dream.

Just like that. Thomas snapped his head from the window and noticed everyone looking at him. Ms. Wentworth was calling his name. He'd been caught not paying attention in class.

"Welcome back, Thomas. I'm glad to see you're so interested in the Universe that you went off to visit it for yourself. Now, like I was asking the class, do you understand what happened in the Indian Ocean?"

"Huh...Oh, do you mean that big wave thing?"

"Yes, I mean that big wave thing. Can you tell me what it was called?"

"I forgot."

"A tsunami. Please try and pay attention in class, Thomas." She looked away and addressed the class. "I would like it if all of you understood what happened and what everyone is talking about, and will probably be talking about for some time. After we finish up with the current lesson on the Universe and Edwin Hubble, I plan to go into this with you in greater detail. However, first, let us go back to what we were doing. Can anyone tell me what four things Hubble is best known for?" When none of the students raises their hands, Ms. Wentworth reminded them. "Hubble's law, The Big Bang, Redshift, and Hubble Sequence. Remember we went over these things in class yesterday."

She walked over to the blackboard behind her desk, wrote all four of them down, drawing a line under Hubble's law. "Edwin Hubble profoundly changed astronomers understanding of the nature of the universe by demonstrating that there were other galaxies besides the Milky Way. He also discovered that the degree of redshift observed in light coming from a galaxy increased with the distance of that galaxy from the Milky Way. The discovery, now named Hubble's Law, helped establish that the universe is expanding. Can anyone remember what the three possible universe types are?"

Not surprising to Thomas, snot-nosed Wendy Kenyon practically threw her arm out of socket in order to answer Ms. Wentworth's question—Wendy the brown-nosing teacher's pet that everyone hated. She not only jumped at every chance to answer a question first, but also thought she was in charge whenever Ms. Wentworth stepped outside the room. It was the popular belief of the class that she kept a log on everyone and everything that went on. She sure was a tattletale on any account. Even though there were other kids with their hand raised, guess whom the teacher picked to answer.

"The three universe types could be open, flat, or closed," Wendy Brown-Nose answered. She looked around the class with a big smile as if she expected praise. One day Thomas planned to put a snake in her bag.

"Thank you Wendy, that's right. We should all remember that these are only theories, and just like the Big Bang, they are unproven, but are educated guesses. What do we call an educated guess? We call them a hypothesis, right. However the universe got its start, it expanded, and the equations of that expansion have three possible results, all of them predicting a different fate for the universe as a whole. Which fate will ultimately take place is unknown, but we can determine the possible theories by measuring how fast the universe expands relative to how much matter the universe contains.

"If a universe is either open or flat, it would expand forever, but in a flat universe, the expansion rate would slow to zero after an infinite amount of time. In a closed universe, it would eventually stop expanding and re-collapse on itself, possibly causing another Big Bang. In all three cases, the expansion slows down, and the force that causes the slowing is called...what?"

"Gravity," answered a few members of the class, including Wendy.

"Well done."

As Thomas sat there and pretended to be interested, he tried to decide if he actually heard the name Frankie, or if it was just his imagination. It had to be the wind.

Maybe when I heard Jay whisper my name I freaked a little. So what? And from that, I heard Frankie, not because Jay said it, but because my mind heard it. As much as Thomas wanted to believe this, deep down he knew what he heard, and from where. By the end of the day, he would have himself believing he never heard Frankie at all. In the background, Thomas heard his teacher talking.

"Our text books, good as they are, need to be replaced." Small amounts of chuckling came from the peanut gallery of the class. "What our books do not tell us, and therefore

won't be on the test, is that in 1998 two separate teams of astronomers concluded that not
only is the universe expanding, but that this
expansion appeared to be speeding up. This
implies that most of the energy in the cosmos
is contained in empty space, a concept that
Albert Einstein had once considered but dis-
carded."

Right on cue, the class token suck up lifted her hand. Thomas really wanted to get
that snake soon, maybe even a few scorpions
to keep it company. When Ms. Wentworth
called her name, Wendy asked, "What would
cause the sudden speed up, Ms. Wentworth?"

"Well, I don't think the acceleration is all
of a sudden. I think they have only just discovered it. The increase is caused from a
form of Dark Energy that nobody understands yet, and it seems to be overcoming the
force of gravity. It looks as if it started about
five billion years ago. Can anyone remember
how old the universe is thought to be?" This
time no one had an answer, and to Thomas's
delight, that included Wendy.

"Some think it could be as much as thir-
teen to fourteen billion years old. See, class,
I'm not really the oldest thing that ever exist-

ed." This started a little laughter and funny looks around the class. Thomas looked up, wondering if he had been caught not paying attention again. He was glad to find they were laughing at Ms. Wentworth.

CHAPTER 26

October 16th:

Around 5:00 a.m., John sat in his office thinking about yesterday's events. He ran Simon prints through the national criminal databases. They came up clean, as far as the Justice Department, and the National Crime Information Center was concerned. Simon had committed no crimes, until now. And so far, his only charge was cruelty to animals.

Of course, not having a criminal record didn't mean he'd never committed a crime, just that he'd never been caught. John ran Simon through both Homeland Security and the Justice Department's OneDOJ system. Not even a speeding ticket had popped up.

John suspected the blood samples taken off Simon and from his bed would not be from another dog. They would be human. In John's experience, people did not sweat blood. If so, his son's night terrors would be a hell of a lot worse.

Simon had a few scratches from the dog. Otherwise, he was unharmed. So where did all that blood come from? John's first thought was a certain young individual that was still missing. He knew how dangerous jumping to conclusions could be. Nothing linked Simon to Jason Benson. Nevertheless, it was hard to ignore these two horrible events happening so close to one another. It was possible the blood on Simon could be non-human.

John hoped he could keep his judgment clear until the lab results came in. He could not assume Simon murdered children because he killed a dog. John, just like everyone else in Harrow, hoped to find Jason and the others alive.

Carl delivered the blood samples to the State Police Barracks in Tamworth for the forensic laboratory. Until those results came back, John had to remain focused and objective.

By 8:00 a.m., John decided it was time to remove the restraints from Simon. He still considered him dangerous, however, Simon had been nonviolent since they brought him in yesterday. The straightjacket was overkill.

The Sheriff's Department would transfer Simon to the Tamerlane State Hospital in Conway for evaluation later today. John was concerned about Simon's complete lack of alertness, his trance like staring. There was no question Simon needed medical attention.

The honor of removing Simon's restraints went to Officers Carl Fisher and Tim Andrews—a job its recipients did not relish. Both sensibly felt a little uncomfortable about this charming task. Tim, who missed the pleasure of being there when Simon was detained, had not seen him with the dog. However, the police report, loaded with photos, was enough for him, therefore he knew how this could go if the psycho returned to the land of the living.

Carl, on the other hand, had participated in apprehending Simon and had seen enough already. He had not seen Simon in over twenty-four hours, and like Simon, Carl hadn't eaten.

Unable to get yesterday's images out of his mind, Carl found that everything, from candy bars to the steak his wife made him, reminded him of Simon. No matter what he tried to eat, Carl saw blood and dog fur on it. Later, he dreamed he ate a maggot and plague-ridden hamburger. He even felt the soft-bodied larva crawl around the insides of his mouth and throat. He woke, vomiting in bed.

Carl had aided John in placing the straight jacket on Simon. He still wondered where John had gotten it from. What other little secrets did their police chief have in his office closet? Carl decided he would rather not know.

Positioned against the back wall, Simon looked as if he had not moved an inch. If it were not for the wet dribble drooling off the muzzle, Carl would question whether Simon was even alive.

"Hey there Allen, you comfy enough?" asked Tim.

Tim tapped Simon twice on his upper forearm, and got no response. "We're here to get that thing off you. You do want that thing off, don't you, Allen?" Tim gave Simon another light tap and looked up at Carl with a comical expression and stepped back. "How should we go about this? Just pull him from the wall and do what we came here to do?"

"Might as well, but I wouldn't count on much help from him. We should turn him so he's facing that wall." Carl signaled toward the wall with the bunk bed.

Tim smiled and shook his head. "I say fuck him. Let him stay like this. If he doesn't give a shit he's in that damn thing, why should we?"

"'Cause John told us to, so that's what we're gonna do. Personally, I wish we could lock him up in more shit. Who knows what the chief's got stashed away around here?"

"Hey, maybe John's got one of those old fashioned insane asylum type head cages, you know, the ones in the movies that look like metal milk crates?" Tim said.

Carl unclipped his stun gun and said, "Let's get this over with, huh?"

"Listen, when I move him, if this son of a bitch makes a move for me, shock the shit out of him. I don't care how restrained he looks, I'm not ending up like that fido from yesterday."

Carl agreed, and waited for Tim to get started.

Tim bent over Simon, took hold of the jacket sleeves, and explained he was only moving him in order to get behind him. He then pulled back, sliding Simon forward away from the wall. He took hold of Simon's left arm, dragged him sideways, and faced him toward the sidewall. Then he quickly let go and stepped back.

Both Tim and Carl watched as the rigid Simon fell to the left. Tim and Carl looked at each other and Tim laughed. "Did you see the way he fell? He looked drunk. Just fell over solid, bang, right to the floor."

"Yeah, I saw it," answered Carl who, unlike the younger officer, found no humor in it.

Tim walked over to Simon and picked him back up. Once Tim let go, Simon fell to the right, his head almost hitting the back wall.

"What the fuck, man? Is he doing that on purpose?" Tim said, shaking his head in disbelief. "Carl, help me move his stupid ass to the bunk or something."

Carl clipped his stun gun back to his belt

and walked over to Tim and Simon. Together they re-sat him back up. Tim held him by the shoulders as Carl picked Simon up by his knees. This was the second time he'd had to pick this asshole up.

On the count of three, they lifted him. Without any resistance, Simon bent in half at the waist. Carl and Tim stood face to face about two feet apart. Tim gave Carl a humorous smile. "Hey, sweetie, promise you won't let something stupid like Simon Allen come between us. You're too important to me!"

Annoyed, Carl inhaled deeply. "Let's just get him on the bed, Tim, can we?"

They carried Simon over to the bunks and laid him down on his back. He stayed in the same jackknife-like position. Tim pushed him onto his right side, facing him toward the wall.

Something was wrong here.

Carl stepped back and unclipped his stun gun from his belt. Tim unlocked and slowly unbuckled the straps. The actual removal of the jacket required Tim to move Simon onto his back again. He pulled down on Simon's left shoulder forcing his torso to fall backward. Only the torso moved. His arms remained locked and folded. His legs did not lift or move at all.

Tim grabbed the extended sleeves and yanked the jacket off. It came away in one swift pull. He saved the mouthpiece for last.

With the jacket now in his hands, Tim looked down at Simon's fixed, straightened arms as they pointed up and angled toward him. The rest of Simon's body looked equally odd and twisted. "What the fuck? This is some whacked shit. I mean, just look at him!" Tim handed the straightjacket over to Carl and stepped closer. "Hmm, I wonder"

"Wonder what?" asked Carl.

Tim took Simon's right arm, lifted it up straight, and let the arm go. It stayed exactly where he placed it. He bent the arm at the elbow, and it held still in mid-air. Tipping the bent hand upward a bit, everything held in place. "Carl, come on, you don't think this is a little odd? Honesty, have you ever even heard of anything like this before? I sure as shit haven't."

"Let's just go. The Sheriff's Department is coming for him today. Someone will take a look at him."

"He's like, I don't know, made of clay or something, or maybe like an opposable action figure. What do you think? Could he be dead or something?"

"Look, I don't know, all right? Everything about him is beyond my understanding. You done playing yet?"

Tim closed the hand he'd been playing with, turning it into almost a fist and raising only the middle finger. "Hey, Carl, Simon says fuck you." And he busted out laughing.

"No, fuck *you*, Tim. I'm outta here. If you want to continue playing with your man of clay, that's up to you. Me, I'm gone." Carl started for the cell door.

Tim finished placing the other hand into the same gesture before getting up to join Carl at the door.

"John's going to love seeing that," Carl informed him.

Tim just smiled and shrugged as he walked past and exited the cell.

CHAPTER 27

Café Wellington on John Adams Avenue was owned by Michael and Kristin Wellington. The theme's inspiration was a mixture of the owners' last name, and their interest in Arthur Wellesley, the first Duke of Wellington. The owners and staff dressed in stimulated early eighteen hundreds British Redcoat attire, even the women.

However, instead of the traditional 33rd Regiment uniforms, they wore red and white dresses. Unquestionably, Napoleon faced nothing like the Café Wellington staff at the Battle of Waterloo.

The café was a favorite of John Moore's, though he preferred coming here for more pleasurable activities—like eating. Today he sat at a booth in the back, scolding Tim Andrews. John was extremely displeased with the young officer. Tim had been warned many times about his practical jokes and unprofessional conduct, but to no avail. Now it seemed he had finally done something that might get him into serious trouble.

"If I didn't need my full force right now, if not for the missing boy and the Harroween Festival coming up, you'd find yourself on suspension, or worse, terminated," he growled. "I could have you brought up on charges for that little stunt you pulled with Simon. Do you hear me?"

Tim hung his head. "Yes, sir, I understand."

"If Simon was more aware than he acted, and he reports your behavior, there will be little I can do to save you."

"It won't happen again, sir."

"It damn well better not. If I hear even one more—"

John wasn't even halfway finished dressing him down when Mary from dispatch interrupted his tirade.

It seemed John was a little off about when the call to the Watson's home would come, but he was right on the mark in that it would.

From the outside the Watson residence, everything looked fine. The house was the same off white color, with baby blue shutters, it had always been. Crushed and scattered beers cans filled the front porch and railing. More cans lay on the ground around the trashcan that served as the beerball net.

The only thing unusual was the quietness. On every other call, John could count on a number of things: the barking dog announcing his arrival, Bill yelling, and Rose crying. He understood why there was no barking dog, but no yelling Bill? Normally you could hear his shouts from down the street. Once reaching the house,

John could always count on a drunken Bill stumbling out his front door yelling for him to mind his own business and leave his property.

This was the first disturbance call with no immediate uproar. Only stillness.

John walked up the porch, kicked cans away, and listened for a few seconds before knocking. Tim stood behind him. John opened the screen door, knocked hard, waited for a response, and knocked again. "Bill, Rose, its John Moore. We got a call. Can you open the door? We just want to make sure everyone's all right."

John got no answer. He knocked for a third time. The Watson's pick-up was sitting in the driveway and as far as John knew, that was their only vehicle. He doubted they went for a walk to "cool" things down. Not these two, not Bill Watson.

A court ordered therapist once told Bill to leave the house for half an hour, take a "time out," to relax, and then talk. Bill told the therapist he didn't need a "time out," what he needed was for his wife to shut up and behave—that was all.

John stepped from the door, moved to the window, and looked inside. There was only darkness. No signs of light or life within. As John's eyes started to adjust, household fixtures became clear. He could see their old fridge in front of him and to the right countertops and a doorway leading to the rest of the house. In the left corner was a kitchen table.

John didn't have a very clear view of the table, but he did have a clear view of the dark wet trail that ran from that table to the doorway across from it. This path traveled through the doorway and into the rest of the house. He jerked back from the window. It was John's second blood trail in as many days.

Bill had hurt Rose a number of times in the past—punched, kicked, pushed, and thrown things at her, but he never injured her to the extent of shedding so much blood. This time Bill's aftermath appeared to be more than smears on Rose's clothing and bruising on her face. John feared Bill might have killed his wife this time.

"Tim, call Mary. We need Carl out here now. We have a situation here."

"What do you see?"

"Not sure yet. I think Rose might be...just call."

Tim blanched. "Is she dead?" He managed to miss the death of Bill's dog, but it appeared he was just in time for the death of his wife.

"Call."

Tim picked up his radio and did as he was told.

"Inform her we're entering the house."

John walked to the front door, removed his weapon, turned the knob at a snail's pace, and carefully opened the unlocked door. Sunlight quickly filled the once-darkened room as he stepped inside.

Tim followed him in. The house was silent and still. A musky, unpleasant odor hung in the air. Tim did not know Rose very well, but within seconds, he could tell she wasn't much of a housekeeper. Dirty dishes were piled all over the countertops, and Tim's feet stuck to the floor. He watched bugs scurrying away from the sunlight as flies buzzed around his head. Going farther in, he stayed close to John, not willing to risk crazy Bill getting the jump on him.

The house was freakishly quiet. There was no other sound than them. No noise came from the obviously old refrigerator, no clock ticked, no appliance hummed, no lights burned, and no people breathed. It was almost as if the house itself was dead. Even the annoying sound from a dripping faucet would be better than that. Nothingness was the sound of death.

John walked toward the table and found a body collapsed face down, with the back of the head smashed in. Blood-splatter covered the table and walls. John looked up and found more on the ceiling. It appeared the attack came from the doorway. Rose never saw the first blow coming.

Lying on the floor, in a thick pool of blood, hair, and other matter, was the three-pound Kobalt drilling hammer Bill used to bludgeon his wife's head. Bloody handprints covered its trademark words: *GENUINE AMERICAN HICKORY.*

The head attached to the body sitting at the table looked like a smashed pumpkin. John could hardly recognize the cranium as human.

The massive level of trauma and blood caused John trouble in making a positive ID. Taking a pen from his pocket, he moved some hair away from what was left of her face. He could not believe the amount of destruction. The most frightening part of all was when John discovered that Rose Watson—was not Rose Watson.

He stepped back and used his pen to lift the robe's sleeve, and there on the left forearm he found the tattoo. Tim saw the expression on John's face and glanced down at the exposed forearm, seeing Bill Watson's Tasmanian devil.

"Whoa...that's Bill! That's Bill Watson, isn't it?" He looked around the room again, confused. "Where the hell is Mrs. Watson? Is she, did she...

"I don't know," John said looking down at the blood trail leading out of the kitchen. "But we're not alone in the house."

He feared he might still discover Rose's body. Tim looked as if he was about to say something when they heard a noise from upstairs. To John's confusion, it was the soft sound of someone singing. Rose. John and Tim exchanged a mutual look of bewilderment.

The song was one they both recognized from childhood. From somewhere upstairs, Rose, who had just killed her husband, was singing a nursery rhyme, the same folksong she sang on the playgrounds.

For whatever reason, John always hated that song. Maybe because its origin came from the black plague. He didn't know, but regardless, he never hated it more than now. The oddness of hearing it under these circumstances made him question what might transpire here over the next few minutes. Rose's tone was soft and harmless, childlike.

However, after what she did to Bill, John had no choice but to consider her a threat.

What had happened since they left his office thirty or so hours ago?

Moving toward the sound of her voice, carefully avoiding the blood trail, John walked through the kitchen doorway into the long hallway. Along the hallway walls, John could see family photos.

On the left side of the hallway were two doors and a set of stairs. One door opened into a closet, the other the cellar.

The stairs led up to the bedrooms and the source of the singing. Tim, who'd once wished the silence away, now preferred it to that eerie singing.

Stopping at the bottom of the stairs, John looked over at Tim. He hoped the young officer had prepared himself for whatever might come. Things could happen fast. John hated to think of Rose as dangerous, hated the thought that his gun might be necessary. He'd known Rose his whole life. She might have had some issues over the years, but she had always been a good and decent person. Bill had turned her into *so* many things—his personal punch line and punching bag to name two, but she always had a friendly word and a smile for everyone.

John hated that things had come to this.

On the floor, trailing up the steps was more blood, not heavily blotched as in the kitchen, thinner, trickles. John knew it was from her hands.

The stairway split into two halves, with a small landing in-between, each set with eight steps. The second set of steps started around a blind corner, and that blind spot made John uneasy. He could no longer hear her singing. She'd stopped about twenty seconds ago, but that could be enough time for her to move in front of the staircase, point a gun, and wait. To reduce the chance of making noise, he carefully placed his foot at the outside edge of the first step and started to climb.

John reached the last step and paused before the landing. The walls of the stairway shared the decorations of the hallway, and he tried to find Rose's reflection in the hanging photographs, but was unable to determine if she was there.

He bent with his head close to the stair case landing and risked a peek around the corner. As he did, Rose started to sing again.

Tim stood behind John with his back nervously against the wall. John told him to wait a few seconds and then follow slowly behind. This way if Rose was waiting with a gun, she could only shoot one of them. Tim was familiar with the procedure and held back. As he watched his chief move around and up the stairs, he regretted being here. He dreaded having to see the dealer of those deadly blows.

Once at the top of the stairs, John heard Rose down on the left side. Having been in this house before, he knew Rose was in the master bedroom.

He took a quick look and was unable to see her. She continued singing like a happy eight year old, repeating the same four lines over and over again.

The time had come to make contact with her. He hoped Rose would agree to come out and this could end peacefully.

"Rose, its John Moore, we received a call that you might need some help. Is everything all right?" He knew damn well nothing was all right. Things had not been all right for her for a long, long time.

Rose stopped singing and the house fell

into a dead silence. Then they heard Rose drag something heavy across the floor.

"Rose, can we talk? There seems to have been an accident downstairs with Bill. Can you tell me what happened?"

The dragging sound changed as whatever it was met the rug. John decided to step closer.

Out of the four doors in the upstairs hallway, the one leading into the master bedroom was the only one halfway opened. He reached the door, waited until the dragging stopped, and called out her name again. "Rose." He waited a beat and added, "It's me, John Moore."

"Oh, hi, John, didn't hear you come in."

"I knocked and called out, 'Rose.'" He hesitated. "Rose, we need to talk. Can we talk?"

"I'm busy. Come back later." She started singing her song again. *"Ring around the rosies, a pocketful of posies, ashes to ashes. We all fall down!"*

He took a few deep breaths as Rose stopped singing and said, "The time of the offering is here, John. I know. A little birdie told me." She laughed quietly. "You know, that sounds a little funny out loud, a little birdie told me, but one did, yes indeed."

John decided to take a chance, opened the door the rest of the way, and stepped through. He immediately saw Rose out on the small back terrace. The little patio was just large enough for a small table and chair, a few plants, and the chest Rose had dragged out there and now stood on. Around her neck was a long orange extension cord that John followed to the solid oak bed frame.

"Rose, please come down. We can talk about Bill. This is not something you need to do. We can work something out."

Rose looked back with clear, bright, happy eyes and smiled. John would never forget that sparkling blood smeared look.

"But I am coming down, John. In fact— we all fall down—just like in my song. I don't think it's going to let us off so easy." She shook her head and smiled. "Fear the storm, John—fear it!"

Rose started her song again. *"Ring around the rosies, a pocketful of posies, ashes to ashes—"* As she sang, she turned and faced her backyard while stepping on top of the banister. *"—we all fall down."*

John made a run for her.

Carl arrived just as John and Tim started to climb the stairs. He was able to hear Rose singing from the front of the house and decided to follow the voice.

Walking around the side, he overheard John and Mrs. Watson talking. When he reached the backyard, Carl noticed Rose, with a cord wrapped around her neck, climbing to the top of the banister as she sang. He ran forward in hopes of breaking her fall.

He did not get there in time.

Rose stopped with one brutal yank, followed by a final twitch. She was dead—fifteen inches from the ground. Carl slipped and fell as the crack of her neck echoed off the side of the house and trees.

PART IV

THE VISITOR

"By the pricking of my thumb,
Something wicked this way comes."

William Shakespeare

CHAPTER 28

October 17th:

This should have been just another New England autumn day. The streets and people of Harrow were looking and acting normal. The local High School football team had taken the field against the Somersworth Hill Toppers. Shopkeepers were keeping to their shops, homeowners raked and piled leaves, and junior weekend warriors raced down streets and sidewalks on bicycles armed with their weapons of play.

There was a clear azure sky hovering above, and with little imaginary skill, one could picture a calm and peaceful ocean above. And coming off this sky-ocean was a cool mild breeze, blowing and lifting dust devils and leaves, twirling and whirling them into a dance. The sun sparkled off windows and car bumpers, reflecting the beautiful crisp day into the office of Chief Moore, where this fall day was anything but normal.

Every news outlet in the New Hampshire area wanted an interview. A few rapacious crews had even taken the incentive to show up and wait. Proving they were nothing short of human vultures, feeding on carrion, scavenging off both the living and the dead.

As inexcusable as they were, somehow worse were the people from right there in Harrow. Everyone in town had an opinion about what happened, in both the event itself and the events leading up to the Watson murder/suicide. They also thought they had helpful information and insight.

The constant calls and messages from every neighbor, friend, and store clerk who had seen either Rose or Bill in the past week had become overwhelming.

Rumors, like weeds, grew wildly, sprouting up and creating chaos. Their seeds spread through supermarkets and drug stores, scattered and budded up in Laundromats, schools and places of work, infecting phone calls and e-mails, turning people into contaminated news carriers. Pubs and bars became nothing more than verbal rag-mag newsstands.

The plain truth, as appalling as it could

be, was not always bad enough. It seemed everyone was guilty of adding little spins and details making events more interesting. Human nature almost enjoyed passing on another's tragedy, and by the time the facts finished making their rounds, it was almost never the truth anymore.

These gossipmongers had turned Rose Watson into a monster, with only madness in her heart, and Bill into a poor helpless victim killed by a savage. Nostalgic, revised stories of Wild Bill Watson had already begun. The same people, who a week ago, spoke about Bill with a "fuck him" attitude, now gave toasts with to "poor Bill," transforming him from a lunatic to a noble husband— remembered as a friend with some troubles, but a decent enough person who didn't deserve to go out in the manner he had.

As for his wife, people started calling Rose things not even Bill lowered himself to. Her name was now cursed and hated. She had become a scar, linked to all things foul and cruel, even to those who had never met her.

These unwanted and untrue anecdotes would only add to the already large Harroween Festival crowd. The Watson house just became another unofficial stop off the hay wagon tour. In time, people would call that place haunted as well. John had already added it to the list of places to patrol.

He sat at his computer filling out the never-ending paper work related to a case such as this. Sunlight and the rapacious sounds of reporters came through the opened window to his left. These news crews had been preying on anyone that dared walk out of the station, or just happened to stroll past it. For many of their viewers, there was nothing better than a good macabre story around Halloween, especially if that story came out of Harrow.

As much as John hated to admit it, Bill's death bothered him. Harrow was a small community and the people in it were a part of each other's lives. They might not all get along or like one another, but each person had an effect on the other.

The manner in which Rose killed Bill and then herself caused John to toss and turn all last night. He, like most law enforcement officers, had been tense ever since the first kid disappeared in Jackson, then Jason Benson—

add in Bill and Rose—and his stress level had raised greatly.

John had the safety of every child in town, including his own, weighing on his shoulders. That burden and liability, mixed with the latest events, only inflamed his already disquieted mind. John's inability to find his son's best friend was taking its toll.

Outside storm clouds had moved in. John's office slowly turned dark and gloomy as shadows crossed the room and sunlight disappeared. The gray of the darkening sky and the glow from his computer monitor were his only light. A strong ozone scent replaced the fresh smell of fall that had been coming through his window. Weatherman Al Kaprielian had forecasted a warm and pleasant day. Kaprielian might be a little wacky, but his forecasts were rarely, if ever, this far off. John didn't know when to expect rain next, but he knew it wasn't today.

Looking away from his report and out the window, John hoped Jane was home and thought to check the home office windows. The last time an unexpected thunderstorm rolled in, the room had been drenched, almost as if the wind had intentionally blown the rain in and aimed for his books. His eyes moved from the opened office window to the phone sitting on his desk. He thought again about giving Jane a quick call, but got up first to close the window.

Standing and looking out the window, John noticed the dark clouds did not look like normal cumulonimbus clouds. Granted he was no expert, but somehow they looked out of the ordinary. Before he could give them any more thought, there was a knock at the office door.

Mary opened the door, looked in, and found John with his hands still on the windowsill. "Chief, there's a Detective Rodale from the Major Crime Unit here to see you. He says it's important."

John let out a soft sigh and nodded.

He'd known that eventually they would come. Harrow was a small town with a missing child and a murder/suicide on their hands. The Governor ordered The Department of Safety to investigate the disappearance of the missing kids in the area. The New Hampshire RSA-106-B:15 determined when a State Trooper could act within a town or city having at least three thousand people.

216

Along with the governor's order, John himself asked for their assistance. What he had not anticipated was Joseph Rodale. If he'd come, things were worse than John expected. Rodale must have the blood results from Simon and his clothing.

"Thank you, Mary. Can you please show the detective in?"

Mary smiled, flipped the overhead light switch on, and left the room. John walked over to a filing cabinet and pulled out the Simon Allen files.

John had only met Detective Rodale a few times, but the man had a reputation for straightforward coldness. Rodale was all business.

Something very interesting must have shown up to bring him up from Concord. The news crews must have liked seeing him pull up. John would have warned Rodale about them if he'd phoned ahead.

There was another knock and again Mary entered with the detective and two other troopers. John extended his hand to greet the lead detective. Rodale was not a large man, but he had strength. His eyes were hard and intelligent, filled with purpose and principles. These eyes looked into John's as they shook hands.

The detective sat down in the same chair Rose had not two days ago. The other two state troopers from the E Barracks in Tamworth stood at the door, book-ending it.

Rodale opened his brief case, removed several folders, and placed them on the desk in front of him. "We have your lab results and they are concerning—to say the least." He flipped through the folders looking for the one he needed first and opened it. "First off, Allen's toxicology test came back clean, he wasn't on anything. Now for the interesting part, the blood traces found on his shorts contained not only the blood from a dog and himself, but from two other humans as well, and I'm sorry to report, one matched positive for Jason Benson." He raised his eyes to catch John's response.

John had feared some of the blood would be human, and would belong to Jason, but another person! Sadly, this other person was probably a child as well. He looked down at his own pile of folders and opened the one containing Dr. Miller's report.

"Questioning the suspect might be a little

difficult, Detective. Mr. Allen has catatonia. He's been in a catatonic stupor since Thursday. The Sheriff's Department moved him yesterday to Tamerlane State Hospital in Conway." John watched Rodale's face, but there was no noticeable reaction. He handed over the medical report, "You weren't informed?"

"I was not. What exactly are the suspect's symptoms? When is he expected to recover?"

"Well, first we noticed Mr. Allen's incivility and refusal to eat. Then yesterday morning two of my officers witnessed and reported some strange waxy-like flexibility. Mr. Allen, when placed in a position, would hold himself in that position, no matter how odd or uncomfortable, for an extended period until he was taken out of the position. I made a judgment call and called Dr. Vassell, MD, and another doctor, a psychiatrist by the name of Miller at—"

"I need any and all information on how to reach these two doctors. Simon Allen could be a very dangerous man. How do you know he's not faking the condition?" Without waiting for a reply, Rodale continued. "I recommend that the parents in this area update their children's finger prints, photos, and have DNA samples taken just in case something was to happen."

John agreed with Rodale. Parents should be updating their child's records. He himself already had. He always kept records of all the members of his family. They were safely stored right here in his office.

"You said two traces of human blood were found, one matching Jason Benson. Is there a match for the second trace as well?"

With a slight nod, Rodale opened another folder and removed a single piece of paper. John could see it was a missing person's poster. Rodale placed it on the desk and using only his index finger slid it across to John. The child's face pictured in the black and white photo looked both familiar and unfamiliar. The little girl on the flyer could have been some performer from a long forgotten television show. She looked familiar, but John didn't know why.

Picking up the paper, John read the black bolded text under the photograph, giving the girl's name, and that made no sense.

"This is Susannah Levi. She went missing

back in the seventies. This is a mistake, Detective!" John tossed the flyer across the desk to Rodale.

"Nineteen seventy-five, thirty-seven years ago this month, actually, and I agree it's incredible, but it's no mistake. The other thing is, in October of '75, Susannah Levi wasn't the only one to go missing. The fall of that year several other kids also disappeared, I believe seven was the number."

John leaned his chair back. He'd forgotten about the other missing kids. "You think they are related? If so, how do you explain fresh blood from someone that's been missing almost forty years on someone born about ten years *after* their disappearance?"

"Oh, I don't claim to have the answers, Chief Moore, just the results." Rodale took out a small flip pad. "The answers are what I'm looking for. Are there any members of Susannah Levi's family still living here in Harrow?"

"Reverend Jack Levi, her brother."

"A reverend, huh? I would like to have a talk with him. Would you by chance have an address?"

John gave it to him without having to

look it up. While the two officers talked, thicker and darker cumulonimbus clouds had moved in. As lightning struck within them, it heated up and expanded the air, producing shockwaves that instantly created a loud, sharp crack. These clouds centered above the Harrowing Hills.

Detective Rodale gave John an awkward glance, shifted his position in the chair, picked up a copy of John's report on the arrest of Simon Allen, opened it, and looked at the pictures.

"Interesting photos. I'm curious though. How did Allen manage to create such a bedlam? From what I read, and see in your pictures, you only recorded tracks of him leaving the apartment. Has anyone considered the possibility that he made another stop before his encounter with the dog?"

"Of course. We searched the area surrounding his apartment meticulously. We discovered no additional blood, other than what was inside his apartment, and certainly no bodies were hidden under his bed, or out in the backyard."

"Don't take my questions the wrong way, Chief. I just find it peculiar, is all. I can assume there's no clarification on where or how that much blood came to be in Mr. Allen's apartment and on his person?"

"No, we still have no explanation," John answered.

"Well, with luck that will change when Mr. Allen's condition does."

The detective was beginning to make John feel uncomfortable and his station inept. He could understand the reasoning and even the justification behind this semi-inquisition, but not having adequate answers made him feel lacking in ability.

"Has anyone at least figured out what the words written on the walls mean?" asked Rodale.

"We had them translated. They are in Latin. Avis means a bird, and the best anyone has done in translating *avi mala* was a bad omen signifying an unknown or undefined fate."

Rodale held up one of the photos of the walls. "So basically, we should read this as saying, a bird signifying an unknown fate, a bad omen? Well that certainly explains the artwork."

Everything electrical shut down as the

power went out filling the room with blackness. The air became heavy with a thickness like nothing John or Rodale had felt before. Both of their chests were thick and congested, making it hard to breathe. John took a deep breath, but was only able to inhale a small amount of air.

Loud thunder exploded and rolled across the sky as lightning flashed, giving the room a split second of additional light.

This storm had everything in common with a severe storm, expect for one thing. There was no wind, and John had yet to hear or smell the coming of rain.

In-between the thunder and lightning, there was a quiet sullenness. The office was completely silent. Everything electrical had stopped working, including the battery-powered wall clock. From outside the sounds of passing cars ceased as they, too, shut down. The only sounds remaining were from people clamoring in wonder.

CHAPTER 29

In her bedroom, Candice thought about her little brother and tried to understand what would make him lie. Could he really hate her so much he would use his missing and presumably dead friend to bust her for sneaking out? That was crazy, wasn't it? Could a ten-year-old boy be so cold and calculating?

Candice held her small MP3 player in her right hand, one finger set on its controls to skip any tracks she was not in the mood for. Pressing, listening, and thinking, she found the black magic techno sounds of Voodoo Velkro.

Lying on her bed, she stared at the ceiling, upset that she had lost the use of her cell, computer, and any promise of going out. Her bitch mother had made it a promise to make sure she got to school and stayed there. No more friends picking her up, no more nothing.

This was her life. Her mother shouldn't be able to control it. In addition, having the Chief of Police as her father was just perfect, was it not? It made it so easy for her mother to use him to enforce her laws. It was not Candice's fault her mother got old. Life sucked. A jealous mother and a hateful brother trapped her in life. The music stopped. She opened her eyes and noticed that not only was her player off, everything was. She removed her ear bud headphones and saw how dark it had gotten outside. Thunder rolled overhead.

The power was out. Okay, but why did the MP3 die as well? She got up, walked over to her desk, and opened the bottom drawer where she kept a flashlight. She pressed the on switch, and nothing happened. She smacked the thing against the palm of her hand and tried it again. Nothing. She looked around the room then out the window. Why was it so dark? She might have lost track of time listening to her music, still it couldn't be much later than 3:00 p.m., could it? So why did it look more like 8:00 p.m.?

She knew the batteries in the flashlight

were new. She changed them herself. The stupid little things get you caught. Therefore, when the Energizer Bunnies died the other night, she changed them as soon as she got home. So why were these batteries dead? Did Thomas take them for one of his kid toys?

She vowed to brain the boy if he had, but if that was the case, why was her MP3 player dead also? Her father made sure all flash-lights had back-ups, and the back-ups had back-ups. Candice was sure that, like her mother, her father had also lost his mind. She walked over to the closet and took out a fresh pack of double Ds, unscrewed the top of the flashlight, and dumped the old ones out on the floor. Tucking the empty flashlight under her arm, she opened the new package and put the contents inside the flashlight.

Candice again tried the on button and nothing changed. She made a scoffing sound, thinking the bulb must have burned out. She tossed the useless light on her bed, walked to the bedroom door, and yelled for her mother. Everything was quiet, except for the thun-derous booms from outside. She stepped out into the hallway and moved down the shad-owy stairs, but it appeared no one else was home. She reached the bottom and found her mother's coat still hanging on the rack. Her car keys were in the kitchen. If she went somewhere, she walked there. Candice believed she must be around, maybe down in the basement with Thomas looking at the fuse box. She hoped their luck with a flashlight was better.

Their kitchen had a duel entrance. On the back wall of the room, a doorway entered into the dining room. In the dining room was the small door to the cellar. The grimy, lightlessness of that subterranean vault had always bothered her. Just the nauseating thought of spiders concealed within the black corners of dirty pipes and wooden ceiling beams made her want to scream, never mind the idea of touching the disgusting floor that unknown numbers of rodents and bugs had probably crawled across.

Candice could not fathom someone willingly going down there in a power outage. Large windows let her see for the first time the clouds that created the gloominess. They rolled and moved like smoke, smothering out the sun and its rays. From the farthest window on the right, Candice caught movement and finally found her mother and brother outside pointing toward the oncoming storm.

Candice stepped out onto the patio and felt how thick the air was. There had been stuffiness in the house, but it was nothing like this. The fresh air the day had started with had vanished with the sun, sucked away with the light. Booming thunder rocked the house as Jane looked back and saw Candice approaching.

"What's going on, Mom? It looks like a fucking tornado or something," Candice said as she reached her family.

Jane could only shake her head to herself. She had asked her daughter repeatedly not to use that kind of language, especially around Thomas. But she already had enough problems with her right now and decided to let this go. She had to choose her battles or they would fight over everything. "I'm not sure, but it's no tornado. This is New Hampshire. I don't think we get them here."

Candice looked from the storm clouds to her mother. "I'm pretty sure New Hampshire can get tornados, Mom. In fact, I seem to remember Keene being under a warning a few months ago."

Jane looked at her. As soon as her daughter mentioned Keene, she remembered. There was something about that a few months ago in Cheshire County. But she would not let Candice know she'd forgotten. "Even if that's true, there are too many hills for one to touch down for very long."

"Whatever it is, it's kinda beautiful, in a spooky sort of way."

"It certainly is something,"

"Dad said it was going to be nice today Mom. What happened?" asked Thomas.

Candice snorted. "Yeah, I don't remember hearing Dad's weather nut going, 'Good Eeeevening, everybody, today we'll have sun followed by a twisted twister, and no chance of normalcy.' Did any of you? I know I didn't. What's up with the power? Did something get struck by lightning or did you forget to pay the bills?"

Jane turned around and faced Candice. This comment she would not let slide. She started to say something when Thomas grabbed hold of her arm and pulled hard. Jane looked down at her son as he darted behind her, pointing up at the storm clouds. Jane looked up and saw thicker, more solid-looking clouds, moving faster and faster in an anticlockwise motion, looking more like hurricane clouds than a tornado. They spun in a circle, building up a small and private storm just for Harrow. These flickering, black clouds stirred around the clear opening of the storm's eye, centered above the Harrowing Hills.

Something thicker, blacker, began to fill the whirlwind clouds, rolling in like smoke or liquid mercury. Later Jane would describe it as if a thicker substance poured into a thinner one, overtaking it and changing its texture and color, like creamer pouring into coffee.

This new entry rolled in, spread out, and started moving in the opposite direction of the storm. As the clouds spun and the lightning within struck, the almost-silhouetted nebula moved clockwise.

This shapeless form defied the force of the storm. As thunder rolled above her, Jane, for the first time since she was a child, was uncertain about what caused the rumbling of a thunderclap.

Forgetting about Candice's off-color remarks, Jane's only concern was to get her children to shelter. "Run for the house!" she shouted.

Candice and Thomas ran without question, with Jane not far behind them. The basement was the safest place in a severe storm, and as much as Candice hated that tomb, she disliked the looks of that thing in the sky even more.

She pulled open the bulkhead doors then she and Thomas ran down the steps leading into the cellar. Jane took one last look over her shoulder. What she saw temporarily knocked her off balance. She stumbled, reclaimed her footing, and ran even faster.

CHAPTER 30

John and his guests went outside to observe the irregular movements in the eclipsed, sunless sky. They watched as a nebula-like thing moved against the current of the wind, a wind still not felt on the ground. This indistinguishable shape appeared to be traveling even faster than the clouds themselves. Electrical devices still weren't working, and this upset the news crews a great deal.

Rodale stood poised with his hands behind his back. John moved to his side and clearly saw that Rodale did not appreciate the interruption. "There's something you should know before you talk to Reverend Levi," John told him.

Rodale turned toward him.

"Jack was with his sister when she went missing. Nobody knows what actually happened, not even Jack. After reading the file, you probably know as much as anyone, but

Susannah Levi is believed to have been kid-napped from somewhere up in those hills." John pointed toward the Harrowing Hills. "That was a long time ago, Detective, and Jack was a young boy then. Whatever hap-pened is in the past. There is nothing you or anyone else can do about it other than expose old wounds. I remember when it happened—Jack was never the same again. I can't ex-plain how Simon came into contact with Jack's sister's blood, but...please, Detective, handle Jack Levi delicately. That's all I ask."

"I'll keep it in mind when I meet with him."

Was Jack now a suspect? John decided to change the subject. "What do you make of that thing, detective?"

Rodale shook his head. "I understand those clouds about as much as I understand anything that's going on here in your town—including this electromechanical failure—which I believe are related to one another," Rodale answered still looking up to the clouds.

All around, people stood riveted in a mix-ture of wonder and dread, making both Har-row's officers' and the State Troopers' jobs harder as they tried to move everyone inside in case the storm decided to turn violent. But for every one person they got under shelter, two would go back outside.

"I don't understand the failure myself," John confessed. "It's almost as if an electro-magnetic pulse had taken place. But from a storm? How can a storm produce gamma rays? It can't, at least not that I'm aware of anyway."

Carl had been standing nearby and over-heard them.

"Gamma rays? Did you just say gamma rays? Is that cloud the result of some kind of nuclear explosion? Is that what's going on? Is that why all the power is dead?" he asked, sounding nervous as hell.

"Carl, no one said anything about a nu-clear explosion, and don't you either. When you're wearing that uniform, anything you might be overheard saying will be mistaken as fact. Watch yourself!"

Carl looked anxiously at his boss, still alarmed about possible radiation from a det-onation.

"There are a number of devices that could achieve a non-nuclear EMP," Detective

Rodale quietly informed Carl. "But let's not jump to conclusions. The last thing we need is the panic of a terrorist attack on our hands. We're not exactly a major city here."

Carl moved in closer, almost kissing distance to him. "What about Seabrook? What if there was a meltdown or something, a leak, you know, at the power plant? What—"

John stopped him before he could finish. "Officer, we can't do this right now. If you need to take a minute and get your composure back, then do so, but do not cause this to get out of hand, do you hear me?"

"Yes sir."

Gasps were heard from somewhere behind the three men, followed by, "Oh my God!" John whirled around as people started to back up. A few even began to run. He turned back and saw the middle of the spinning clouds start to form a cone-shape. A spiraling funnel lowered from the center of the storm and connected itself to the Harrowing Hills.

The dark nebulous thing disappeared from the clouds and into the cone, blackening it, and then it was gone.

The whirlwind clouds slowed down, the

lightning and thunder stopped, and the heaviness in the air thinned out. John and Rodale both were at a loss over what they'd just witnessed.

Finally, John felt the air loosen. He took a long-needed deep breath and said, "Now what are we supposed to make of something like that?"

Detective Rodale had no answer.

All of a sudden, a low, prolonged sound of pain and suffering filled the air. An ominous and unearthly moan came from the Hills. The sound slowly increased and vibrated the ground as a pulsation traveled like a shockwave across Harrow.

CHAPTER 31

Eyes wide open
Open and alive
Alive but dead

October 18th:

J ack sat out on the porch of his Winter
Street home. One hand held a glass of
water while the other clutched the arm-
rest of his chair. With his eyes closed and his
head tilted backward, he thought about the
past week and what might be happening to
him, to his sense of reasoning. He had to
consider the possibility that he needed professional help, that these day and nightmares
could be a sign of serious problems. That his
mild case of neurosis might be developing
into a psychosis. That he may be losing his
ability to determine what was real, and what
was not.

That he could be suffering from a serious mental illness and the birds were only an illusion.

Jack lifted his tired head off the chair's back, opened his eyes, and brought the glass of water to his mouth. The wetness felt refreshing as it touched his lips and tongue. For a brief instant, Jack wished it were something warmer and stronger. Something that burned as its passed through the body, numbing feelings and thoughts, heating the chest the way only the bottle could do.

He lowered his glass and the desire was gone, lost, but for a second, he could smell and taste whiskey. While putting the emptied glass on the table next to him and getting up from the chair, Jack realized it had been years since his last AA meeting—hadn't felt he was in need of one—but maybe with all that was going on, he should think about attending a few just in case. He was sure they still held them in Conway, but thought it might be best to find one not so local, maybe over the border in Maine.

He stepped over to the waist high railing enclosing the porch, placed both hands on top of it, and leaned forward, becoming aware of how many leaves had fallen again. It felt like just yesterday that he'd raked them up. He caught a whiff of someone in the neighborhood burning their own, and thought about heading to the backyard shed for his rake. He could use these leaves. He already had quite a few bags tucked away in that old shed, but he could use a little more.

Jack thought twice about it. For one, his doctor told him to take it easy over the next few weeks, and two, Lisa was home and surely not very far away. In fact, she was probably watching him right now, knowing just what he'd been thinking, and was just waiting for him to do some damn foolish thing like raking these leaves.

He did not want her questioning the collection.

He understood he shouldn't push his luck after what happened Thursday morning, even if it was only a mild heart attack. But the thing that caused the attack made the leaves all the more important.

The doctor told him his heart was still in fine condition, and that it was most likely stress that caused the attack, rather than a weak heart. Jack knew what triggered the attack, and he supposed the doctor was right about it being stress-related. After all, something masquerading as a bird did almost scare him to death. But did he actually see that raven? He believed so, and that was where his problem lay. If that thing really did exist, O'Brien would have seen it—right?

It could have flown off as his car pulled up, or maybe the thing simply had not registered to Sean as anything more than just a bird. Of course, maybe the damn thing was never there to begin with.

Either way, Jack felt the need for the leaves, and knew he should not gather them himself. He would hire one of the local boys from down the street to take care of them.

Jack had not gone for a run since his ordeal the other morning, but he started walking yesterday, and now decided to go on a short one. Nothing more than a few houses down or at the most to the end of the street. But with a little luck, he would run into one of the Wallace boys and ask him about managing his leafy predicament.

He stepped away from the railing, looked up and down the street, and scanned the rooftops and trees, hating the fact he felt the need. He wanted nothing more than to believe those wicked little things were only in his head, and with a little help, he could be free of them.

He opened the porch door and yelled in to Lisa that he was going for a walk up the street to ask Justin or Ronald about raking up the leaves. After her normal warning about being careful and not going too far, she told him goodbye.

His wife had always been overprotective, at least ever since they had kids, but she'd been especially cautious after his attack. Or should he be thinking of it more like an assault? The last couple of days Jack felt more like her son, than her husband. He appreciated her loving, worrisome ways, and he recognized she was only trying to keep him safe because she loved him. He just wished she would ease up on it at times.

Walking, as with running, was a way for Jack to think things over, get them organized, cleared. Sitting around, over-thinking only made a situation worse. This had complicated matters in the past. Moving helped keep the cobwebs from forming, allowing him to sort most problems out.

This bird predicament—no matter how fast he ran or how far he walked, he could not sort it out. From where Jack stood, there was no light at the end of the tunnel. His darkened passage ran deep, and Jack felt so alone. However, he was not. Others were feeling, stumbling, and tripping their way throughout this charnel house in search of light and answers. But this chamber held no solutions or peace for them, just broken bones and bodies of pain and sorrow.

CHAPTER 32

Among normal, everyday people were the deeply depressed, the walking dead. Blood may flow through their hearts and in their veins but life was not with them. These people no longer walked among the living. Instead, they were lost, submerged in a sea of melancholy, and buried in a pit of despair and pain—a desensitized, living corpse yearning to complete their deaths.

Lying in a sarcophagus of foam in a mausoleum called the Phuket International Hospital, Bruce was one of these living dead. A bed acted as his coffin, but a tomb was still a tomb.

In this grave of his they told Bruce she was dead. They told him it happened a few days ago. They told him it was the tsunami.

Bruce heard her voice, smelled her scent, and heard her footsteps—and the little ways she moved around a room. He had felt her next to him, watched her at night, standing in the dark corners.

Still they said she was dead. They said it happened a few days ago.

They said it was the tsunami.

They told him they were sorry.

Nightmares... of things crawling on floors, things crawling on ceilings, things crawling on angels, things eating angels, things eating Liz, eating him, eating picnic baskets, killing dreams, killing love, taking his promises away—taking her away!

Blackness... was all Bruce had now. His eyes could open but they saw nothing— nothing that counted or mattered—nothing to live for again.

Bruce did not see Liz, and though his heart still beat, it no longer existed. All that remained was the hollowed hole where it had died with his love, his life, his Liz.

From her upstairs bedroom window, Lisa watched as Jack walked up a street he'd have preferred to be jogging down, searching for someone to gather up leaves he would rather be heaping himself. She had no idea why Jack wanted all those leaves anyway. All week he had been bringing them home and putting them in the old shed. She could not bring herself to worry about it. If Jack wanted leaves, he could have leaves. Out of all his odd behaviors this week, she could deal with that one.

The past few days had been hard on him, but today was probably the hardest. It began with him sitting in the pews and not handling the morning homily himself. Lisa could see how much it hurt him, but it was just too soon. Chances were he would have done fine. Both of them knew this, and Jack's doctor probably would have agreed. But they decided it was best for Jack to sit and rest.

Lisa had feared Jack's stress level was high and related to his nervous condition, but never in a million years would she have predicted he would end up in the hospital as he had. Her husband was in excellent shape and never showed signs of heart problems in the past, not in one single test or physical. Whatever was going on, he could not handle it alone.

Therefore, without telling Jack, Lisa

made reservations for an Inn in Vermont and planned to leave Tuesday morning at dawn. She would make sure they were back by Saturday. By then Jack would have had plenty of time to rest and would be ready for his sermons come next Sunday.

She had a double agenda in mind for this trip. Yes, she wanted to go back for the maple activities, but just like her husband, she too needed some time away from Harrow. She'd puzzled together every covered bridge Vermont had to offer. Now she wished to see them again in person. The small one over Merriam Brook was just not cutting it anymore.

More importantly, she hoped the time away would loosen those stubborn lips of her husband's. A lot had gone on in town the past few days, and she knew her man well enough to know it was bothering him. Lisa realized Jack and Bill Watson had become practically strangers over the past twenty years or so. But they had been childhood friends. Too bad things, and people, had to change so much

No matter what kind of man Bill turned into, at one time, he was only a boy, and they grew up together. Things might have changed over the years, but you never forgot the bond you had with your childhood friends. Never again in one's life were the friendships as true and strong as the ones you made as kids. She knew it upset Jack that someone he'd known his whole life was now dead—and had died in the manner that he had.

Jack was the town's pastor and a sensitive man. It wouldn't have mattered if he'd never met the Watson's before. Something like this would have pained him just the same. But Jack had not even mentioned what happened yet. That was unlike him, and it was among the things that worried her.

Lisa moved away from the window as Jack waved to someone and faded past the house next door. As she left, something black landed on the roof just above where she stood. It also had been watching Jack. Once again, this atrocious thing spread its horrible wings and took flight, soaring off the Levi home and away from Jack. From across the street four more ravens followed and together they traveled above this confused countryside community.

The five fiends passed over the reverend's church without discomfort, but avoided Father O'Brien's house of worship, continuing their journey through neighborhoods where few still wondered about yesterday's outlandish storm. A few still questioned, but the majority had already put the storm, and the moan that followed, out of their minds. The ground-shaking moan was passed off as thunder almost as soon as it was uttered. The storm itself was remembered only as something weird and frightening.

The weekend was ending and real life was starting up again. People had a way of moving past some things while holding on to others. The oddness of a storm, even with a total electrical failure, could not compete with the Watson stories. Come Monday morning, the true powers of the rumor mill would start up again.

The Malign passed over Mrs. Wentworth's home as she prepared for the upcoming week's class work. She was just one of many who did not give the storm much thought after the lights came back on. Her mind was on other things. Her heart reached out to the Benson family for the loss of their son, and she worried about the Moore's son Thomas.

She understood how hard it must be for him. Jason was his best friend and—at ten years old—that meant something.

She wished there was more she could do for him. She'd already decided to reassign Thomas to a new desk first thing tomorrow. It may not be much, but at least it was some-thing.

She probably should have done it before now, but the loss of one of her students had affected her a great deal, had affected the whole class in fact.

She would feel better having Thomas sit-ting in front of her desk, and she couldn't think of a better place than right next to Wendy Kenyon. Everybody loved Wendy Kenyon.

As the schoolteacher thought over her plans for Thomas, the five iniquitous ones moved past, going about their way, shifting their course transversely across Harrow and heading out of town.

These devices of deception now dashed their way toward a State Hospital in Conway.

John moved, more slowly, toward that same location, to see the same patient.

CHAPTER 33

Voices in the dark
Voices speaking of promises
Promises of answers
...and revenge!

Ninety-one hours, fifteen minutes, and an unknown number of seconds ago was when they said Liz died. They said it was the tsunami, they said there was nothing Bruce could have done. They told him he was lucky to survive. Bruce told them to leave, that if Liz died, then he died with her. He told them to hurry up and bury him beside her. They gave him something to relax him, and he faded away into the pills they made him take—into the numbness, the nothingness he had become.

Bruce woke, speaking of angels, of demons. He told them he remembered what happened. He told them of clattering mandibles, of things crawling across floors and ceiling.

They told Bruce of post-traumatic stress and survivor's guilt, of denial, of coping, and "all in good time." He told them she came to him in night. That sometimes Liz stood in the dark corners of this very room. They told him that was not possible. Bruce told them to leave.

From the corner, a voice spoke of need, the needing of him. This voice spoke of saving and helping, of retribution, of reckoning, and taking reprisals for, about retaliation, and taking revenge...of requital.

This voice, did it belong to Liz? Was this who visited him in the night, who stood in the darkened corners? Was this the women he loved? Was this his love, his life, his Liz?

Time-released pain medication reentered his system, and Bruce drifted back to sleep.

Waking again, Bruce expected to be lying in the bedroom of the resort and for Liz to be next to him. Again, he was disappointed, finding himself in the international ward of a hospital with four other patients. Looking around, he remembered where he was, and why. His bed was the second from the left wall and the fourth farthest from the room's door.

Bruce had requested to be moved closer to the entrance a number of times, with no results. The nurses respectfully told him that all the beds were full in this and in all of the other rooms, but if something came up, they would consider moving him. Bruce wished they understood his need to be near the door.

The hospital staff moved in and out of the room as they attended to the patients. Out of the five in here, Bruce suspected he was the only one who spoke English. The others sounded European—Italian and German. Bruce wondered if any of them had seen or heard the thing in the room's corner. He supposed not. This visitor was his and his alone, and the words were for his ears only.

He did nothing but stare into the off-white colored wall in front of him. When he was not spacing out on its cracks and lines, he slept, trying to pass his life away, falling into small patches of death and emptiness, looking for peace and release from Elizabeth, from wanting to be with her sweetness. From the need to see her again, from the need to see those blue eyes again, the way they glowed, the way they shined when she told Bruce how much she loved him.

If he could only see that love again.

He remembered how she would look at him, her smiles, her eyes, how they made him feel. That the rest of the world could continue without her was unimaginable. A vital part of life was gone and nothing looked or felt the same. Could the rest of the world not see this? Could they not feel the loss, not notice how food had lost its taste, how the very air itself had lost its freshness? Could they not see and feel the cloud of smog and haze that had fallen over everything?

He heard the nursing staff moving about the room, talking with other patients, attempting to talk with him. He remained unwilling to join them, frozen. The world could move on around him, but Bruce just wanted to lay there and not exist.

Off in a distant land, another patient

waited the return of visitors. The catatonic Simon had other things in common with Bruce. They both stared off into nothing, but the difference was that one felt dead, while the other had never felt more alive.

The little speaking unknowns had returned. At first, their soft mumbling was unclear and unwanted, but in Simon's lost and clouded mind, they, and the other presence, became all be knew.

He no longer heard guards or nurses. He no longer feared the presence living within, but welcomed it, becoming a part of it, becoming something new. The Being that Simon once felt under his skin was *becoming* his skin, and very soon, there would be little of Simon left.

Outside the building, perched again in a tree, were the five ravens. Together they spoke to the presence overtaking Simon, informing him that The Black One had arrived. As these wicked little things filled Simon's head with imagery of a new time and "now," the floor of his room begun to change.

The random smudge and grime marks reminiscent of Rorschach inkblots moved and changed form, becoming disturbed and

distorted heads of unknown creatures, drag-
ons, and insects. Each tile square developed
shapes of disarray and confusion. Haunted,
off-centered eyes looked up from the floor,
twisted and lost. Human and non-human
skulls snapped and bit, shook and rolled.

The floor blots increased in size, connecting. The filth and encrusted stains began creating a shape that quickly consumed the
floor. The skulls and heads merged, and the
floor markings solidified into a forest of
large, uncanny trees. Unrecognizable living
fruit hung in anguish from their limbs.

The trees enlarged and moved apart creating a solid blackness between them. As the
spot grew, it formed into a pathway. A figure
materialized inside. Simon's eyes cleared
and focused, his mind alert, aware. The path
spread over the entire floor and standing
within was the life sized outline of a boy.
The boy's head lifted as his arms stretched
out in welcome.

A new time was coming—the new "now"
was soon.

CHAPTER 34

With both hands, Thomas pulled open the basement bulkhead door. Daylight revealed the cellar's inglorious surroundings. The smell of dirt and old wood flowed up as he stepped down and entered the cellar.

His father's wood working bench was on the left, along with all his tools. The dangerous power and manual tools were kept in a locked cabinet at the end of the bench, but sitting out was a forgotten hammer. Thomas walked over and picked it up. He looked around for a few scrap pieces of wood and picked a few chunks from a pile in the corner.

The pieces were small. One was roughly a foot long. The second was about half that length. Both bits were only a few inches wide. Not that Thomas cared. He just wanted to nail something—anything—together. It was the banging and hitting that he liked. He placed one piece over the other making the easiest thing that came to mind, a cross.

Centering a nail over the boards, he pounded hard—too hard. The nail drove through both pieces of wood and into the table.

Thomas tried to pry them apart before his mother came down. He knew he was not supposed to be playing with this stuff by himself. He could help his father, could even make his own things, but he was never to use anything alone.

Thomas knew his father had a lot on his mind lately and had left the hammer out by mistake. If he found out Thomas was down here playing, he'd ground him for sure. Thomas worked the hammer under the wood and pushed down. It did not come free. He tried again and still couldn't pry it off.

Turning around, he saw his bicycle on the other side of the basement then tried the wood again, but he was still unable to pry them apart. Thomas panicked, tossed the hammer on the worktable, and ran for his bike. If he had not been going through his own stress, he would have just gone upstairs and apologized, but instead, he grabbed his bike, hauled it up the old wooden steps, and rode off in a getaway.

Just as he pedaled away from his home, his father arrived at Tamerlane State Hospital for an appointment with Dr. Miller, the doctor covering Simon's care. As the driver's side door swung open and John stepped out, five shadowless black birds sailed overhead, unnoticed as he walked toward the hospital entrance.

Thomas rode across town, still not realizing that what he had done was not so terrible. Yes, he broke one of his father's rules, and yes, he knew how seriously his father took the rules, especially the ones put in place to keep him safe.

Thomas left without any place in mind. He just rode. Sometimes on the weekends, kids put together a ballgame at the field behind the school. That was if the older kids hadn't already. He rode to the large browning baseball field, but other than a few leaves blowing around, it was empty.

He decided to find Ronnie. The Wallace's lived a few streets away from Thomas, but believed he would have no problems getting to Ronnie's unnoticed. Thomas and his friends enjoyed pretending they were spies behind enemy lines, or bank robbers dodging the cops, any scenario where evasion and avoidance was necessary. They even mapped out "secret courses," called snowball escape routes that ran through the neighborhood.

The first of many backyard obstacle courses had been created when a car was accidently caught in the cross fire of a snowball fight.

When the car stopped, Thomas, Jason, and Ronnie took off running, searching for somewhere to hide. The three jumped or slid through fences, climbed trees, and when needed, scaled over woodsheds, doing anything to escape whoever was chasing after them.

Of course, nobody had been chasing after a bunch of nine year olds, but the excitement of the experience stayed, and they spent the next few weeks mapping out their escape routes in case it happened again, hoping it *would* happen again. There had even been a few cases of throwing a snowball or two at moving cars just to make it happen again, but mostly the backyard itineraries became a normal way to each other's homes.

Today however, Thomas was on his bike and was skidding to a stop outside of Ronnie Wallace's house.

Mrs. Wallace answered the door and let Thomas go upstairs to Ronnie's bedroom where he was playing video games with his older brother Justin.

Justin—an eighth grader—would never speak to Ronnie or Thomas outside the house.

In some ways, Justin reminded Thomas of Candice, only a little funnier. Thomas decided that all teenagers were mean to younger kids, but there were times when at least some of them could be friendly. Justin could be, as long as none of his friends were around, unlike Candice, who happened to be cruel all of the time.

"What's up, squirt?" said Justin as Thomas entered the room. Thomas smiled a little and sat down on the bed behind the two boys who played *F.E.A.R. 3*, a game Thomas only played over here. His mother would not allow him to own that kind of game and probably wouldn't want him playing it over here either.

"After I'm done blowing the snot out of

him, I'll take you on, Moore. Ronnie here is like playing with a girl."

"Maybe. I kind of wanted to play ball somewhere."

"You can play ball afterwards. It's not like I'm going to kill you for real. Besides, I'm sure you'll last about as long as my sister here anyways."

"I'm not your sister, you Buttwipe," replied Ronnie.

"Buttwipe, huh? Maybe I should tell your friend's sister about that little crush you have on her. How would you like that?"

Ronnie laughed. "My crush? Don't you mean your crush? After all, you're the one with a picture of her in your room."

Justin's face turned red with embarrassment and he punched his brother in the arm. "What are you doing in my room? She gave me that picture. She wanted me to have it."

Justin looked over at Thomas.

At first Thomas thought Justin was about to hit him next, but then he turned back to his arm-rubbing brother.

Ronnie smiled and looked over at Thomas. This time, Thomas understood what the look meant and got ready to run.

"Did she want you to keep it under your pillow, also?" Both Ronnie and Thomas laughed as they ran from the room.

"Yeah, did my sister also want you to kiss it goodnight?" Thomas called and then pretended to kiss a picture in his hands.

Justin dropped his game controller and ran after the two smaller boys. And just as he was about to grab Thomas from behind, Mrs. Wallace came up the stairs, saving them with the magic words of "Stop running in the house." Thomas and Jason slipped past Mrs. Wallace with a smile and headed for the front door, overhearing, "And Justin, since you have so much extra energy, take out the trash."

Justin stopped and picked up the trash bag.

Once the two boys were outside, they hopped on their bikes and took off down the street. Justin could hear the last of their taunts as they rode away.

Placing the trash by the street curb, he watched as the two boys disappeared over the hill. As he turned away, Jack Levi appeared from the other direction and waved to Justin with a smile.

CHAPTER 35

Bruce woke again to the bliss of medicated fuzziness and freedom. The bird-egg-sized pain pills given to him deafened the intensity of his shattered rib cage, and for the time being, suspended his neck pain and headache altogether.

During these short periods of relief, Bruce not only got a break from his pain, but from himself as well. The medication allowed him to forget the things that haunted his every thought, permitting him to forget who Bruce Wren was for a while.

Like most drugs, there were side effects. These god-like pills made him unable to understand and grasp his surroundings. He doubted, and questioned, everything in his dreamlike and unclear world.

This was one of those times.

It was nighttime again. This was the only reference Bruce used for time keeping now—it was daytime or it was night—other than that, time had become the enemy. A second was too long; a minute felt like an eternity. Bruce wished he could smash every clock and set fire to every calendar, to destroy and disregard all forms of time keeping.

The room was dark with little moonlight shining through the windows near the balcony. Bruce hated that balcony and could not believe they had not relocated him yet. Was there no empathy here? Did they not realize what had happened to him, that the very existence of that thing was a constant reminder of his tragedy? He tried to get his bearings while hardly being able to keep his eyelids open. Sometimes the nighttime nurse left him a large cup of water if she found him asleep. At least there was one good-hearted person in this compassionless hospital who understood what Bruce was going through.

He found and pressed the up button on the bed's remote control, and his upper body slowly lifted to a semi-sitting position. Without moving his torso or head, he angled his eyes sideways. Using his peripheral vision, Bruce found the cup placed on the bedside table at his left. He reached out and grabbed hold of the large lidded plastic cup, and as he struggled to bring the long straw to his mouth, movement caught his eye.

Carefully, he lowered the cup and looked. Standing just outside the dreadful balcony doors was Liz.

Bruce lost his grip on the cup as she stepped in. A scent filled the room as water spilt down Bruce's chest and onto the bed. He'd sensed her presence a number of times before, had heard and seen her standing in the dark, but never had she stood so out in the open. And like the times before, Bruce wondered if she was really there. He now questioned if he actually wanted her to be.

Many people had attempted to visit with him, wishing to pay their respects and show sympathy. However, Bruce did not want the condolences from the hotel staff or the local government, nor did he wish to see other guests from the hotel. Once, even the rubber tree man tried to see him, but Bruce wished to see him least of all.

Deep down, he did not blame the rubber tree man. He couldn't. Nevertheless, when something terrible happened, blame went out by the fistfuls, and that included to the client and the company who brought him to this god-forsaken island. Bruce did not care how Mr. Rubber Tree Man managed after the tsunami. In fact, he hoped he lost everything—just as Bruce had.

Out of all the unwelcome visitors, Bruce was most unsure of the one he saw now—his visitor who no longer stood in the corner, this visitor who was supposed to be dead.

As he watched Liz's silhouette glide gracefully across the floor under the soft moonlight, Bruce closed his eyes and wished his head would clear. He wondered if he could possibly be asleep, but he was unable to convince himself of this when the sound of water dripping to the floor and the chilled pinch of it seeping beneath him, told him otherwise.

He opened his eyes.

Liz continued to move slowly toward his bed. The earthy scent of flesh flowers and spring air drifted off her. Bruce had smelled the aroma when she first stepped through the doors, but now it was much stronger. He had never smelled anything like it before, pure and natural, unlike anything manufactured and put in a bottle. Did spirits have a scent?

Bruce quickly pushed the question from his mind. Seeing her now only confused him more. How was he supposed to comprehend that Elizabeth Bernhardt's ghost might be standing at the foot of his bed.

"Liz?"

There was no answer from her. The darkness of the room hid her features, but Bruce knew Liz's mannerisms and he could still make those out, even in the lightless shine of the moon.

"Is that really you?"

He waited for her to say something, anything. No matter what she had to say, it would be better than her just standing there looking him over. She started to walk up the right side of his bed, sliding her hand along the edge. Bruce's heart pounded with both fear and excitement. Even if this happened to be her spirit, did that mean it was Liz?

After everything he had seen, how was he to know this apparition, this Manitou, was not evil?

"Liz...is that you?" he asked in a parched voice. Now more than ever, he could use that spilled water.

Liz stopped beside him and, as he looked

up at her, an overwhelming feeling of peacefulness flowed through him. His mind and body relaxed and tranquility took over. As his eyes adjusted to the moonlight and focused on Liz's face, he saw that the eyes looking back at him did not belong to Liz. They belonged to a woman he had never met before, to the only face in creation more beautiful than the one he'd expected to see. From the shadows, her hair had looked as dark as Liz's, but as she leaned closer, her tresses turned blonde.

All feelings of depression and desperation left him, including forlornness. This unknown woman reached down and ran a pretty finger across his forehead, moving sweaty strands of hair away. He could feel a warm, almost tingly, sensation fill his head as she relieved him of his headache.

In a soft voice she said, "No, Bruce, I am not your Elizabeth. My name is Sariel."

The news that this woman was not Liz should have stirred a mixture of emotions within him, confusion, fear, sadness, relief, disappointment, and anger to name a few, but it did not. Without feelings of confusion or misunderstandings, he just simply accepted. She said her name was Sariel, and that was all he needed to know.

Her full lips smiled as the moonlight exposed her light blue-green eyes before they marbleized to black. "How are you feeling? Are they giving you what you need?" she asked him. Bruce was unsure how to answer the questions. "I might be able to help you," she continued. "In some ways at least."

Placing both of her hands on Bruce's bandaged chest, she said, "Don't be afraid. Things are going to feel better physically for you. But sadly, not even I can fix all that pains you."

A warming sensation hundreds of times stronger than when she ran her finger over his forehead filled his entire body, causing Bruce to shiver and arch his back upward as he lifted off the bed. A white flame quickly brightened the room, and all his pain was gone. The white blaze turned spectral blue as his body lowered back to the bed.

He instantly felt the need to take a deep breath, and as he inhaled, he knew his rib cage was no longer broken. In fact, he could not remember ever feeling more vigorous in all his life. His muscles felt somehow different, actually stronger. He knew this was no pill related vision.

Although awed, Bruce accepted the welcomed change. Feeling both physically and mentally improved, he believed anything was possible in her presence. He had no idea who this Sariel was, but he loved her just the same.

Not in the way he loved Liz, but in a way that made him feel completed and part of the cycle of life—him a part of her, and her a part of him.

Bruce realized Sariel was more than he could ever understand—that she was not only a tool of peace and love, but also an instrument of death. He sensed the sanguinariness within her.

How he suddenly knew these things about her, he wasn't sure. He just did. The knowledge was within the changed blood pumping through his veins. It flowed through every new breath he took.

"You should feel no more physical pain Bruce, for you have already suffered and lost so much, and for that, I am sorry. But there will be more to come—a lot more, if you do not aid those who need your help."

Understanding her effect on mortals, Sariel paused briefly and waited for Bruce to pay attention to her words.

"Before your Liz died, you made contact with an angel. Do you remember him?" Sariel waited, knowing the changes in Bruce's body were distracting him.

"Bruce, do you remember Ezziel?"

Ezziel. The name snapped Bruce back into the hotel room. He more than remembered the name. He remembered the beast he first heard speak it.

Strangely, however, the memory did not trigger off the usual anger and resentment that he normally felt from memories of that day. This time, he simply nodded his head yes.

"By misfortune, or fate, depending on which you choose to believe, he happened to be discovered by you. There arc those who believe it was not just chance that it came to be so."

Bruce looked at her, unsure what she was telling him. Then he remembered the words Ezziel spoke, and one of them had been—

"Sariel, he said your name. Ezziel muttered the name 'Sariel.' His new, stronger heart stopped and started pounding harder than ever before.

Sariel slowly nodded her head. "Ezziel and another named Abaddon were amongst a group coming to me for aid when they were attacked by the demon Báalzbub. We believe only those two survived, and after being separated from one another, Abaddon found me and you found Ezziel. Báalzbub was the demon that followed Ezziel and killed your Liz."

"They were seeking you?"

"Yes. Ezziel and Abaddon were once of the order Cherubim, the second highest rank of angels, and were among the over one hundred and thirty-three million that turned and waged war against our kind. This horrible war happened eons ago, and since that epoch, many of those cast from Heaven wished for a cessation of hostilities. In exchange for this possible armistice, Abaddon offered information that must be attended to—the very fate of us all is threatened."

"You are telling me that the angel that washed up on our balcony had been among The Fallen? Then—wouldn't that make him a demon also?" asked Bruce.

"No, negative energy is negative energy, as positive energy is positive energy. Demons have been a part of everything from the very beginning, as we angels have been. The angels that waged war are still angels—in a way—but they are no longer pure positive energy. In terms of Light and Darkness, the fallen ones are grey, neutralized."

"The Fallen are not evil then? I thought The Fallen One, Lucifer, was Satan?"

"There is no single Being named Satan, only negative energy. Satan is the name mankind created for the collective whole of negative energy, the Dark God, the co-creator of everything."

"What do you mean the co-creator of everything?"

"There are two Gods that oversee the laws of this Universe, both being supreme architects of this existence. Together each half equals the one whole. One cannot subsist without the other. There is good and evil, and it is a part of all life, all things of nature—in this existence and all others—but it is also a choice. One makes the decision whether or not to harm another. It is those decisions that define each of us. Some of the fallen ones became evil because they chose to become evil. I knew Lucifer, and he was no God. He broke my heart. Ezziel, Abaddon, and a few others, made a choice to repent, and made a good decision, one that will hopefully save us all."

Feeling strong, Bruce tossed back the covers and sat on the edge of the bed. "Sariel, why tell me any of this? I don't understand what it is that you want from me. You said earlier that the one named Ezziel might not have washed up on my hotel balcony by chance. What did you mean by that? Also, you speak of a danger to *our* existence, implying there is more than just our existence." as Bruce spoke, he stood and stepped away from Sariel. "I'm sorry, but I don't understand any of this."

"Báalzbub and his swarm's assail and pursuit of Abaddon and Ezziel caused the earthquake and tsunami. Those waves could have brought Ezziel anywhere, to another beach—or continent for, that matter—but they did not. They brought him to you, someone from Harrow.

"There are a vast number of other universes, Bruce, many close to our own. The event known as The Big Bang occurred, but it was not just here. It created a *multiverse.* No *god* understands *everything* that is. After all, at some point, something created them as well. The threat to our universe—our existence—comes from one of those other universes, one very different from our own. With different energy and laws, with different atoms and matter, one with its own *gods,* a darker *god* that has been seeping into this universe unnoticed for five billion years— with the help of Báalzbub."

Dumbfounded, Bruce gaped at her. "What?"

"Think about this. If God and Heaven had no enemies before Lucifer and the fall, why did we have an army of angels in the first place?"

Bruce had no answer.

Sariel stepped closer, and Bruce stepped backwards into a wall. Her small frame stood in front of him. Her naturally exotic and intoxicating fragrance of Mondi flowers, Gardenia, and Almond oil caused a wave, similar only to a drop in a roller coaster ride, to flow through him. Pinned to the wall Bruce was unable to move as Sariel brought her lips to Bruce's ear. "I need you to come with us."

"What are you, Sariel?"

Sariel moved back a step to relax Bruce. "I'm part of the embodiment which mankind thinks of as the Holy Spirit. Bruce, I do not know the part you have in this or what help you could be, but Gabrielus has asked for you." She stepped backwards some more. "At the very least, maybe he wants to give you your revenge. The change in you, the transformation, is a gift from him, not me." She turned a walked toward the balcony. "Gabrielus awaits us in Harrow."

"I need revenge for Liz more than I've ever needed anything before."

"I believe you, and if things go well, you shall have it." As she walked across the floor, Bruce noticed for the first time she was barefoot. Her soft, beautiful feet moved soundlessly and elegantly over the floor. Never had he seen, or would have believed, a being could look so stunning. He watched as this amazing creature reached the doorway. She stopped and looked back. "Well, you are coming?"

Bruce dressed quickly and walked toward the angel.

"Do not be frightened," she said, leading him outside. "But I am not alone."

Before Bruce could ask, he discovered her companions. Out on the balcony waited a fallen angel. His cynical, black eyes stared at Bruce.

Bruce lost all interest in the fallen one as two large grotesque monsters lowered their heads in submission to Sariel. He watched as she petted the teeth ridden heads of these biomechanical-appearing monstrosities, as their sharp-pointed tails affectionately curled around her. They both had four lethal humanoid arms. The top two ended in a three-fingered rending claw. The lower two were simply long scything talons at the end of a short limb. Hefty tusks and huge leathery wings filled their backs.

Dog-like, these things obediently fell back when Sariel motioned them to. She faced Bruce again. "I would like to introduce you to Abaddon, sole survivor of the rueful fallen, and these two are members of my cohort. They are Valkyrja. Get used to them, there are more."

Abaddon nodded and Bruce noticed that, like the angel from his hotel room, his wings were gray. From Sariel's back, however, two large white wings appeared. Drifting off them was an aromatic hint of vanilla scented baby powder.

Taking one long quick stride, Sariel was gone. Her two Valkyrja followed. Only the mixture of her sweet and delicate fragrance remained behind.

"Please, turn around. I mean you no harm."

Reluctantly, Bruce did as Abaddon asked. Arms wrapped around him and the fallen one lifted him into the air.

CHAPTER 36

The main lobby of Tamerlane State Hospital was larger than John expected. From the outside, the building looked small, but the inside was spacious. Fake trees, real plants, sofas, lamped end tables, and a coffee machine decorated the soft-lighted reception area, giving it a feeling of warmth and comfort. On the left wall, adding life, was a large saltwater fish tank. Centered on the front wall was the hospital's reception desk. John walked through the lobby and signed in.

He arranged in advance to interview several members of the staff before he met with the Dr. Jonathan Miller. He wanted to hear what the people who tended to Simon on a routine schedule had to say.

There had been a few unusual changes in Simon's condition. Changes John could not have anticipated.

After the staff interviews, John went into

another, smaller, waiting area. Unlike the larger one downstairs, this one was cold and impersonal. There were no plants or trees, and instead of soft large couches, this room was lined with hard wooden chairs with a bare minimum of cushions. On the small wood table, centered in the middle of the room, were none of the normal publications one expected to find in a doctor's office waiting room. For that, John was grateful. He found it hard to trust any doctor who would allow the sort of celebrity gossip found monthly in grocery checkout lanes and hair salons into his office.

As John waited, he reflected on how so many cases were oddly linked together and surrounded Simon. First off, four children were missing from the area, the latest from Harrow. Then a normally calm and mild tempered man appeared and, wearing nothing but blood and boxer shorts, attacked and killed a dog. This attack seemed completely random. But why? Then there was Rose Watson. She was walking the dog when the attack happened, and then thirty-six hours later she killed her husband and herself.

Next was the blood. At the time of Simon's arrest, the blood of young Jason Benson and the blood of another missing person, Susannah Levi—a girl that disappeared from Harrow thirty-seven years ago this month, almost to the day—covered him. The existence of that blood was still unexplained. The remaining blood found belonged to the Watson's dog, which was to be expected. The only person who could enlighten John on this was Simon Allen himself.

Finding these kids had become a personal mission for John. These families deserved to know what happened to their children, and they deserved closure. Every lead and trail had run cold until the blood samples found on Simon made him the first real suspect. John was not about to let his one and only link to these kids go easily. He did not care if Simon was faking his condition or not. He would be held accountable for his actions.

It was not John's responsibility to determine guilt or innocence, nor was it his responsibility to determine whether Simon ended up in jail or in a mental institution. His responsibility was to keep the public safe, gather the proper information and evidence, and follow it to wherever it may lead, and right now, it led to Simon Allen. Though Detective Rodale was not ruling out Jack Levi as a suspect. It was his sister's blood found on Simon, and Jack was with his Susannah when she went missing. Now thirty-seven years later, it had started happening again. John hated to think it, but the detective had reason to question Jack.

Dr. Miller's office door opened and a middle-aged couple exited. The doctor waited until the couple was gone before he invited John into his office. Dr. Miller was a small, fragile looking man with a balding head. He walked with a slight slouch and seemed to have more than one thing on his mind.

The psychiatrist's office was small and cluttered with barely enough room for the two of them. Hanging on the walls were diplomas, awards, and other certificates showing his credentials.

However, his walls and desk lacked any personal photos. The doctor was either unmarried or he kept his private life completely away from work. On the other hand, his family photos could be lost under the disorder encumbering his desk.

Sitting in a chair just as uncomfortable as the ones out in the waiting area, John took out his notepad and flipped through it.

"Thank you for meeting me, Doctor. I understand that you can't break patient confidentiality, but I hope you can shed some light on Mr. Allen's condition. What is catatonia exactly? Will he ever be able to answer my questions?"

"As I told Detective Rodale earlier, I'll answer what I can, but there are some things I can't discuss with you, at least not without a court order. But I don't think it'll come to that. Most of what I have to say is general information about common symptoms for this sort of syndrome, which includes psychic and motor disturbances."

"Such as the stupor and rigid poses he showed back in Harrow?"

"That is correct. Catatonic stupors are very common with this disorder. A subject's motor activity may be reduced to zero. They make little or no eye contact, become mute, and initiate no social behavior. There is also the opposite reaction in which an individual becomes extremely hyperactive with no purpose to it. They can also become aggressive, showing violence toward themselves as well as others."

"I understand a member of Allen's treatment staff quit yesterday. What can you tell me about that? It's my understanding that Mr. Allen came out of his state of unconsciousness."

Miller opened a folder he had on top of his mess. Apparently, it was some kind of an organized chaos, at least for him. He looked over at John and closed the file. "Yes. We had an RN leave her position last night. She overreacted to some movements of Mr. Allen's, but I assure you they were common movements. However, I do understand her reaction. Mr. Allen has a very strange and difficult disorder. Hopefully, we will be able to convince her to return."

John looked down at his notebook and read, "Simon Allen was pacing back and forth on his tiptoes, making odd and repetitive movements with his fingers, repeating the phrase '*navis navis*' over and over again, only stopping to make animal noises." He looked up at the doctor. "Are these also common?"

"Essentially, yes. As I said, catatonia is

very hard to identify. There's a variety of symptoms associated with it. The one called echopraxia is the imitation of the gestures of others. Another is echolalia, the parrot-like repetition of words spoken by others. Other symptoms include violence, assumption of inappropriate postures, selective mutism, negativism, facial grimaces, and animal-like noises. Tiptoed walking, and what we call ritualistic pacing, are also ways we make a diagnosis. Trust me, there is more, all of them strange and abnormal to someone who does not truly understand the condition. In addition, if it helps—the words '*navis navis*' that Mr. Allen spoke were Latin for vessel."

"So let me get this straight, someone who just a few days ago who couldn't, or wouldn't, move was now getting up to speak Latin and walk around like a ballerina. Is he coherent? Can he answer any of my questions?"

Dr. Miller shook his head, no. "I'm sorry officer, but Mr. Allen's condition is not improving. We have him on medication, benzodiazepine, which is the preferred treatment. Normally catatonia responds quickly to medical intervention. So far, he has not responded, but it has only been a few days. I'm afraid it may be a long time before Mr. Allen will be able to answer any questions you have for him, and sadly, he may not remember the answers to them—if he ever had them."

John rubbed the back of his neck in frustration. He had the feeling his only link was slipping away.

There had to be something they could do for him, and fast. Simon might be the only chance anyone had of saving these kids.

"What if the medication never takes effect? What can you do then?"

"Well, if this medicine doesn't work, there are others. There are barbiturates and antipsychotic drugs, but the antipsychotic ones often cause the catatonia to worsen. Electroconvulsive therapy has been beneficial for those not responsive to the medications, but it's too early to think about that yet."

John stood up. "I still have a few questions, although I'm unsure if asking them will help me much. I believe I am starting to understand what we are facing here. However, I do have a last request, and you are probably expecting it. I would like to see Mr. Allen again, to verify his condition hasn't changed."

Dr. Miller escorted John down to Simon's room, only to discover that their catatonic patient had somehow managed to escape the locked, windowless room.

CHAPTER 37

After Thomas and Ronald escaped Justin's clutches, they tried to find that ballgame Thomas wanted so much to play. Their luck was no better together than when Thomas was alone. Even if the boys had found a game, what were they planning on doing? Neither one of them brought their own glove, bat, or balls. This fact did not stop them. Someone would surely share their glove, or so they hoped, and if not, Ronnie would go home and get his.

However, they were unable to find a game. In fact, they were unable to find any other kids at all. It was as if they all had ridden their bikes off the face of the earth. Though, the odds were better that everyone's parents had shortened their leashes, keeping them closer to home.

The boys decided to look in one last spot. The place their parents had told them to stay away from. These ten-year-olds had adopted the "what our parents don't know can't hurt us" attitude last summer and pointed their BMXs toward the Harrowing Hills.

The main body of the Harrowing Hills climbed high and deep before joining with the mountains behind it. The State Park resided in the center of a curvature that was most noticeable while entering the parking area.

The city of Harrow locked the parking lot this time of the year and only reopened it to prepare for and host the festival. It had become impossible for anyone to overlook the decorations that hung on streetlights or turn the radio on without hearing ads featuring the Harvester of Harrow's spine-chilling voice.

Thomas and Ronnie glided their way up the pedestrian walking path. As they rode, they saw small groups of people scattered along the tree line and the dirt road leading up to the camping area. As the boys watched them prepare for Harroween, they passed the old wooden vegetable wagons used to carry people through the woods. The horses were nowhere in sight.

The ball field was on the far left side of the parking lot, and although it was still some distance away, Thomas could tell that like their school, only fallen leaves inhabited the browning-grass field.

Parking their bikes behind home plate, Ron regretted leaving the house without his ball and gloves. If he had managed to grab them as he ran out, they could at least toss the ball back and forth. As it stood now, there was nothing for them to do here.

Thomas walked over to the aluminum bleachers as the festival staff's hammers ricochet off the trees and hills. Thomas wondered if his sister's boyfriend was among them. He remembered overhearing that Bobby's mother was on the committee and that Bobby and his brother sometimes would lend a hand. Thomas was sure Bobby Benito's idea of helping out came at a price. Who knew what kind of havoc he would perform under the cover of night and a mask come Halloween night.

Thomas had climbed halfway up the bleachers when a gust of wind blew. He held onto his Red Sox cap as small deadwood objects flew into the air. A tiny speck of dirt found Thomas's eye, and he instinctively closed them and started rubbing hard. As he frantically chafed the dust away, he heard a low whispery voice calling out his name.

Thomas stopped moving and reopened his eyes. All he saw was Ronnie standing at the fence with his fingers wrapped through the links while slowly kicking the bottom.

Apparently, Ronnie heard nothing.

Thomas looked around for whomever had spoken. He knew they were close because the voice sounded completely different from the echoing hammers on the other side of the park.

Someone could be hiding with some sort of voice changing device. Thomas had seen those things in movies and on cartoons, but never in real life.

The wind blew again, wafting Thomas's hair across his face. He turned and faced the oncoming wind, making his watering eyes worse. He tried wiping away the moisture, but his vision remained blurred. Every time he blinked, his eyes re-filled, and tears ran down his cheeks. Through his wetted vision,

Thomas saw a flash of red move behind a group of trees.

He looked back to Ronnie, but he was still looking out across the empty ball field.

"Ron!" Thomas called out then looked back to the trees. Nothing was there. He called Ronnie's name again. This time Ronnie stopped kicking the fence and turned his head.

From behind Thomas came an unarticulated whisper of a young girl, causing him to look back. This one sounded different from the one calling of his name. This was starting to remind him of the other night.

"Did you just hear that?" Ronnie asked Thomas.

As he turned back around, Thomas could see a strange, alarmed look on Ronnie's face. His eyes were focused and intense, and his skin color was turning lighter as Thomas watched. Ronnie looked as if something invisible had just reached out and touched him.

"Yeah, I heard something. I've heard it a few times now, can't really tell who or where it came from. Can you?" Thomas pointed toward the decorators. "Could it maybe be them?"

Believing, knowing, that the voice came from the Hills behind them, nevertheless, Thomas was hopeful Ronnie would say yes. Then maybe he would be able to convince himself.

However, he could see that look on Ronnie's face, and all hope of pretending was gone. Ronnie pointed into the woods and said what Thomas feared, "Over there somewhere, it came from there."

Thomas scanned the woods. The tree line was about twenty feet away, and as the two of them listened, a twig snapped—someone, or something, was just beyond their sight, moving in the shadows unseen. Watching them.

Ronnie, not wanting to be alone, left the fence and joined Thomas on the bleachers. A red flash moved from one tree to another. Both boys scurried backward across the bleachers, looking at one another. There was absolutely no question about whether or not the other saw it, saw him. Ronnie looked as if he were about to start crying.

"You saw, right? You saw him, too, didn't you? Thomas, please tell me you saw who I think I just saw?"

Thomas nodded his head yes. There was no point in saying otherwise. "Yeah, I saw him."

"It looked like—" Ronnie stopped and swallowed the buildup of saliva that formed in his mouth. "—it looked like..."

"Jason, yeah, I know," Thomas finished for him.

Ronnie did not move or say anything. He just stared off, watching for, but not wanting, to see that flash of red again.

His family told him Jason was probably not coming home anymore, that he might even be dead. Both Ronnie and Thomas knew that Jason was wearing a pair of jeans, a blue Patriots T-shirt, and his red hooded sweatshirt the day he went missing. They'd just seen that hoodie, and even with the hood pulled up, they knew it was Jason.

The whispering voice came once again. Ronnie shimmied farther down the bleacher seat and then slid underneath. His brother Justin told him about the voices of the Hills, told him they were ghosts and witches, and something called a siren. Justin said a siren would sing her songs, leading men into her lair. Ronnie didn't know what a siren was, but he knew what witches and ghosts were, and he was not following them or anything else, anywhere.

"Tom, I want to go home, please Tom, can we leave? I want to get outta here."

Thomas looked through the bleacher seat and foot planks and found Ronnie tucked down with his knees up to his chest and his arms wrapped around them. He looked up at Thomas with his scared reddened brown eyes and said, "Please," again, this time in the pitched sound of someone trying not to cry.

"Get to the bikes and take off."

Ronnie started crawling out on his hands and knees. Before he reached the end, he looked back and saw the woods through the bleachers' support beams. The tree line grew darker, the dimness looked...wrong, and so did whoever stood unmoving inside the shade.

Turning his head away, Ronnie crawled faster, digging his hands into the graveled dirt, bumping and hitting every piece of metal or sharp object as he went. From above, he could feel and hear Thomas stepping from plank to plank, moving down.

Just as Ronnie exited from underneath the

bleachers, he heard Jason say hello to Thomas.

Ronnie stood up and looked towards the dark tree line, and standing there in the shadows was Jason Benson. His face and features were hidden, but it was Jason's voice. There was no mistaking it.

Ronnie ran over and got on his bike. He expected Thomas to be behind him doing the same. In fact, Thomas probably should have beaten him to the bikes, but he had not. Instead, Thomas stood at the foot of the bleachers looking at the figure in the dark, and then he started walking toward it.

"Thomas, what are you are doing? Don't go over …don't go near him!"

Thomas kept walking.

"Something's not right, even you know that."

Thomas gave Ronnie a slight look back and smiled. A smile like that normally would reassure Ronnie, letting him know that everything was going to be all right. That Thomas knew exactly what he was doing. Yet, it did just the opposite. Something in that smile was more daunting than the creepy voices he heard. Thomas looked nervous but unable to stop himself. Ronnie let go of his bike and ran to his friend. He thought about what his brother said about sirens and wondered if Jason could be one. Could someone become a siren? Were they like vampires in some way? Ronnie had no idea. He just knew he had to stop Thomas from following Jason into the woods.

He caught up to Thomas and grabbed him by the arm, stopping him.

"Hey, don't!"

Thomas smiled again, even wider this time, but there was still unease in it. Ronnie tried to pull Thomas back and could not, discovering he was unable to force Thomas backward. Even if he could somehow knock Thomas down and drag him to his bike, he could not make Thomas climb on it and ride away.

Thomas shook free and started walking again.

"If you don't stop, I'll tell your dad you were out here. You know he'll ground you, maybe even lock you up for not listening to him."

Thomas stopped, turned half way around, and looked at Ronnie. Blankness had taken over his face. Ronnie started to walk towards him, hoping that talk of his father had gotten to him. He quickly found out he was wrong.

"Go ahead, you dickweed tattle tale. I don't care. The only reason I'm not allowed here is because everyone thought Jay was kidnapped. Well, look right there." Thomas pointed to the dark figure. "There he is, and he looks pretty okay to me."

"I don't think that's Jaso—" Ronnie tried to add, but Thomas cut him off.

"And when I bring him home later, nobody's going to give two shits that I was up here. In fact, they're going to be glad I was and glad I found my best friend. *So go if you want to. I—we don't need you anyway*!"

Thomas started walking again, even faster than before. The figure inside the tree line stepped backward, becoming more unseen.

From somewhere behind the bleachers came that soft whispery voice of the young girl again, calling out Ronnie's name. Ronnie looked, saw nothing, and ran back to his bike.

Thomas reached the edge of the woods and shadows. Jason moved deeper back, forcing Thomas to step farther in. Thomas called out Jason's name, and from some-where inside, Jason called back.

Ronnie got on his bike and started pedal-ing faster than he ever thought possible. Looking back, he watched Thomas vanish into the shadowed trees.

"I'm telling, Tommy. I'm sorry but I have to." Ronnie raced away as Thomas walked deeper and deeper into the darkened woods.

PART V

DEPARTURE

"I became insane, with long intervals of horrible sanity."

Edgar Allan Poe

CHAPTER 38

The last thing John expected was to discover Simon Allen's room empty. The first thing he did afterward was call the Harrow Police Department. He had little doubt as to where Simon would be heading, the only question was how? John had been working in law enforcement a long time and had come across more than his share of atypical cases, but the characteristics of this one were proving to be even more than he could understand.

How could anyone in Simon's alleged state vanish from a locked and windowless room? It just did not make any sense. Simon Allen could not just "tiptoe" past two State Troopers like a ballerina in Madam Butterfly.

Detective Rodale arrived and took over the search of the hospital. John couldn't envision Simon making it off the grounds. Then again, he couldn't have predicted Simon escaping his room. In all reality, how far could a sick man wearing nothing but a hospital gown get? He had no money or means of transportation.

Around the time Rodale was taking over the search for Simon, the phone was ringing at the Moore home. Before the call, Jane had had a better day then she expected. This morning she actually managed to round up all four Moore's for church. Jane had prepared for a battle with Candice, who took a stand on every little thing, but she was surprised when her daughter only mildly disputed. She guessed Candice finally realized she had caused enough trouble for herself this week and did not want to risk getting in deeper. She did still have the Harroween festival to lose after all.

After Father O'Brien's Mass, the family went to lunch.

Once home, Thomas changed his clothes and was off to do whatever boy's his age did, and Candice, unable to leave the house, just went to her room. John went to his meeting at Tamerlane State Hospital.

Then the horrid call from Mrs. Wallace came.

John's heart and feet stopped at the sound his wife made when he answered her phone call. He knew that sound, that mournful outcry only a mother could make. John heard it every time he told a mother that one of her children would not be coming home. Now, that sound came from his wife, for one of his own.

Jane did not, could not, believe her son's dead best friend led him into the goddamned woods. She'd never believed in ghosts or the paranormal, but living here in Harrow it was almost impossible not to hear ghostlike stories. However, right now the improbability of the supernatural, or the super-unnatural, did not seem so far-fetched to her. As much as she did not want to believe it, there was something wrong with the Hills of Harrow.

And her baby was in them now.

Jane tried to tell John as much as she could get out. It was not very intelligible or coherent but John grasped what she was trying to say. He called headquarters and told Tim Andrews to pick up Jane and meet him at the Hills' softball field. John wanted Jane to stay back at the house in case something turned up that he did not want her to see. But she'd insisted on going and there was no talking her out of it. John understood why, but there was one decision she would have to agree with. She was not going into the woods. On that, he was adamant.

Tainted, unnatural eyes watched John arrive shortly after Jane and Tim Andrews. Jane's cries filled the woods as John's car approached, and they were like mournful pieces of grief-stricken music to the Malign' ears, a harmonic dirge of sorrowfulness. The creatures listened gloriously as her life crumbled into dilapidation.

These onerous and merciless things watched as Chief Moore and Andrews left Jane alone and stepped into the woods. These heartless tormenters followed along in the treetops, going from branch to branch, chortling silently as they did, knowing whom they searched for, and what awaited for them to find.

As John walked deeper into the woodland, he could still hear Jane. Her disconsolate cries were as saddening to him as the fact that Thomas missing was. He couldn't see how Simon could have anything to do with this. From what he could put together from Jane's call and Ronnie Wallace's story, Simon disappeared from the hospital around the same time Thomas got to the ball field.

John didn't trust Ronnie's account of what happened. It was not that he thought the boy was lying, just maybe confused. He knew his son was having trouble dealing with Jason's disappearance, and he was sure the Wallace boy was also.

John couldn't say what really happened out here, yet, but it was not Thomas following Jason Benson into the woods. It did not take John and Tim long to spot what the Malign had wanted them to see. Near the base of an old stump were the fragments of Thomas's Red Sox cap. Bits and pieces were scattered across the ground, torn and ripped apart.

John ran over and picked the pieces up, holding them out in his hands, not wanting to believe what he saw. Under the blood soaked visor, was the name "Thomas Moore" written in his son's own hand. John's legs let go, and he dropped weakly to his knees. From all around, caws of amusement filled the air. Tim put on a pair of rubber gloves and placed what he could find of the hat into small plastic bags.

John looked up at him, holding out the visor with his son's name written on it. "My boy, Tim...My..."

Tim bent down and took the hat fragments from John. "I know, sir, I'm sorry. We will find him, John. We'll find your son."

The Malign flew off, expressing their pleasure and satisfaction, enjoying their role in the tendering of death and the deterioration of life.

Shortly afterward, volunteers gathered in the center of the softball field for Thomas Moore's search party. The group consisted mostly of the Harroween people at first. One of the ones gathered, and among the first few to know about Thomas and his walk into the woods, was Reverend Levi. Jack found out just minutes after it happened, but he had feared and dreamed about this long before that.

Justin had been raking and bagging Jack's leaves when Ronnie turned the corner and raced down the street. Seeing his older brother, Ronnie slammed on his brakes and came crashing uncontrollably into Jack's yard.

Hearing Ronnie's story, Jack felt like his head was shrinking. He could actually feel squeezing pressure and knew his nightmares were coming true—and that if anyone was going to find young Tommy Moore, it was going to be him. The question was: before or after his death. After the Wallace boys left for home, Jack walked unsteadily around to the back of his house, slowly pulling a bag of leaves behind him.

The sound of the bag dragging caught Wolfgang's attention. His ears perked as he watched Jack tow this noise-making object toward the old wooden shed. As the bag passed, Wolfgang ran from his hiding place in the garden to the safety of the back porch. Once underneath it, he observed Jack fish a key from his pants pocket and unlock the creaky weathered door. Deciding to improve his hideaway, Wolfgang backed away to the end of the porch as Jack opened the door and stepped into the shed, closing it behind him.

The shed had no electricity and, as unsafe as it was, Jack kept a kerosene lamp in there. Long dark shapes lined the walls. Once Jack lit the lamp, its golden yellow glow brightened the musky-aired shack. The shapes began to take form, revealing Jack's hard work and preparation, his tools of discouragement—bird frighteners for an immemorial amount of time, the protector of crops and, Jack hoped, Harrow's salvation.

These stuffed human figures hung off all four walls. Their intimidating faces stared blankly off at nothing. Jack walked over to a table, swiping away flies as he went. Sitting on the floor was a headless and unfinished scarecrow, his last one. Jack, for a number of reasons, named his creations, and this last one was Tattie Bogle.

Seventy percent of Jack's scarecrows were dressed in the traditional ragged clothing of overalls, patched pants, and plaid long-sleeved shirts.

However, not all. Some special scarecrows were clad in the black slacks and long-sleeved shirts of a clergyman, others in black double-bell sleeved Geneva gowns with an undecorated white linen mitre placed on their heads.

Jack bent down, picked Tattie off the floor, and rested him on the table. He finished stuffing leaves into a pillowcase head and attached it to the body using safety pins and bailing twine. Underneath the table was a small wooden trunk. Jack reached in, took out a set of rosary beads, and put them around Tattie's neck.

Six dead crows—the inspiration coming from Daniel Defoe's novel *Robinson Crusoe*—hung securely upside-down above Jack's head. As he pulled down these lifeless birds one by one, flies filled the air. He positioned the crows' stiff bodies side by side on the table next to Tattie's feetless legs.

Jack removed Tattie Bogle from the table and moved toward the right side of the shed. Leaning up against the wall were several crucifixion-styled stakes and pillars waiting for their mannequin sacrifices.

Hidden somewhere within these pointed posts was temptation, an enticement left by the very things Levi wished to discourage.

Eric Henson

Once the scarecrows were mounted and fastened to these palisades by bailing twine and positioned around the Levi homestead, Jack left for the Hills.

Now walking in the middle of the search party heading into the Harrowing Hills, Jack hoped to save ten-year-old Thomas. He took with him only his lingering nightmares and the bag slung over his shoulder.

CHAPTER 39

When Officer Mark Greene arrived at the Harrowing Hills State Park there was a tingle in the air, a charge. He found John standing off to the side holding his wife. Soon after finding the pieces of his son's cap, John decided to hand the helm of Harrow's law enforcement over to Mark until the location of his son was known. There was a chance this situation had nothing to do with Simon, or the other missing children. Kids did wander off all the time.

On the other hand, too much had already happened for a town with the population of only thirty-five hundred people. Something was going on. Every ounce of John's body felt it. He didn't trust himself to act in a professional manner. If he came across Simon with his son, could he be unbiased? No, it was impossible to detach himself when it came to family. Right now, there was nobody else John wanted heading up the search for his son more than Mark.

The searchers split into three groups. Mark and Carl each took one each, while John and Tim took the third. Carl's team went in where Tommy went in. John and Tim went off to the left of where Thomas entered. Mark's philosophy was that if Thomas did not head straight, he probably walked to the left. If he went right, the Harroween workforce would have spotted him. There was no guarantee in this, but Mark had to trust his instincts.

There was the risk that Moore's team could find Thomas's trail. If that were the case, Mark would relieve John as soon as he could.

Mark knew he was better off spending a limited amount of time searching and more time overseeing. Therefore, he led a small team toward the right side, just in case the workforce had missed Thomas somehow.

Dusk came upon the Hills. The setting sun reminded everyone of where they were.

The three teams had set out over two hours ago and the only trace of Thomas, or of his direction, had been the bits and pieces of a baseball cap. So far, all their calls and bellows had gone unanswered.

While aides searched and yelled out for Thomas, the mischievous and intensely cruel Malign watched from above, guffawing in amusement. To the ears of the unsuspecting below, their harsh cries of boisterous laughter were only birds protecting their ground.

Walking alone—hands tucked in the front pockets of his pants to keep them from shaking, and then only managing by balling them into fists—was Jack. And like everyone else, he heard the crackling caws from above. However, unlike everyone else, Jack knew their source and understood how vicious and sadistic they were. He knew they watched in mirth as everyone ferreted for something they would never find.

Jack walked slowly, waiting for his chance to wander off on his own, believing he was the only one with any hope of finding the Moore boy and that dreadful path.

Mark and his small group made their way through the hayride's thoroughfare. Mark had attended, and worked, several of Harrow's Harroween festivals and never enjoyed it. He preferred the park keep to its intended purpose. Growing up, his family made weekend camping trips here. He always intended to do the same with his own children, but time ran short and he never had any.

He knew the town didn't intentionally keep the road dirt specifically for the event, but Mark had to admit it wouldn't have been the same with a paved road. The temporary old shacks and barns would've looked out of place. The same went for the large cast iron cauldron that reminded him of Macbeth's three witches.

Something above the road sparkled in the fading light. Mark looked up and saw a wire stretching from one side of the road to the other. Stopping underneath the peculiar wire, he saw that one of its ends rested in the tree next to the old iron pot.

Curious, he moved over and looked up, and found a wire quick-linked to an eyehook. Tracking the wire to the other side of the road, Mark saw what looked like a hanging body.

Upset, he heaved a deep sigh and walked

across the road, glanced up, and saw a pair of shoes dangling freely in the air.

"Puppets," someone said behind him.

Mark turned around and found Bobby Benito.

"Excuse me?"

Bobby smiled and pointed up. "In the trees. Puppets. I personally hung that one," he said, actually proud of his handy work.

"You put 'puppets' resembling kids in trees? Do you have any idea how injudicious something like that is—how dangerous?"

"It's only a joke, you know, to scare people, and I thought with all that's going on, the customers would get a kick out of something like that."

"Son, I think you're the one in need of the kick." Taking out his notepad, he asked, "You have any ID, boy?"

"Why? I didn't do anything wrong."

"That's a matter of opinion. You may not have done anything illegal, but you unquestionably did something wrong. Now again—your ID!"

"They're only puppets. We swing them across the wires at the passing wagons. We've been doing this kinda thing for years.

It's all part of the experience, to get them all worked up, their blood pumping, before they reached the haunted pumpkin patch." Bobby pointed up the road. "Where the Harvester of Harrow finishes the ride."

"You should've had the brains not to make the puppets look like kids. It's unacceptable and offensive. I'm only asking you one more time—your ID." Mark held out his hand. Bobby gave in and handed over his driver's license. "Robert Benito, the same Bobby Benito dating Chief Moore's daughter?"

"Yes sir."

Mark looked hard at the brainless teenager. "You are aware it is Chief Moore's son— your girlfriend's brother—that we're out here looking for? You do, don't you? And still you smile and brag about your infantile stupidity, and to a law enforcement officer?"

Mark wrote the boy's information down. He would let Moore deal with this one. He handed Bobby back his ID. "Go home. Your presence here is an insult. I want these puppets taken down tomorrow. If I come back here and find them, I'll find something to charge you with. I promise you."

Bobby took his ID and ran off down the road. The last thing Mark saw of the boy was his Mudgett Auto Repair jacket disappearing into the crowd.

With daylight fading fast, Mark made the decision to call the search off until morning. He had already begun to move his small team out.

He radioed John and wasn't surprised when he did not reach him. He continued trying to contact John and Tim with no response.

Either the two officers had walked out of signal range—something he highly doubted—or, more likely, their radios were turned off.

In the background, his search party left the pumpkin patch and started back down the dirt road.

Mark noticed Revered Levi lingering in the back, as his radio squawked out his name.

His first thought was that John had finally decided to report in. Instead, it was Carl informing him that his team was heading out of the woods.

When Mark looked back toward Levi to wave him in, he was no longer there.

CHAPTER 40

John trailed behind the majority of the volunteers with his thoughts broken like shattered glass, every memory shard from the past week sliced into his sense of sagacity, splintering any unity and integrity he once believed life had. His family, this town, were both in a state of disarray, and everyone's feelings of confusion and hysteria were only going to grow and worsen.

The searchers stretched into smaller groups and called out for Thomas every few minutes. John was grateful for them all and hoped their efforts would pay off. John did not know how he would cope if Thomas was not found, and Jane would never recover if their son was forever lost to them.

He moved through the difficult terrain. Every cocklebur and thorn bush found and pricked him as he went by. Pausing to clean off his clothing, John heard his son's name whispered. He stopped and listened.

He did not notice the black bird in the spruce tree and completely disregarded the pyramid-shaped evergreen altogether. However, the bird did not overlook him and again, softly spoke Tommy's name.

This time, John pinpointed the sound's location and looked up into the tree, seeing the raven. He looked hard at the bird. He'd heard rumors that some ravens and crows could mimic, but he never heard it personally.

While he was staring at the bird, it tilted its head sideways. Rose Watson's words suddenly came back to him. *'The time of the offering is here, John. I know. A little birdie told me.'*

A little birdie told her, that was what she said. The bird slanted its head to the other side, hopped a few inches down the branch, and straightened its head upright. John watched as the pigmentation washed from the bird's eyes. While John tried to account for the new whiteness—a blue tongue flickered.

John now tilted his own head and started nervously wiggling his fingers. He heard the rustling of footsteps over dried leaves, and then Tim stood at his side. "You holding up, Chief?"

John shrugged his shoulders, looked at Tim, and said, "Honestly, I don't believe I am."

Tim tapped him lightly on the back. "We'll find your son, Chief, I promise. I know I have my faults...but my head and heart are with you in this." John still looked toward the spruce tree, so Tim followed his glance. "Wow, once upon a midnight dreary. That's one big, goddamned bird."

The thing softly spoke again. This time both Tim and John watched as the raven uttered Thomas's name.

"Did that thing just..."

"Yes."

Tim was shocked. "How?"

"Look at the eyes. Do you notice anything out of the ordinary about them?"

"I once heard that if you split a raven's tongue it could mimic words. Guess it's true. I hear they also impersonate other bird calls."

"Tim, the eyes. Forget about everything else for right now, just tell me what you see."

Tim finally did as asked and centered his attention on the bird's eyes. The thing started pacing side-to-side, bobbing its head again.

"Is it blin—" The blue forked tongue flashed out and caught Tim off guard. "— What the hell?"

John drew his firearm and advanced toward the bird. Although the Malign had nothing to fear, it took flight, creating a whirring sound as the wings fluttered.

It landed in another spruce tree and let out a loud throaty *kruk* sound. Tim was visibly petrified, causing him to appear younger than he already was. John continued toward the bird. Hesitantly, Tim followed.

As the two men advanced, the Malign again flew off to another tree, always staying near and visible, wanting the humans to see, wanting them to chase.

Putting his firearm into its holster, John realized the bird was leading them somewhere. If this thing *somehow* could pilot him to Thomas, he would gladly go along with it.

John looked back at his frightened officer. The young man was so nervous he could hardly walk without tripping over every rock and branch. The expression on Tim's face alone told John that he disagreed with this decision.

"Tim, you don't need to back me on this. There's no way of knowing where I am going, or what I'll find when I get there. I simply don't know what's going to happen."

Tim looked at his chief for a second and said, "You told me I needed to spend more time with you, to learn how to properly conduct myself as an officer. Isn't that what you told me? Well, that's what I'm doing."

John was about to tell him this wasn't what he meant, but Tim protested before he could speak. "Yes, I'm scared, and yes, I would rather not follow this blue-tongued speaking bird deeper into the woods, but...I'm coming, John, and that's that. I'm coming because I told you I would find your son, but most of all because I'm your friend, not just your officer."

John humbly nodded his head in thanks.

Tim caught up and said, "Let's go find your boy."

CHAPTER 41

Every movement made him feel suspicious, like a criminal. The more Jack thought, the more paranoid he became. His attempts to look natural only made him feel odd. If he was going to slip away, he had to do it soon or lose his nerve. Jack ducked into the woodland, unseen, and crawled away from the others.

Once out of everyone's sight, he stood and ran like a criminal expecting the entire Harrow Police Force to be chasing him, the child-napping reverend. He ran until his breath ran short, and then he ran some more, only slowing when his heart warned him he had to.

Resting his back against a tree, he gasped for air as strong feelings of déjà vu swept through him. He had been here before. Even though he had not been in these woods for almost forty years, he recognized where he now stood.

His dreams—he had been here in his dreams!

Slowly, he turned his head to the left and looked up, finding what he feared and expected to see. Perched in the ash tree was the raven. Jack looked away as he heard the other call from the right. This had all happened before. He carefully reached his hand into his shoulder bag, expecting to grab hold of a dead crow. Instead, he grasped the familiar squared shape of a Jack Daniel's bottle. His hand stopped. He had thrown that bottle away, smashed it, in fact.

The birds sat quiet and content in the skeletal tree. Was it possible they placed this bottle both in his bag and in the shed, tempting him? Jack knew it was so, and it was starting to work. Never had he wanted, nor needed, a drink more. Suspecting his life was soon coming to its end, Jack looked at the Tennessee whisky and twisted the Lynchburg bourbon's cap off.

The old and once loved smell of the drink's aroma made his lips dry and his throat arid. Unable to control himself, he smelled the cap. Powerless, he licked. He closed his eyes at the familiarity of the taste.

The bottle lifted as Jack opened his eyes and he looked down the opening to the dark liquid inside. Before it reached his lips, he caught himself, tightened his grip around the glass bottle, and threw it at the closest raven. Then he turned toward the others watching him. He walked toward them, knowing exactly what lay beyond the cluster of white birch trees they sat in.

As he entered the strange clearing again, he realized that not only had he been here in his dreams, but also as a boy as well. This was where it had happened. This was where his sister disappeared thirty-seven years ago.

He stepped across the greenish-yellow soil. Its sulfurous scent replaced the sour mash taste of Old No. 7 in his mouth. Ahead, through the twisted bare-boned trees, he could see the tree line on the other side of the clearing. Unlike the dreams, there were no ravens, but still he felt watched, tolerated. They were allowing him to pass. Reaching the finger-laced trees, Jack stopped.

No ravens landed on the side boulders and no shape lingered inside the darkened path. He waited. He expected ravens, and maybe Thomas, but he found neither. He yelled out Thomas's name but his voice fell dead and flat, muffled as if he bellowed into a pile of pillows.

Jack heard the sound of fluttering wings, turned, and faced dozens of white-eyed ravens. Their heads bobbed as Jack backed away, turned toward the path, and heard, "Hello, Shepherd."

He stumbled to the right and backed away from both the path and the birds. He turned around, planning to run, but stopped. Standing thirty feet away was his sister Susannah, and in her arms she carried Thomas Moore.

"Suzie?" Jack said softly, knowing what he saw was as much his sister as the thing behind him was Jason Benson. The shock of seeing her image was hard and painful, and Jack knew he was too late. How could he have been so foolish to think he could save this boy, that he alone could have stopped this from happening?

His chest tightened as a sharp pain ran down his back and arms, the beginning of his second heart attack in less than a week. He fell to his knees, clutching his chest, as his bag slid off his shoulder.

From behind, Jason Benson walked out of

the path. "Having trouble, Shepherd? Here, let us help you."

Jack slid around to face the thing decoying as a boy. He watched as the mischievous sprite moved toward him, hoping his heart killed him before it could. He shut his eyes and thought of his Lisa's face, wanting her smile to be the last thing he saw. As her image filled his mind, stillness filled the air. He heard the disembodied spirit stop approaching. Jack opened his eyes, but large white feathers blocked his vision.

A soft peaceful voice spoke. "I have you, Jack."

A warm feeling filled his body. His heart eased and relaxed. Jack bent in half, placing his head between his knees. His subconscious had not felt so serene, so meaningful, so welcomed, since leaving the safety of his mother's womb. As strong arms wrapped around him, Jack looked up.

The face looking down at him was recognizable, but at the same time, not. It was a younger, stronger, face of an old friend.

"O'Brien?"

"You shouldn't have come here, Reverendus. We must leave."

"The boy, get the boy. Leave me."

"Sorry, Jack, the boy's been taken beyond the path and into The Crescent Realm. I cannot enter there, and you don't want to."

"Am I dreaming, or am I dead?"

"Neither."

Without any change of sensation, not even one of movement, Jack found himself in the air, traveling straight up and fast. He did not feel it, but he had reached a height unnatural for man. Looking up he saw large white wings coming from his friend's back.

"Who are you? You're not Father O'Brien.

The same soft, calm voice said, "Father O'Brien was how you came to know me. My real name is Gabrielus."

Jack looked into the black eyes of the smiling archangel.

In her backyard, Lisa stared with wide, shocked eyes at the mess her husband left, realizing Jack's mental state was far worse than she feared. Her home and yard were in total chaos. Everywhere she looked a scarecrow hung from a stake or cross. And lynched from the rain gutters and roof were large black birds.

Calling for her cat, Lisa feared Jack just sat back and watched these things die. Slapping her leg and calling Wolfgang, she prayed Jack had not strung up something that was a part of their family.

From under the backyard porch, she heard the cry of her cat. She walked over and saw green eyes looking out at her. Reaching under, she picked up Wolfgang. Forget Jack, she and this cat were getting away from here.

Going up the back porch, she stopped before entering the house. What if Jack was inside? Bravely, Lisa opened the door, stepped inside, and listened for any sign of her husband. Hearing nothing, she stepped farther in and called out Jack's name. She got no answer. Lisa went upstairs and threw a few things in a suitcase. She did not know yet what had happened here, only that Jack did it. She had no plans to go far. She would just grab some cash and get a room in North Conway. From there she'd call Jack, and if everything was better by tomorrow, or the day after, she would come home. Jack would understand her reaction. If for whatever reason, things were still not under control, she'd go to Peter's in Kennebunkport.

As she packed her bag, Jack was traveling in the arms of the Divine, viewing Harrow in a way he never would have imagined—flying above it with an angel. His whole life he had been loyal and dedicated to the church. Never had he expected to truly experience, never mind meet, a heavenly being. His convictions alone had kept him faithful.

Now with Gabrielus, even after seeing that doppelganger of Susannah, Jack felt at peace. He closed his eyes and let the angel take him where it wished. Although Lisa did not know it yet, her Jack was whole once again, maybe for the first time since he was a boy.

He was unable to change the past. The pain he caused Lisa years ago was unforgivable, but he could use the rest of his life making that up to her. She was an amazing person, thankful and understanding, Jack couldn't think about what he could have become without her. He couldn't imagine his life without her.

Jack saw his old friend was taking him home. For a moment, he considered his friendship with Sean—the number of years they had known each other, all the dinners and talks, the card games and walks. Sean O'Brien always had something special about him. But no one knew how special.

Jack descended toward his Winter Street home. The scarecrows and birds he unfortunately placed around the home were still there. Seeing them now made him feel foolish. How could he have fallen so fast into such desperation?

As Gabrielus flew over the roof, Jack caught a glimpse of Tattie Bogle's headdress and was embarrassed that this angel had seen what he had done.

They landed in the backyard unnoticed by any of the surrounding neighbors, but they were seen by Lisa as she gathered her belongings. Dropping the sweater she was folding, she moved to the window, unable to believe her eyes. Lifting a hand to her mouth, she backed up, bumped into the bed, turned, and ran down the stairs.

Jack, still daunted, took a step back from his friend, looked him over, and smiled. His years of faith had not been for nothing. Then he remembered what had transpired in the Hills, and his smile faded. There was no more doubt about the evil flowing within them.

"The boy, will you save him?"

"If we can. Jack, I, like you, am very fond of the boy and his family, of all the families here in Harrow. However, there may not be time, and we could already be too late. Rest, you need it. I suspect you will find sleep a little easier tonight." The angel moved away from Jack and looked up into the darkening sky. "Others wait on me. I must to go." He looked back at Jack. "Take down these things and stay out of the Hills. You need to control yourself better from now on. I will not always be around. If you foolishly re-enter the Harrowing Hills, you are on your own."

Hovering above the ground, Gabrielus smiled one last time at Jack. "Go find your loving wife. I feel you have some repairing to do by her." And Gabrielus was gone.

Lisa ran out the back door in time to see Gabrielus. Jack, hearing the door swing open and slam, looked over. Lisa was running to him. He opened his arms and told her every-thing was all right, that everything was going to be okay.

If only that were the truth.

CHAPTER 42

In the place once known as Mystery Hill, Bruce Wren sat on a four and a half ton ancient stone slab. Tracing his middle finger along a carved groove cut around the edge of its surface. An unusual mist crawled across the desolate hilltop as the day's last light faded into the clouds.

This table's gutter led into a spout, making it hard to ignore the inference something such as this gave, of the long-forgotten ceremonies that required the construction of such a slab. How much life bled out along the channel of this sacrificial stone and poured from the drain onto the ground?

Surrounding this center point were thirty-acres of four-thousand-year-old megalithic structures, low straggling walls, and primitive cave-like tunnels built by some ancient unknown. Stones weighing up to eleven tons had been erected with meticulous precision, positioned to predict solar and lunar events.

This was not the first time Bruce had been to these ruins, and he was confused as to why Sariel had brought him to Salem, New Hampshire. Turning around, he watched the strange angelic creatures and remembered when Liz and he first discovered the one they called Ezziel. Even barely alive they feared him, and now Bruce found himself with two strong and healthy ones, never mind the two Valkyrja, which scared him more than he'd ever thought possible.

Nevertheless, as deep-seated as that fear might be, it did not match the entrenchment of his hatred for the Thing that killed Liz, and right now, that hatred was evenly split between that Thing and those who brought It to them in the first place.

Abaddon and Sariel glanced over at Bruce. He was not surprised their conversation included him. He only wished he were a part of it. The horrors that followed Sariel like pets perched themselves on megalith formations like rooftop Gargoyles in the Plaza area of what was now called America's Stonehenge.

Their scythed bladed limbs were tucked up and under their lower arms. Both of their large, full-bodied, frames tilted forward as they leaned on their massive, clawed hands. Even from this distance, Bruce could see them digging into the rock below them.

The enlarged teeth and horned, armored chest of the Valkyrja looked even more unnatural in the day's dying light, and due to their homogeneous kindred with Báalzbub and his horde, everything about these creatures screamed death. They were once the darkest side of the supernatural, and now, they were the shadow cast upon it.

Abaddon walked toward Bruce. He could feel the Being's power as he approached and could not be anything but intimidated, knowing how helpless he was against this destroyer. From an enclosure housing eight alpacas, came high-pitched and shrieking whines. The group of camel-like animals retreated to the furthermost corner, and as Abaddon passed, a few brave males screamed a warbling, birdlike cry, attempting to terrify the terror.

As Abaddon reached Bruce, the fallen angel took a deep breath and looked up at the early evening sky. After studying the stars and the bright, visible moon, he lowered his head to Bruce. "Look above you. Do you understand what is beyond this world? Have you given any real thought as to what's happening beyond your own vision?"

Bruce looked up "Yeah, and—"

"That is what all of this is about. Keep looking up, human, because one day it may not be there to see. Maybe not in your lifetime, maybe not even in this planet's lifetime, but the time will come when our universe will be gone. That is, unless we do something about it." Abaddon stretched out his wings and re-folded them. "Let's say you humans were to last, and on this planet. Eventually, your observable universe— everything that you can see—will shrink. Humankind can use all the technology they can muster, but the only things they will be able to find is black nothingness, and why? Because as gravity weakens, it will no longer hold the galaxies together, and they will separate from one another. Our universe will ultimately fade into nothingness in approximately fifty billion Earth years from now."

Bruce lowered his head. "Fifty billion years?"

In the background, an annoying "wank" sound came from an alpaca.

"The universe, not this planet. That won't last even close to that. In fact, Bruce, if we do not reach The Crescent, your Earth may not exist in a week from now. Besides, for my kind, fifty billion years is a lot shorter than you might think."

Bruce glanced past Abaddon and noticed Sariel had stopped in front of the enclosure. A posted sign read: *PEOPLE-FOOD MAKES US SICK...* In the middle of the sign was one of the long-necked animals, then, *PLEASE DON'T FEED US.* Bruce watched as Sariel lifted up and glided over the fence, landing inside the enclosed space. He glanced back to Abaddon.

"Let's get a few things straight. We—" Abaddon spread his arms out to indicate he meant Sariel, The Valkyrja, and himself, and not he and Bruce. "—don't like talking monkeys, and I don't care for, and cannot trust, what Sariel did to you. I am not trying to save your life, and by your life, I mean your species. But if Báalzbub gets his way, and The Black One implodes this rock of yours and creates another black hole, it will only permit more of this Phantom Energy to enter, accelerating our end."

Bruce was tired of just listening to this fallen one. He stood up and looked into Abaddon's dark eyes, "I don't understand what the hell you're talking about, but fair enough. I don't need any of you. As far as I'm concerned, you can't be trusted, and if I didn't want revenge on that thing that killed Liz, I wouldn't help you at all. That is my price. In return for whatever reason I was brought along, I want that thing dead. In case you haven't been paying attention, the only thing I cared about is now dead, partly thanks to you. Thanks for that by the way!"

Abaddon surprised Bruce with a smile.

"First, I don't believe we need you, and second, you only *think* you want Báalzbub destroyed. You have lost only one. I've lost scores more than that, one of which was my only son Zacre. My kind is still betraying and killing one another over that beast. I will do all I can to meet your terms, but only because they fall under conditions I have already set for myself. Nevertheless, destroying the Lord of the Flies will not end our pain, and in the end, your woman and my son will still be dead.

"Even if we accomplish our goals, kill

Báalzbub, and somehow stop The Black One, what have we really achieved? At some point, another envoy will come. We will have only postponed the inevitable. And for you, Bruce, your pain will only grow. After Báalzbub's death, what then? Let us hope Sariel changed you enough to deal with that, because at some point that anger is going to destroy you."

From the alpaca enclosure, Bruce heard a new sound, one of friendly submission. Taking his eyes off Abaddon, he glanced over and saw Sariel patting the heads and backs of the alpacas as they made "click" and "clunk" noises while flipping their tails over their backs.

"Do not be fooled by her beauty. Sariel is a conundrum even among our kind. Never has a Being been so capable of both peace and devastation. She is the Angel of Death, Bruce. I have witnessed it firsthand."

Bruce shifted his attention back to Abaddon, noticed the way he was looking at her, and remembered the primordial history between the two.

"She has captured countless hearts and imaginations of your kind. Your Italians named her Venus, and the Greeks once called her Aphrodite. Others have called her by Anadyomene, Cypris, and Cytherea. Your Norsemen wrote songs and poems about her. To them she was a Valkyrie. They saw her as the chooser of the slain, but it was her subordinates that flew over their battle fields." From above, Gabrielus broke through the dark skyline and drifted down to them. Seeing him caused the intonations of Abaddon's voice to lower. "It was the Valkyrja who they first saw as demons of death."

Bruce noticed the slight pause and the change in Abaddon's voice. He looked up as Gabrielus landed inside the alpaca enclosure and walked toward Sariel. With a disdainful smirk, Abaddon said, "You can all relax now. Your guardian angel is here." And he walked down the pathway to the site's oracle chamber.

Bruce watched in shock as he recognized Gabrielus. Things were becoming more complicated. They brought him along because their Gabrielus was his O'Brien. At least now he understood the significance of Ezziel washing up on his balcony and how it would affect Harrow and Father O'Brien.

Bruce flicked a twig off the top of the slab, and as the stick bounced off a large fin shaped stone, he walked across the stoned altar, confused.

Everything that had, and was, happening around him was beginning to take its toll. The stress and complete insanity of being with them at all was mounting and on the verge of becoming too much. Finding a tree, Bruce lowered himself to the ground and felt unavoidable sorrow creep in. His eyes watered and, without caring if anyone heard, Bruce finally wept for Liz, for the life they had, and for the one that had been taken away from them.

It was different being on the outside looking in. These Beings that humankind called angels did not feel or experience life the same way humans did. Bruce believed them to only have the ability to empathize, but not truly understand.

His life might be short, but it had been becoming meaningful. He'd felt whole, and happy, not simply content. He'd no longer just been going through the motions of life. He'd been living it. He'd been in love. Some believed love was not real, that it was nothing but a delusion, that people only convinced themselves that it existed. Bruce himself had thought that same way, that like God, rational, intellectual people did not believe in it.

Bruce now believed in both. Love was stronger than he'd ever thought it could be. The other, maybe he was better off never knowing, but now, he was unable to pretend anymore. He was unsure if the universe was better off with a theist, deist, or pantheist god. He just wished They had left Liz and him alone.

Hearing something behind him, he wiped his eyes the best he could. Standing on the other side of the tree were Sariel and Gabrielus. He looked at Gabrielus and could see the characteristic features of Father Sean O'Brien, only stronger and younger—except for the black marbled eyes. Gabrielus gave Bruce the same smile he had been giving him his whole life. Sariel came around the tree. As striking as she was, his attention was still lost in the longtime friend of his family.

"Hello, Bruce."

"Hello, Father O'Brien."

"Please, call me Gabrielus if you can."

He gave Sariel a momentary look and said, "I understand how difficult things have been for you, and I was profoundly sorry to hear about your friend. I wish I could be standing here as your priest, and that I was here to give you all the support you are so greatly entitled to, but sadly, I am not. Selfishly, it is I who needs you."

Looking away, Bruce carelessly whispered, "My help?" and looked back up at the archangel.

"Yes," said Sariel softly. "Gabrielus and I cannot enter The Crescent Realm. However, you can, but of course, not alone."

"Abaddon. You want me to go somewhere with Abaddon?"

"Yes. The Crescent Realm, a place others have named Zebub or Jotunheimr, the heim of giants—for reasons of Báalzbub and his plot."

"Heim of giants did you say? And am I to understand that *neither* of you two can come with me. That I am to enter this unknown place, alone, with a fallen angel?"

"Giants yes, the Jotnar, a race of nature spirits, dryads. The Crescent Realm is a land of high mountains and dense forests, a realm of mist and darkness. My two Valkyrja will also accompany you."

Bruce remembered the way they looked upon the structures, their claws and teeth, their whipping tails. "Are they any safer than Abaddon?"

"Abaddon can be trusted and, even if not, Sariel's Valkyrja will protect you. I assure you, Bruce, they most certainly can be trusted," answered Gabrielus.

"Why can't the two of you go? Why me? It's more logical that the two of you go."

"We cannot enter. Have you ever attempted to force two opposite halves of a magnet together, and no matter how small the pieces were, no matter how hard you tried, you were unable to put them together? Well, this is the same. It is impossible for the two of us to enter that realm. Abaddon and The Valkyrja can. They are no longer pure energy of either force," explained Sariel.

"Because they have been neutralized," remembered Bruce. "How do we reach this Crescent? Are we going to Harrow?"

Sariel touched Bruce's shoulder as she stood up. "No, there are other passages. Báalzbub's worshippers built this place and others around the world to watch and mark astronomical events. They waited for The Black One. Abaddon knew of this secondary passage."

Heavy vibrations shook the ground. Bruce stood, as the center of the three-sectioned V-hut and east-west chambers area opened into a black empty hole. He looked at Gabrielus in horrified shock. The two Valkyrja landed behind him, while Abaddon landed near Gabrielus. "We need to enter quickly. It will not take long for the opened portal to be noticed." Abaddon looked at the Valkyrja, "One of you takes the human."

"Wait!" protested Bruce as large arms wrap around him and a heavy snort filled his ears.

Together, Gabrielus and Sariel looked at him as both Valkyrja lifted off. Then they turned to Abaddon. "Another has come for The Black One. You deal only with Báalzbub. If things become too much for you, send back a Valkyrja," instructed Sariel. "He will return with a multitude."

"Will I recognize this entity here for The Black One?"

"I'm sure you will. Think of him as The

Bright One if you wish. Just stay clear of them both."

"Also," interrupted Gabrielus. "There may be other humans as well. If achievable, rescue them."

"If they are attainable, I will. One thing, Sariel. Was it wise, changing the human into a nephilim?"

"He is not full nephilim."

"Bruce was transformed at my request, a gift from me," Gabrielus said.

Abaddon bowed his head in respect and joined the Valkyrja going into the void. Sariel and Gabrielus took to the air themselves as the hole disappeared and solid ground returned.

CHAPTER 43

Still stumbling over shrubs, bushes, and small-growing trees, Tim stuck with John as they moved through more thorny underbrush. The chief's pace was becoming more and more difficult for Tim to keep up with, and at times he fell behind. Not expecting John to slow down or stop, Tim pushed himself harder.

The strange bird dashed from one branch to another, moving from tree to tree, maintaining its distance. From the surrounding trees and the air above, others joined the bird as it guided Tim and John to the unknown.

Tim watched as these white-eyed things flocked and spiraled around each other, moving in such a fury they sometimes collided, smashing together, causing small aggressive skirmishes.

Tim realized these fiercely violent creatures meant them harm. If these things knew where Thomas was, it was because they brought him there. But how could one man convince another to stop pursuing his only lead for his son? He couldn't. Therefore, no matter how unpleasant things became, Tim would stay at John's side. What other choice was there?

More birds flocked around them. The surrounding trees looked as if their leaves had turned black. The flock had grown to several dozen, maybe even a hundred or more. No longer did just the one bird lead them, now they all did. They rotated around each other, moving from side to side, up and down, creating turbulence. The chaotic force, made of talons and wings, moved faster and faster, blocking out everything around and beyond them.

The intensity and strength of their energy bent and swayed the surrounding trees, rocking them back and forth. The tumult of wind, wings, and bark breaking made it impossible to think of or hear anything else in the hurricane-like wind as hundreds more ravens joined in. Branches fell and hurled all around them while the noise level reached that of a jet engine.

Both of the officers lay on the ground,

curled into a ball, shutting their eyes tight while pressing their hands hard against their ears. Just when neither one of them could handle the noise and wind any longer, it all stopped. One moment it felt as if their heads were about to explode, and the next was completely calm and quiet.

John opened his eyes and the whirling birds were gone, the surrounding woodland destroyed. Trees lay uprooted and spilled over one another. Only the rocks planted the deepest remained in place.

Tim stood. "What the hell was that? And where did they go?"

John shook his head. He had no answer for him. He noticed Tim staring off past a patch of broken shrubbery. John walked over and saw the clearing through the now dis-carded trees not more than a hundred yards away.

"Want to check it out?" asked Tim.

"Maybe, yeah..." John's eye caught movement. "Hold on, Tim."

The same flock that had moved fast enough to create a severe windstorm was now descending at an impossibly slow and silent speed. Their approach came in one single, fluid, and unnatural motion. It was like nothing John and Tim had seen before. Standing between the odd trees these things landed in and an even stranger pathway, was a man.

"What the hell is Levi doing out here?" mumbled John.

"Maybe he found your son's trail and followed it here," responded Tim, but even as he said the words, they didn't sound true.

The dark woodland path stood directly before the reverend. They watched as Jack turned and found the ravens then backed away and turned toward the path. The two officers could not see what Jack saw, but they watched him retreat from both the pathway and the birds, spin around, and then stop.

John tried to see what brought Jack to a standstill. Tim moved closer to the clearing, hiding behind what remained of an ash tree, and looked at John. The expression on his face told John something was very wrong. "What is it?"

"It's Thomas. He's being carried by some—young girl."

John ran the distance between them. Not

more than forty feet away, his son draped, unmoving, in the arms of Susannah Levi. And she looked no older than he did. John removed his firearm for the second time since he entered the woods.

As he advanced, Tim forcefully grabbed his arm. Without stopping, John smacked the grip away, giving Tim a wrathful look over his shoulder. In that instant, John hated Tim as much as he hated whatever was holding his boy. All his rage and frustration loaded into one cantankerous look, an inferno of odium as deadly as the gun in his hand. If Tim had been looking at John, he would have seen a man he never knew existed.

However, he did not. What he did see stunned him into the blind siege of John's arm. Even in his state of mind, John noticed the total blankness that came across Tim's face, the stupefaction that filled his eyes. John turned and saw a winged human figure wrap feathery appendages around Jack. Bewildered, John tried to distinguish if what he saw was real or some figment of his imagination.

Unable to remove his eyes from the inconceivable form, John did not see Thomas taken down the dark path. Mesmerized, both John and Tim watched as this implausible thing took hold of Jack, skyrocketed off into the heavens, and raced across the darkening-gray sky like a shooting star.

As the angel escalated off the ground, the Malign swarmed bat-like onto the path. Tim took his eyes off the skyline long enough to watch them fly over and around Jason Benson. He heard a distorted hissing as they entered.

He lowered himself to the ground and, overwhelmed, brought his hands to his face as he fought to hold back the tears. Overtaken by shock and dread, he feared he would be unable to stem the tide.

Hearing movement, he lowered his hands. He watched John step into the clearing and walk toward the path. Although Tim did not want to move, he picked himself up and followed anyway. John stopped at the spot where the winged humanoid had swept up Jack.

"John, what the hell is going on? What the fuck did we just see?"

"All I know is that my boy's somewhere beyond that path. As for everything else, I have no idea." John circled the area looking for a trace, a mark, some sort of visible sign confirming what he had just seen. The only things left behind were the reverend's footprints and a duffel bag.

"What was that...an angel? Did an angel actually just fly off with the reverend? John, what should we do?" Tim studied the path. "Where does that thing lead to? I bet it's the Black Forest."

John glanced at the sky and back down at the ground. He bent down and touched a footprint. It clearly belonged to the reverend. The other made not one mark. There was no proof of anyone but Jack being in the spot. John turned his head toward the path.

"I'm not interested in Black Forest stories, theories, or anything else right now. What we're facing here is real."

"The Black Fore—"

"*Tim,*" John barked. "Please, enough."

Tim clenched his jaws hard, forcefully pressing his back teeth together. Tightening and straining the muscles along his jaw line, he sighed heavily. "What then, huh?"

"I'm going after my son. I think it's best if you stay put out here."

"John, I'm coming with you. It's probably a mistake, but I'm going. I don't think either one of us should go heading into the Black—into that pathway. But I can't let you go alone, especially not after what we've just seen."

"I'm thankful you came this far with me, I am. But, things are different now, Tim." He paused and finished with something he would have preferred not to say. However, this was not the time to be worrying about hurt feelings. The only thing important now was Thomas. "Frankly, I don't think you can handle this. I have to concentrate on my boy now. I can't be concerned about your safety as well."

John started toward the path. Tim stood there watching him go. He called out John's name and got nothing back until John reached the threshold of the path's entrance.

"If I don't return, tell Jane and Candice I love them—and never tell them what you've seen here today. And most of all *never ever* bring them or anyone else here."

John stepped onto the dark and nothingness path. The air was thick, black, and breathless. Vertigo struck, and the lightheadedness almost caused him to pass out. He reached out for trees he could not see, but knew must be near, only to discover there was nothing but more emptiness.

Unsteady, he walked in total and complete darkness, hands stretched out in case he stumbled across something in the pathway. The air had absolutely no smell, not a scent of tree or dirt. Not only was there no trace of anything familiar and recognizable, but nothing unfamiliar as well. The atmosphere lacked everything, including taste and sound. John moved in a void, as if he'd walked off the face of the Earth and into the abyss.

Unexpectedly, John's body became weightless. He lifted off solid ground and began to float. He hovered for a moment then slowly started to move forward, feeling a force surrounding him, pulling him increasingly faster and faster through the unknown darkness. He opened his mouth and yelled out Thomas's name, but made no sound. John knew he was traveling at an elevated rate of speed, but felt no wind—only the tug.

CHAPTER 44

Tim stood outside the entrance wondering what he should do. His mind raced with several thoughts and ideas, and he tried to differentiate between the good and bad, the brave and the cowardly.

He could do as John told him, just turn around and leave. Nobody would ever know he left John behind. It would be easy. He could just say he lost him, or that John took off when he wasn't looking. It was even believable. There would be no questions, no blame. When asked why he and John left the search group in the first place, he'd answer that he had seen John slip off and he followed him, all the time working to get John back.

It wouldn't be leaving him behind. It would be following orders, right? Tim guiltily asked himself. He walked over to the bag left by Jack Levi and picked it up. Holding it, he thought about how easy it would be to toss this thing into the pathway behind John. Instead, he put the strap over his head, flipped open the flap, and reached in. His hands fell on a number of objects, but the one he removed was the strangest. Tim looked at the bird tied lifelessly to the end of the rope. The dead thing was too small to be one of the things he and John had come across, but the resemblance was unmistakable. Just what did the reverend know about what was going on? It was not coincidental that he ended up here with a bag of dead crows.

The sun had set and night was upon him. However, the night did not scare him. Knowing what he should do—that was another story. Putting the bird back in the bag, Tim forced himself to look at the path again, unsure which he hated more, his thoughts of leaving or the idea of walking down that thing.

Tim believed his story would be convincing. John running off, looking for Thomas, was very plausible. In fact, that was what had happened. Nevertheless, he couldn't do it, and now he faced a problem. He believed John was not coming back, and if he followed, he too would never return from whatever rested at the other end.

Where was the logic in both of them dying out here today? There was none. So why did Tim find himself walking back toward the path? Because even though he ought to—wanted to—he just could not leave.

John felt his whole body spinning in a circle with his head acting as the pivot point. Around and around he went. Turning his head was like rolling a boulder and it took immense willpower to force his eyes open and discover that he was not actually spinning.

In fact, he was lying motionless, face down, on the hard, cold ground. He rolled over and saw, through blurred vision, the outline of a reddish glowing light coming from somewhere above him.

Lifting himself up John wondered how long he'd been lying here and, more importantly, just where *here* was. Carefully, he got up and looked around. However, it was too dark to make out anything with certainty, only shadowed objects, just enough to know they were there.

John knew he was inside something. There was hollowness to the place. He got an overwhelming temptation to yell out his son's name. Yet, he resisted. He had no idea where he was, never mind what was nearby. Finding Thomas was important, however, in order to do that, John first needed to find himself. He had to move. He came here somehow, so there must be a way out.

He retrieved his cell phone from his pocket. It had a full charge. Even if there was no signal, the screen light might make the difference between finding his way out, or not. John pressed the power bottom and nothing happened. Disappointed, but not surprised, he put the useless thing back into his pocket.

Even without a light, he needed to move. Placing his hands out in front of him like he had in the pathway, he moved them back and forth, feeling for anything that would give him direction.

After about ninety seconds, his hands finally landed on a rock wall. Continuing to feel his way slowly, John walked along the stony object. If he was inside something, then there must be a way out.

The wall was tall and wide. The stony substance was unlike anything John ever had felt before. It was warm and moist, almost sweaty. The surrounding air was thick and humid, but also somehow dry. John did not think the air caused the wall's dampness. Oddly, it was part of the wall itself.

As he moved, he wondered more about the reddish glow above. What was the source and origin of that light? The dimness indicated it was far above, but how far was impossible to tell. He stopped. If the glow was far off, just how large was this place?

Removing his hands from the stony surface, he went approximately fifteen feet, reached back for the wall, and stopped again. He turned and looked for the red glow and did not see it. Suddenly nervous, John frantically whipped his head around, searching. That glow should be there. He had not moved far enough to lose sight of it. Then his eyes caught a glimpse of it, however, not from behind him, but from his left. Had the light moved? He waited and the light held still. John stepped forward and the glow moved in the opposite direction. When John stopped, it stopped.

He moved slowly while keeping his eyes on the red glow, and again the glow moved away from him. He turned and walked in the reverse direction. This time the glow moved toward him. The wall went in a circle, enclosing him. John now understood how trapped he might be. This place was shaped like an enormous smokestack, and that glow above could be his only way out.

He continued moving back toward the light while the question of how he ended up here remained. This place somehow was the end of the pathway. Dragging his left hand along the wall, John considered if maybe he fell through a hole. That the red light above could be the sun rising. There was no shortage of caves in the Harrowing Hills. Could it be possible that he stumbled across weak ground over an underground tunnel?

He estimated that light was at least a hundred feet up, possibly more. A fall from that height, landing on this hard rock bottom, would have killed him. Forget broken bones, his head would have smashed. So again, how did he end up in here?

The last thing he remembered, before awakening on the cold ground, was the feeling of lightheadedness and being pulled through the air. In the dark, he could have mistaken those same things for falling. Had he fallen into a hole after all?

All of a sudden, he tripped over something solid and fell on what could only be a flight of stairs. Unhurt but confused, he stretched his hand out until he found the wall and regained his footing. Placing his hands back on the steps to make sure they went upward, John slowly started to climb. Unsure how great an idea it was to follow them up into the unknown blackness, he crawled on his hands and knees in case the steps suddenly decided to end.

PART VI

HARROWMENT

"Old vision wake thine opening eyes
Gleam black with clouds of other skies,
And as from some demoniac sight
I flee into the haunted night."

H.P. Lovecraft

CHAPTER 45

Within The Crescent Realm, Simon Allen was suspended in agony from long, drooping limbs. He was fully aware when the sharp hooked branches dug under his skin and wedged themselves into his ribcage. His arms and legs dangled freely, his open-eyed and clear-minded head snapped backward, in a resurrection like pose.

This place, the things he'd seen, filled his head as he hung, remembering a floor he'd never seen before, open into a pathway. How the boy inside had invited him to enter. The visions of birds and something only described as a walking void being the worst of all. Simon misplaced days at a time, living in a trance-like state, then waking to find drawings and writings on his apartment walls.

Worse than the graffiti was the feeling that someone, or something, had taken over power and controlled him. Then even after

371

he regained command of himself, this thing still lingered inside.

Frightened of what was happening to him, Simon stopped leaving his home, and never allowed anyone to enter, fearing he might hurt, or be hurt by, someone while under these spells. Something was wrong with him—something Simon was both embarrassed by and afraid of.

After the first few weeks, he lost his job, his friends vanished, and his girl left him. At the time of his last blackout, Simon was losing his apartment. Not that he needed it anymore.

When Simon saw the movement on the floor, he thought his mind had finally given up. When the movement formed into a pathway, Simon hoped he had at last died, and that the boy was there to finally give him peace. He was wrong on both accounts.

Above the Blood Tree, and the draping Simon, was an oxidization-colored sky with black clouds. Even through the thick branches and other victims, the sky was visible. Simon tried to look past the strange unknown organisms that swung and swayed, decaying above him, and focus only on it. He attempted to ignore these suffering and rotting things in all their stages of undying decomposition.

He didn't want to acknowledge The Blood Tree feeding off him. Simon's body, like the others, would die and be reborn repeatedly. His body would bloat and turn green from putrification. Simon would darken from that greenish color into black, as his mouth, lips, and tongue swelled. His skin would mummify as his organs continued to rot. Simon's voracious host tree would then suck and swallow the spoilage that he would become.

Simon, like the others, would never reach the final stage of decomposition and would always remain mindful. Would feel when his body died and know when his skin painfully adhered to his bones.

The anguish of life was next, the torture of everything growing back and regenerating.

The tree's dark, purplish-blue/red roots waited on the ground to devour whatever skin or muscle that happened to fall loose. The heights of these hellish trees reached hundreds of feet into the rust colored sky, with grisly and exaggerated characteristics similar to that of an ancient Ankerwyke yew. And like the great yew, these trees had large deracinated roots breaking from the ground and spreading across the land, covering everything as they searched. However, instead of water they sought prey.

These predatory roots traveled distances of a mile or more, and like their long thick branches, they also snagged life from the ground.

Warped skulls and faces entwined throughout the bluish-black bark of these abominable trees, trapped and transformed, becoming large twisted knots and lumps. These knots buckled back and forth pleading beseechingly for release.

Simon wondered if he'd followed the path into Hell. Looking for the red sky, he could only see the trees' Keepers moving above him. Simon watched as they rummaged around, hunting for foragers. Their sunken corpse faces looked momentarily from one place to another. Twigged fingers stretched out from legless-torso bodies, grabbing any unwanted scavengers from the tree and placing them within the obtruding roots that made up the rest of their body.

Simon realized that if this were real, he would spend unending time in a Hell even Dante Alighieri could not have depicted. How many others had abandoned all hope after they entered here?

The Keepers moved from Simon's limited vision, but he was still able to hear their screeches of triumph as they went about their work.

CHAPTER 46

In another part of The Crescent Realm, John came to the end of his climb. The staircase he'd stumbled upon spiraled up the towering walls. Unable to see until he was more than three quarters of the way up, he expected to find empty air each time he placed his foot. The red light grew brighter with each invisible step he mounted.

The tower narrowed toward the top, and the closer he came, the better he could see the opening leading to the world outside. A world, John feared, that was not his own.

The stone stairway led to a small cavern antechamber and crevice. Lowering to his knees, John removed his firearm, crouched, and carefully looked out the opening.

As he edged his head forward, a sound echoed up the shaft walls. A scuffing noise— a footstep—something was coming up the stairs behind him. Looking and only seeing darkness, John decided to depart the narrowed passage. There would be little chance of defending himself here, and if he did not escape now, it could be too late.

Creeping out, he discovered the horrid tropical forest of The Crescent Realm. Looking up into the closely spaced tree branches, he saw the red light through the dense canopy ceiling, and learned it was the sky. Movement within this jungle's over-story caught John's attention. Within the exceedingly tall trees were the rotting remains of countless indescribable and unnamable creatures, things belonging only in the imaginary minds of H.P Lovecraft and Arthur Machen. The site of their unspeakable nightmarish bodies brought John back to the lurid memory that something was moving up behind him.

Looking into the darkness, John listened and heard nothing. After thirty long seconds, he relaxed, convinced that nothing approached. Then heard the sound again. Something was on the steps and moving closer.

John jumped out of the opening, touching the sulfured soil, as sounds echoed off the rounded narrow walls. Unwilling to go any-

where near the trees, he moved around the
mouth of the shaft to the rocky hillside. Hol-
stering his firearm, he jumped up and
grabbed hold of some dark roots sticking out
from the hillside. Bracing himself, he dug his
feet into the unearthly earth and climbed up.
As he scaled, reaching from root to root, digging for safety, he looked over his shoulder
for whatever wickedness coming his way.

Without warning, the very things John
depended on to bring him to safety turned
against him. The roots grabbed and pulled
him down. Fighting frantically, John kicked
and swung, screaming every antagonistic ob-
scenity that filled his head.

With his one free hand, he managed to
get hold of his firearm and shot the root
clinching his right leg. Blue-sappy liquid
sprayed from the root as it recoiled back,
snake-like. From the sky above, half-bodied
monstrosities flew toward him, dropping
equally disgusting things from their rooted
bodies, as they approached, shrieking.

John took aim as one closed in, but before
he could pull the trigger, it snapped away in
pain as the same blood liquid splattered from
the thing's side.

Without questioning it, he took aim at the next one.

This time he heard the gunshot. However, the blast did not come from him, but from somewhere below.

Kneeling on the ground, ten feet below, was Tim. He continued to fire, covering John as he fought to break free. The roots lost their hold and John slid down next to Tim. The two officers exchanged confused looks before they got up and ran.

The Keepers chased them.

John and Tim looked for somewhere to hide. The only things around were strange ivy plants, orchids, and other low-growing vegetation. Nothing that could provide the cover they needed. As they ran through shrubby and small juvenile trees, John realized they should have retreated into the cavern, but things happened too unexpectedly, and now there was no other choice but to flee into the uncanny mammoth trees that surrounded them.

They heard thousands of lugubrious cries from the sufferers trapped in the macabre bloodcurdling trees and felt the gruesome presence of each morbid dryad that held them captive. Their strangler roots blanketed the landscape, covering the gloomy jungle floor, enveloping everything. The aerial roots covered every obstacle in John and Tim's way.

Climbing over an enclosed boulder, Tim looked over his shoulder and saw three Keepers, two traveling up the right and left sides, flanking them. The third hounded straight up the middle and was gaining on them. Tim turned as a beast with vestigial wings filled his vision. Unable to stop, he and John dropped to the ground as the beast flew overhead, killing the Keeper behind them.

John grabbed Tim by his shirt, forcing him to his feet, and ran.

From above came another primal scream as a second abominable creature landed before them. Even as unnatural as the thing looked, the unsuspected sight of what clung to its back was somehow even more disturbing. Between two rows of jutted tusks was a human male.

CHAPTER 47

John and Tim watched in horror while this person stepped to the forefront. The creature swung its ghastly tail out and leaned forward like a gorilla.

With no chance of escape, both officers backed up while raising their weapons in defense. From behind, the first beast threw what was left of the Keepers' corpses next to them.

Tim quickly moved so John and he were back to back. With both the front and backside covered, John locked eyes with the human who at first did not look familiar. Then after a few moments, the man's face became recognizable.

However, it was not Bruce's face he identified with, but his father's.

With the arrival of the Valkyrja, every Keeper, including the other two pursuing John and Tim, fled from the area. Now the Valkyrja focused solely upon the officers with their guns drawn. Grunting and slowly moving forward, they waited.

Bruce stepped closer toward John holding out his hands. "Easy, officers, easy. Please put those things away before...before something regrettable happens."

"Back off! Back, back!" John shouted.

"I recognize you. You're from Harrow. You knew my parents, Dennis and Carol Wren. I'm Bruce Wren. Don't you recognize me?"

"I know who you are. That changes nothing! If you're here, and a part of this, then you're *far* from the man your father was!" John yelled. *"What do you know about my boy?"*

His hands tightened around the firearm. Desperation controlled him now. His reality crumbled beneath the actual and the real, and now despair held a gun in sweaty hands and fretful fingers. "I want my boy, that's it. I need my boy so I can bring him home to his mother. Please."

Finding these law officers from Harrow confused Bruce, but knowing one of their kids was here also complicated things.

They had not just happened upon this

place. They entered willingly, and with a strong purpose.

"John. Your name is John Moore, correct? I don't know where your son is, but if he is here, we will help you find him. But first you need to lower your guns."

"Why in hell should I trust y—"

A blur slammed into both the officers and lifted them, dropping them hard enough to daze them. John, unable to breathe or defend himself, looked up at Abaddon standing over him and weakly stretched his hand out for his fallen gun.

The Valkyrja grunted in excitement, banging their tails and bringing their scythed-like limbs into attack position. Bruce ran over and The Valkyrja slowly moved as well. The question, Bruce feared, was which side were they on, Abaddon's or the officers'?

"Abaddon stop—don't hurt them!" Bruce attempted to stop the Valkyrja with hand motions. "He's just looking for his son. He's scared, that's all."

Abaddon frowned, puckering an eyebrow. Gabrielus had said there might be humans on this side. He watched the pathetic thing grasp for a weapon almost as useless as he was. Scowling, Abaddon bent down and picked up the gun before John reached it, thinking how pointless it was even bothering with these humans at all.

"I'm not going to hurt them. I just saved them. How long were you expecting Sariel's minions to allow them to hold a weapon on you? They're under orders to protect you. I'm surprised they hadn't butchered them already. Luckily for them."

John forced himself to his feet while Tim kicked away in a cloud of dust and gravel. Inhaling deeply, John faced the fallen angel.

Abaddon smirked.

Knowing he couldn't win, John still stood his ground against the threat. If he was to die here and now, it would be on his feet, fighting. Tim could die anyway he felt comfortable. John raised his fists, and waited.

"I admire your spirit," Abaddon said. "It is one of the few intrinsic qualities I respect in your kind. It's almost as impressive as your ability and willingness to kill one another."

"Look who's talking," John replied

Abaddon knew John referenced the war

in Heaven. "I am not your enemy but, I assure you, everything else you encounter here will be. You might want to save your—" He smirked again. "—strength."

Tim saw movement through the dense trees behind him, and like before, he found John's son in the company of evilness. Thomas was no longer in the arms of a young girl.

Instead, long-limbed, muscular, lime-green and yellow, goblin-like creatures hastened him across the backcloth of this strange and evil land.

Reminded of why they were there, Tim regained his dignity and stood up. A new-found feeling of self-possession filled him. No longer frightened by the blackened, monstrous creatures or the winged man John foolishly squared off with, he moved to John's side. "You can't fight everyone, John, but look behind you."

Reluctantly, John did and saw the goblins with his son. Ravens flew slightly above them.

"Shape-shifting Malign. Not many things are more insidious," Abaddon said. "They are among the most pernicious beings ever known, baleful and detrimental to everything seeking contentment."

John looked back at Abaddon. "You say you're not my enemy. Then what are you?" He looked at Bruce. "You said you would help me. Will you?"

"Yes," answered Bruce.

Abaddon turned toward Bruce. "We need to remove these two. There are more important matters concerning us. I will send them back with one of the Valkyrja. Their doorway must be close."

"Remove who—me? I don't think so. My boy just went past us, and that's where I'm heading." John reached his hand out. "Give me my gun!"

As Abaddon handed John the firearm, he shook his head in disbelief. "This is useless here. I hope you understand that."

"I'm going with them," said Bruce, and before Abaddon could protest, the Valkyrja moved off with him.

John and Tim had already begun running toward the Malign and Thomas. Bruce watched them and looked back at Abaddon. "They cannot save the boy alone. You know that better than I do. We need to help them."

"Fine, but we need to do this quickly. By now, Báalzbub will know of our presence here, particularly the Valkyrja and mine." Abaddon moved past Bruce. "Let's hope their path leads to our own."

Abaddon flew off, scooped up the two running officers, and went after the Malign.

CHAPTER 48

The black clouds overhead slowly merged, darkening the reddened firmament above. Screeches echoed back as the Keepers moved farther away. The pains ailing Simon had changed. He no longer experienced the excruciating agony of the tree. Instead, a new, heating sensation grew within him. It started in his chest and spread throughout his body. As his body temperature escalated, everything from Keeper to desperate scavenger fled from him. Nearby Blood Trees nervously swayed as their dryad wished they, too, could uproot their gargantuan trunks and relocate themselves.

The blackening sky above was the last sight Simon ever saw as his eyes crystallized blue/white, and the rest of him followed. The overtaking entity left no vestige of the man-vessel behind, no mark, trace, or visible evidence of any kind remained. Simon Allen simply no longer existed. The transformation was almost complete.

White-hot and singeing the branches hooked into the life-form that once was Simon, an incandescent form floated freely in the air. Luminous with intense heat, bolts of compressed energy discharged from the shape, igniting the trees. As the fires blazed, the inarticulate groans of those still enslaved developed into moans of relief. A few hamadryad themselves shrieked out in the release.

Blinding light traveled from the form, creating an orb of energy. As the sphere increased in size, electric currents sparked inside the orb. Twisted, rope-like, magnetic structures of purple, yellow, blue, and green filaments violently struck inside. The bubble engulfed the area, incinerating everything in its path.

The engorging orb swelled as it completed the transformation, delivering the mathematical opposite of The Black One.

Jumping, hopping, and climbing, the Malign avoided Abaddon. Their ability to change shape made the task of catching them almost impossible. Like a game of keep away, the goblin-shaped Malign passed Thomas around like a baton, while the raven-shaped Malign slammed into the humans.

Gunshots lit the darkening woods.

The Valkyrja dropped Bruce a safe distance away and plummeted into the chaos, vigorously hewing to pieces every Malign within reach, coursing directly towards the devils holding young Thomas. Disarrayed by the unexpected danger of the Valkyrja, the rancorous Malign—fearing the bladed limbs and rending claws—scattered into the trees where large ligneous branches waited to pluck them from the air and ground.

From the back, Bruce watched in disbelief as skyscraper-sized trees came to life, reaching and swinging their massive limbs back and forth, clinching. He could see John and Tim's hysteria as they yelled and shot and, like him, struggled between what they saw and what they believed to be real. Caught in same perpetual nightmare, they might never escape. In horror, Bruce observed roots break through the ground and wrap around Abaddon's legs.

Sariel's words, '*...the heim of giants*' came powerfully back to Bruce.

A shimmer moved in the distance, simmering like a heat-haze, causing tree trunks to vibrate agitatedly as it passed. Incessant, it traveled unnoticed toward them.

Frustrated, he was unable to manage these things alone, Abaddon gnashed his teeth as a sword of flame formed in his right hand and instantly struck down both Malign and branch. Clawing, biting, and scratching, the turbulent Malign desperately fought for their escape. Wild with fear, they turned on each other, forcing weaker ones into the path of the Valkyrja and Abaddon.

Sounds of madness came from a fatefully-doomed goblin struggling to free itself. Senseless, it intensely slammed back and forth, smashing itself, and Thomas, hard against the ground. The creeping root constricted tighter as the wretched creature gasped for air. Its large eyes bulged in the building pressure. The Valkyrja hewed the incurable hold of the ensnaring root that dragged the two across the ground. Once severed the root shriveled, desiccated into dried-up power, and withered away. Enraged, the now freed Malign let go of Thomas, took advantage of its mutability, and changed back into a raven. Fluttering its wings, it bounced on the ground twice before the Valkyrja stomped on it.

John ran to his son. Unsure how to thank something that looked as the Valkyrja did, he gratefully nodded his head, lowered himself to the ground, and kissed his son.

"Is he all right, John?" asked Tim as he knelt at his side.

Uncertain, John was hesitant to answer. His young son lay motionless in his arms, maybe breathing, maybe not. "I—I can't tell." He looked at Tim then glanced at the creature still standing over them. Angst-ridden, he repeated. "I just can't tell."

Tim understood, began to check Thomas for signs of life, and discovered, although faint, the throb of a pulse. Lowering his ear to the boy's mouth he felt breath and gave John what he hoped was an encouraging smile. "He's alive, but I can't say for sure if he's all right." Looking at the blood soaking through Thomas's clothing, he continued. "But John, he's alive."

John, with tears in his eyes, placed a

trembling hand on his deputy's shoulder. "Thank you."

"You have nothing to thank me for. Come on, we have to get your son to a safe place, preferably home."

"Is it—I mean, should we move him? What if—"

"John, we can't stay here. There's more of a risk for him, and us, in staying here."

A lulling voice called John's name. He looked up and saw Bruce staring down at him.

In a nervous, but soothing tone, Bruce said, "Let me help you. Come, we need to get out of here." Bending in front of Thomas, holding John's eyes and attention, Bruce calmly slid his hands under Thomas.

"*No*! Don't touch my son!"

After wiping dirt and hair from Thomas's face, John started to lift his son. Bruce rose with him, keeping his hands beneath Thomas.

"There's another boy."

Tim followed the angel's gaze and saw what appeared to be red and blue clothing. Abaddon found Jason Benson suspended from another tree.

Immediately, Tim turned his eyes to Abaddon, who guffawed sardonically, "Why not? It's not like we have more pressing matters," and flew off toward the tree canopy.

"I understand you don't trust me yet," Bruce said. "But I believe I can help your son."

Without waiting for John's reply, or consent, Bruce slid his arms farther under Thomas and lifted him, only lowering his eyes from John long enough to ensure Thomas would not slip out of his grasp.

"One thing I do know for sure is what Officer Andrews said. We all need to move, and fast."

"You're no doctor, Wren. I trust in that much!" John answered rudely as he stood. "So what do you suppose you can do that I can't? You're what, a broker or whatever. I'm in law enforcement. At least Tim and I have first aid training."

Tilting his head down to the chief's son, Bruce simply smiled and said, "Sariel, that's what I have."

"Sar-a-what? Give me back my son before you cau—"

John was blown forcefully backward as

he attempted to grab his son. Landing a short distance away, stunned, he saw Bruce hovering above the ground.

John stood quickly as an iridescent sheen reflected off Bruce. When he stepped closer, he felt warmth. Bruce's body was giving off heat and a rainbow-like glow. His eyes were radiant with life.

Tim didn't notice Bruce change, or his role model being pulsed backward. What he did notice, and the others missed, was the great void traveling in their direction. The once shimmering haze had transformed itself into the nothingness that was its true nature.

The Blood Trees sensed this living shadow's approach, lifted their wooden limbs, and extracted their roots back into the ground. The already-panicked Malign's fear intensified into total chaos. Tim watched as their frenzy amplified and was horror-struck by the opaque pestilence drawing near. The mere sight seized Tim's mind and voice.

A human-shaped shadow moved toward him, looking as if a gingerbread man had been cookie cut from the dough of reality, or someone had run through a door in an old Tom & Jerry cartoon, sucking the environment into itself like water going down a drain.

Inconceivably, Tim advanced forward.

He started firing rounds into the form. His bullets disappeared into the walking abyss until his Glock faded into empty clicks. Tim looked down at the useless weapon and threw it at, and into, The Black One. As it vanished, the words from one of Father O'Brien's sermons rang in his head, and he softly mumbled, "The light shineth in the Darkness, and the Darkness comprehended it not."

When the strange intra-abdominal tugging first started, Tim assumed it was due to over excitement and shock. He then felt an almost pleasant and comfortable stretching throughout his body. Confused, he ran a hand over his chest and down his thigh. He looked up and into the hollowed faceless Being, and felt It looking back into him.

Abaddon reached the other boy and swallowed hard, questioning the oddness of finding this second boy so easily. Carefully bracing his left hand under the center of the boy's lower back, he hesitantly cut Jason free.

The tree's spirit within shuttered as Abaddon slowly lowered the boy. With Jason freed, he turned and found a situation far beyond anything he could handle.

No matter what your view of The Black One was, It looked the same. With no sides, no top, and no bottom, all could see it facing them.

Tim heard voices in slow speed yelling out his name. He turned and everything around him moved in a stop-action motion. Puzzled, he wondered if time somehow slowed here in The Crescent Realm. Then pure undiluted terror filled his stomach with icy fear.

Time only slowed for him.

Attempting to back away from the Black Hole, Tim found it was too late. His body suddenly bowed forward as unbelievable pain replaced the short-lived comfort and the gravity point of his midsection became stronger than that of his upper and lower body.

When the tidal force of The Black One exceeded the molecular bond of Tim's body, his bones, muscles, and organs could no longer remain whole. Tim ripped in two between his chest and waist.

With his time slowed, Tim was aware of what happened, however, being torn in half was only the beginning. As the difference in gravity continued to grow, so did the number of parts of Tim. Both his upper and lower halves split in two, becoming four. Then those segments separated, making him eight, then eight became sixteen, and so forth, bifurcating Tim into an ever-increasing number of parts, shredding him into tiny organic fragments.

Then those tiny parts succumbed to the rising tidal force and divided, creating a flow of atoms that branched off until Tim was nothing but unrecognizable particles.

The Black One constantly moved forward, forcing Tim's body, and parts, to stretch like spaghetti into Its center point, extruding Tim through space and time.

CHAPTER 49

To those for whom time moved normally, Tim was there one second, and gone the next. Vanished into the tenebrous hole unknown to them a moment before.

John knew Tim had lost his life, attempting to save his son's, and that he was responsible for that loss. He never should have allowed Tim to follow him in the first place. It was against his better judgment, yet he'd let Tim talk him into it.

The young man was just that, too young. He'd still had his whole life before him, and if his actions in the last few hours were any indication of the man Tim was going to be, it was a greater loss than John wished to imagine.

Both Valkyrja stood behind him, while Abaddon floated above. For that moment, even as The Black One pulled closer, they all looked at Bruce.

Sariel told Abaddon she'd changed Bruce partly into a nephilim, he just did not know to what extent...until now. Bruce floated back to the ground and Thomas opened his eyes.

Bruce handed Thomas to his father. An understand-able expression of compassion and concern filled John's face. Abaddon landed next to John, looked down at Jason. "Can you heal this one as well?" Bruce nodded that he could, and Abaddon handed him over. "Good, but it will have to be as we move."

Somewhere within the deleterious jungle came a foreboding shrill. The poisonous, deathlike, sound filled the air as an odd twitching noise, followed by the vile smell of horror, came from the trees. Scurrying like insects, Báalzbub's horde made their way along the landscape, crawling over land and trees.

One Valkyrja wrapped its arms around John and Thomas, while the other swept up Bruce and Jason. Abaddon followed as they retreated toward the cavern where John had entered The Crescent Realm.

All around them the trees groaned their

eerie song and the lost within moaned their sorrowful cries. Thousands of Keepers hung upside down and screeched from branches as they passed beneath them. Hundreds of unknown creatures and scavengers raced from branch to branch, tree to tree, waiting to pick the remains from their bones after the horde caught them.

As their cavern hillside came into view, John did not remember it looking, or expect it to look, as it did. The structure's high peaks, hollowed middle, and darkened trees made the rock formation look like a mixture of Arnold Böcklin's five *Isle of the Dead* paintings.

The song of misery grew louder, with the grisly creatures hanging and climbing within the horrible trees adding to the distressful sound.

John and Thomas's Valkyrja broke through the tree line entering the clearing outside the cavern, only to discover the horde crawling over the rock formation hillside. Behind them, Báalzbub's sordid creatures infested the jungle's edge.

The Valkyrja stopped in the center of the opening and put the humans down. Abaddon hovered above, turning in a circular motion watching as the numbers increased around them. How, he wondered, did Sariel and Gabrielus expect him to defeat such overwhelming odds? To accomplish with just two Valkyrja what his group of defectors had failed to do. As Báalzbub's horde engulfed the area, Abaddon realized surviving the end of The Beast was never part of Sariel's plan.

The Valkyrja placed the four humans into a tight group, with the two young boys positioned between the men. The creatures themselves took defensive postures in front and behind them. Sariel knew Abaddon would have to make a decision, and these pets of hers did as well. Even now as they protected the humans, Abaddon knew they waited for him to make it.

That was the reason they stopped. They waited on him.

There was only one choice, only one thing for Abaddon to do, and damn those who had made him choose it—the Angel of Death most of all. She'd always known his true nature, which was why she met with him in the first place. Abaddon looked at the hollowed hole within the hillside.

"Go, get them out of here."

When he looked back at the jungle's edge, he saw the worst thing he had ever known, Báalzbub himself.

The Blood Trees groaned their song of misery as Abaddon moved forward, almost feeling the Valkyrja's satisfaction as he did. They'd used him. He knew this now, and a small part of him wished to turn around and smash those humans, beg Báalzbub for forgiveness, and return things back as they had been. But it was too late for that. There was no going back, there never was. Abaddon understood this now, too. He was no longer a fallen angel, but a lost one.

He knew this was how it had to be. He deserved nothing more. Let his last act be for, and from, his first nature, to die doing the right thing.

Not bothering to watch Abaddon, the Valkyrja reloaded the humans, placing them all with the larger of the two. John and Bruce held on to the back tusks, while the creature's upper-clawed arms took Thomas and Jason.

Their grunts became more furious as they moved toward the cavern. John glanced back. This was the second time he watched another move toward certain death. He realized these Valkyrja were doing the same thing in order to save them.

Compelled, John strained and lifted his head as high as he could manage.

"Sure you want to do that?" yelled Bruce from beside him. John, leaving the remark unanswered, pulled up, brought his head eye-level with the Valkyrja's shoulder, and discovered Bruce was right.

CHAPTER 50

Nothingness moved through the jungle, soundlessly breaking down and pulling matter into itself. Hundreds of Crescent creatures, including Keepers and Malign, fled in the direction of this blackened Envoy, trapped between two opposite forces, as the Being that once was Simon Allen locked tidal forces with The Black One.

Relentlessly the two pulled toward each other, dooming everything within their path.

The humanless Valkyrja battled its way into the horde, hewing, slicing, and chopping a path for the one carrying the humans to pass through.

Both took on a barrage of lethal blows.

Using only scythed limbs, the back Valkyrja did its best to defend itself and its cargo.

However, with the two children in front, those limbs became more sheld than weapon.

The horde closed in, creating an inescapeable noose. The lead Valkyrja unexpectedly stopped and stood its ground. Moving with lightning speed, it took on the spawn, butchering as many of the bevy as it could.

When the back Valkyrja reached and took hold of the others tusks, they advanced as one, plowing through the horde. The cavern slowly came closer.

The lead Valkyrja pushed and fought to stay alive long enough to reach it.

When they finally made it through the split, the leading Valkyrja collapsed, dead. Stepping over the burning-ashed body of his fallen kin, the other Valkyrja tossed the humans to the side, turned, and attacked the on-coming adversaries as they funneled at the crevice. Picking themselves up off the ground, John and Bruce grabbed the crawling boys and backed away toward the spiraling staircase, watching as the horde fought their way in.

Somewhere within The Blood Tree jungle The Black One and the "Orb of Glowing Light" incressed speed as they traveled toward each other, one pushed forward while the other pulled in, causing any in-falling matter to be simultaneously sucked up and ostensibly receded away, pulling them in, splintering the in-falling atoms, then re-emitting them destroyed.

The two forces, one blackenend, the other luminous, connected at their event horizons and melted together—nothing bleeding into nothing—then suddenly emploded, bursting inward into a brief stillness before they violently detonated in a burning light, destroying everything within their path.

This deadly and cleansing flash quickly traveled through the forest, toward the clearing and the cavern opening.

Outside the cavern, Abaddon moved toward the fearful Lord of the Flies. Memories of pain, tragedy, and betrayal rushed back to this lost angel as the weapon of flame once again formed in his right hand.

Báalzbub stood motionless as his dipter-ous-like creatures rushed forward. Their ran-cid stench filled the air as they passed with no engagement, disregarding Abaddon com-pletely.

The lost angel did not care whether their interest lay with him or with the humans fleeing somewhere behind him as he swung his sword, feeling the vibration of its power, accepting that it would be the last time. He gripped the hilt tighter as Báalzbub extended his wing-like appendages and lifted off the ground bringing his flamed spear to life to meet him.

Stopping and hovering, Abaddon waited, no longer lashing out at the drones that buzzed past him. He dropped and rested his arms at his sides, confident.

Off in the distance a bright light flashed, causing Abaddon to cross an arm over his face and close his eyes. When he re-opened them, dark afterimage spots filled his vision. He quickly squeezed them shut again, know-ing it would help him achieve a better sense of the color in its true aspect.

The largest of the spots remained black: Báalzbub waited.

The Beast's wings slowly flapped as the demon carefully started to circle. Abaddon blinked rapidly hoping to restore his vision as he turned, attempting to keep Báalzbub in front. As the two circled, Abaddon glided backwards keeping a safe distance between them. The Beast countered his movements by moving forward.

"You always seem to be heading away from me, Abaddon. Why is this? Weren't we once friends?" asked The Beast as he tilted his head to the right, looking at Abaddon almost sideways.

"We were nothing but a mistake."

If The Beast could grin, Abaddon was sure he was doing so now. "Not all of your kind feels as you do, especially a certain one close to your heart."

"If you speak of the one who betrayed us, I assure you he is not close to this heart," Abaddon said, as he pounded his chest where his heart would be."

"What is this that you are doing, moth? Look at you, playing the sacrificial lamb. Little late to become a martyr, don't you think?"

"I've felt like a lamb among wolves for a

long time, but that's about to change. This ends between us now. You will die for what you did to my son."

"Your son? You mean Zacre? You might want to rethink what you know about that one."

Abaddon stopped his backward dance and moved forward at the noise of The Beast speaking his slain son's name.

He was surprised when Báalzbub backed up. Abaddon tightened his grip around the hilt. "You killed Zacre. Don't speak as though you knew him."

"Still the foolish moth. You really haven't figured it out? Well sadly, let me be the one to inform you that your son is not dead. But—" Báalzbub held up one finger. "—it truly is my delight to inform you that it was Zacre, your son, who led you lambs into the mouths of my wolves."

"Liar!" Abaddon sprang forward and struck a blow at The Beast, aiming his flamed sword for Báalzbub's head, only to miss.

The Beast easily knocked the enraged blow to the side.

"Who did you think those Malign worked

for, me? I have no need for such weak and pathetic creatures."

"You lie. My son would never do such a thing." However, already Abaddon feared it was the truth. Knowing Zacre always took to the dark side a little too much.

"You sure about that? Even I can hear the doubt in your voice." Báalzbub laughed, stopping as he turned his attention briefly toward the advancing light. "In the end, it was all for nothing. Zacre and his slaughter, you fleeing helplessly to your precious butterfly for protection. What a waste. It would appear The Black One and I won't be meeting after all."

"You have that right at least," said Abaddon. Taking advantage of The Beast's focus on the blinding light, he struck another blow. Before Báalzbub was able to raise his spear in defense, Abaddon's sword found its mark.

Abaddon watched with great pride and pleasure as the Beast's head fell toward the ground, burning to ash while his spear of flame died out.

With thoughts of Zacre, Abaddon looked toward the cavern and decided to exit The Crescent Realm the way he came in.

Carefully, with a hand on the cave wall, John led the way down the stairs. With Thomas riding piggyback, he stepped slowly down into the dark, hoping not to lose his balance.

Behind him, Jason clung to Bruce and together the four of them moved down, with the dark gruesome outline of the battle happening above them.

As they rounded the back wall, a large shape fell from above, smashing against the feeble stoned stairs, causing them to fracture, knocking Bruce into John.

All four tumbled off the side into darkness.

Red cracks of heat splintered across the remains of the Valkyrja burning ahead, making this the second time John followed a red glow through this hellish shaft.

The only difference was the source and direction.

Below, the Valkyrja incinerated into ashen flakes that floated past them like burning paper from a bonfire.

Above, the echoing song of the trees'

stopped as a bright burning light filled the shaft.

Numbness again overtook John.

Then everything went silent and black.

EPILOGUE

October 23rd:

Mark Greene, usually with Carl Fisher and the NH Fish and Game conservation officers at his side, relentlessly searched the Harrowing Hills. Understanding if they did not, Jane Moore would. Losing both her son and husband in the same day, to the same woods, was more than she could bear. No wife and mother should have to cope with such a thing, and with Jane's bloodshot eyes and unwashed face, it was easy to see she was not doing so very well.

Mark believed Jane had not slept without aid in the five days since her family went missing and was on the verge of a breakdown.

Her pain compelled him.

On the morning of the twenty-third, Carl met Mark at the Café Wellington, sitting only a few tables away from where John and Tim had sat when the Watson call came.

In the days between that call and this morning, the town of Harrow buried both Bill and Rose Watson, in two separate services. Their memorials shared the standard amount of flowers, prayers, and remorse. Both had eulogies and memories of the past, and both had Father O'Brien. However, one service was full, while the other consisted of more prayers than mourners to smell the flowers and hear the eulogy.

Bill had a large service, filled with condolences and pity, and stories of how he was trying to turn his life around. Rose's funeral was colder and more impersonal than the ground she been laid to rest in. Only her immediate family and a few loyal friends, who remembered how miserable and despondent life truly was for Rose, attended hers.

Finishing their breakfast, Mark and Carl quietly paid their check and left the café for another long and disappointing day of searching the Hills for their friend and Chief of Police.

Sunlight and the smell of morning air woke John. Again his head rolled like a bowling ball. He found Thomas lying at his side. Forcing himself to sit up, John saw his son's best friend curled up where a pathway that never should have existed no longer did.

The pathway was not the only thing missing. The once sulfurous, greenish-yellow soil, was now plain old normal earth, and the once haunted, bare-boned trees now swayed in the light breeze like every other tree of the Harrowing Hills. Come springtime, they should bloom leaves for the first time.

Then he noticed the absence of something, or rather, someone else.

Bruce Wren was no where to be seen.

He remembered Bruce picking up and carrying Jason, and he remembered the last of the Valkyrja knocking them off the stairs. Did Bruce continue to fall, if so, where to? Did he hit bottom, did he exit where he entered? It was possible Bruce woke first and left. Rubbing his face, John stood, unable to blame Bruce if he had taken off. In a way, he envied him. Besides, Bruce would be just another thing for him to explain. As it was, John had no idea how he was going to explain Tim's disappearance or how he found both his own son and Jason Benson.

The truth, unquestionably, was not the answer.

The truth was something John did not understand anyway, and that was probably for the best.

Bruce might have been a son of Harrow, but the town would still question his sudden reappearance, and with Simon unaccounted for, people would speculate on Bruce's involvement.

After Simon's escape from the hospital, his story would be general knowledge in town, and although the evidence against him was inconclusive, the townspeople would condemn him.

The only question anyone would have was whether he worked alone. It would be almost impossible for John to convince people of Harrow, and Detective Rodale, that he just happened to come across Bruce in the Hills. If the town decided to point their fingers toward Bruce, John would be unable to change their minds.

John woke Thomas and then Jason. Both of the boys looked as confused as he was. Their questions started with where and how and ended with the two crying. John hugged them and did his best to soothe the lost and found boys, but he knew there was only so much he could do for them.

Their mud-streaked faces looked at him for answers he did not have, for the support and comfort they so needed and deserved, and that he would do his best to provide.

He smiled, took each one by the hand, and started to lead them out of the Harrowing Hills.

After leaving the café on John Adams Avenue, Mark and Carl returned to the Hills, entering near the baseball diamond again this morning.

Their conversations were nothing more than small talk, rambling about television programs they watched the night before, and how much they wished their wives would make something different for dinner than the same old dishes every week. And since Boston was out, they didn't care who won the World Series, as long as it wasn't the Yankees.

Then something happened that made this morning anything but another day of disappointing search. Their Chief of Police walked into view with not only his son in hand, but the long-lost Jason Benson as well. John had found them.

October 27th:

Upstairs in the Levi home, Jack carried a sweater from the hallway closet into the master bedroom, folding it as he walked. At the end of the bed laid an opened suitcase. While placing the folded sweater inside, Jack smiled as he thought about past trips to Vermont. Granted, the trips had changed over the years, but the need for them never had, and the needing had never been greater than now.

This trip, however, would be for more than just the normal rest and relaxation. This trip was more about gathering bearings and leaving Harrow. Jack and Lisa never planned to return. They had put the house up for sale, and their son Peter had agreed to pack and store their belongings. Jack and Lisa intended to stay with him and his family in Kennebunkport until the house sold and they found a new place to call home, one as far from Harrow and as close to their grandson as they could get.

On one of the bedside table lay a white twenty-four-hour desire chip from AA. Jack walked over and picked it up. He had not started drinking again, but with all he had been through, especially with that bottle appearing repeatedly, he decided it might be a good idea to get some extra support. He had endured much over the past few weeks. Until he put his mind at ease, he would attend the meetings.

He rolled the chip over, read the serenity prayer written on the back, and again prayed for courage and wisdom. From his window, he saw Thomas Moore ride by on his bike, no doubt heading to the Wallace home. Jack put the chip in his front pocket as Jason Benson coasted past. He'd seen both boys a few times over the past few days and made every attempt to avoid them and the town's police chief as well. Jack did not wish to know the horrors they'd seen, nor where those horrors took place.

There were many unanswered questions, and very soon, John would have to answer them. People were more than a little curious about where Tim was, and how John found the boys.

Jack watched the two boys ride past and turned from the window. On the other side of the room, Wolfgang the prowler rested on the adjacent windowsill. Jack strolled over and stroked his hand down the cat's back. Peter would also be taking the family feline away with him.

Outside the window, Jack saw another thing he dreaded—his pile of scarecrows. He stared at them in disbelief. So many. Come trash day, Justin would properly dispose of Tattie Bogle and company. Until then, they could remain piled outside the shed.

The sound of the front door opening and closing traveled up the stairs and into the bedroom. Jack turned his head toward the hallway. He'd missed Lisa pulling up in the driveway, which was odd. Normally he heard the engine through the open window. Running his hand one last time down the cat's back, he returned to the roadside window. There was no car. The driveway was empty.

Frowning, he wondered if something happened to the car on her trip to the store. He moved to the doorway and heard Lisa opening cabinets, putting away the last minute items she wanted for the trip, and making sure Peter had plenty to eat and drink while taking care of the house.

"How was the trip?" he asked as he stepped down to the lower floor. "Did you have car trouble?"

Lisa stood by the sink with her back to him. He looked to help put the groceries away and noticed she had already finished with them. That was fast.

"Was there a problem with the car?" he asked again,

Lisa only raised her hand, dismissing the question. Clearly, whatever happened she didn't want to talk about. Fair enough. Jack saw no point in rattling her cage.

"I'll call Horton Mudgett. Hopefully, he can fix whatever it is today. I really don't want to postpone our departure time by much," Jack said walking over to the food cabinets. "Is it at Bill's market or somewhere in-between?"

He opened a cabinet, hoping for a surprise can of Pringles, but instead found a single black feather.

Slowly, he reached in and picked it up. The thing was warm to the touch. Dropping it, he quickly opened the next door and came across another. Jack stood there frozen, looking at it. Dumbfound he opened the next cabinet door and found the same.

From behind, he heard Wolfgang release a low growl. Jack turned.

Lisa stood in the middle of the kitchen with her head down and her hair hanging low. "Lisa?"

She lifted her hollowed face, twisted her mouth into a ghastly grin, and said, "Hello, Reverendus."

I would like to thank everyone who read the HARROW manuscript and helped along the way. However, a few people deserve special mention: My parents, David and Robin Henson, for always believing in me—even when I did not, Dana and Shannon for being my brother and sister. Genevieve Bartal for her early editing and help, Melissa Wolverton for everything under the moon, Igor Vukojevic for his website expertise, Joe Chatman and Brad Mitchell for their cameras. Lauri, Mike, Faith, and Gibby from Black Opal Books for all their hard work.

Thank you all again—nobody writes a novel alone.

-E

About the Author

Eric Henson was born in Salem, Massachusetts. Although he has lived the majority of his life in New England, he currently resides in the Atlanta, Georgia area. Henson has always wanted to be an author. He loves the feeling of connecting his head to his hand and bringing a tale to life, watching it take shape before and behind—his cycs, and allowing it to grow legs and run where it wants. However, his chosen profession is a double-edged sword with another sharper and more painful side—the jagged edge caused by severe dyslexia, a learning disability that impairs one's ability to read, speak, and spell. Over time, as the itch—the need—

to write remained strong, Henson managed to overcome many of these hurdles. Being an avid reader helped, as did his desire to inspire others suffering from dyslexia not to give up on themselves.

HENSONFICTION.com